Praise for Dollar Signs

"A high-speed storyline full of twists and turns upon a stark background of reality as lawyers might really experience it. Manning Wolfe is one of the up and coming legal thriller writers of this generation. Read her and enjoy her, but don't expect much sleep!"
— John Ellsworth, Thaddeus Murfee Legal Thrillers

"Manning Wolfe's new legal thriller is filled with great local color, fascinating characters, legal shenanigans, and plenty of action. A great read, and Texas crime fiction has a new star."
— Bill Crider, Dan Rhodes Mysteries

"A legal thriller not to be missed, compelling and action-packed, with vivid characters and an authentic Austin setting. Manning Wolfe just put herself on my list of must-read authors."
— Mark Pryor, Hugo Marston Novels

"Dollar Signs is an "out of the gate" legal thriller that captures everything I like to see from an experienced author. A heroine with a small legal practice takes on a big Texas law firm and gets caught up in arson, murder, and threats to her life. A fast-moving plot and well-developed characters will leave you wanting to read the next thriller in the series. The eyes of Texas will be on Manning Wolfe."
— Rick Polad, Spencer Manning Mysteries

DOLLAR SIGNS

Texas Lady Lawyer vs Boots King

a novel by

MANNING WOLFE

STARPATH BOOKS, LLC

Starpath Books, LLC

Austin, TX

Library of Congress Cataloging-in Publication Data

ISBN 978-1-944225-00-1

1. Texas Law—Fiction. 2. Psychological—Fiction. 3. Murder Mystery

FIC Wol 2016

PS3557.R5355 W58 2016

2015917317

Cover City Art by Aaron Wolfe, SkyWolfe Aerial Photography

Manufactured in the United States of America

10 9 8 7 6 5 4 3 2 1

For my darling Bill and magical Aaron.

DOLLAR SIGNS

Texas Lady Lawyer vs Boots King

I think that I shall never see
A billboard lovely as a tree.
Perhaps, unless the billboards fall,
I'll never see a tree at all.

—OGDEN NASH

1

The smiling head of Greg Lee Wood burst into flames. Each animal surrounding him caught fire and burned. Two dogs, three cats, a sheep, and two goats all went in a giant ball of fire. Neither the director of PETA nor the animals made a sound, but the giant billboard buckled and groaned as the metal twisted and broke from the scaffolding holding it to the creosote columns erected into the sky. Falling pieces of wood broke windshields and car windows forty-five feet below. Three cars were crushed. Their gasoline tanks leaked fluid and exploded in the dark Austin night.

Tarantella 'Tireman' Estevez dangled from a metal halogen light, which was tearing away from the catwalk of the twisted scaffolding. As the metal ripped rivet by rivet, he dropped closer and closer to the flaming mayhem below. The sharp edge of the fixture cut into his skin as he looked down into the mess he had made. From this height, the cars below looked like flaming Hot Wheels.

His eyes searched South Congress Avenue, but did not find anyone walking about in the middle of the night. While he wanted help, he hoped he could free himself without being seen. If he called for assistance, there would be a witness to his act. He'd never intended to burn the cars, just the billboard. But here he was hanging and hoping and regretting.

He dropped another foot toward the ground as he heard voices yelling and coming closer. *Would he break his bones if he fell? Would he die?* His blood mixed with his sweat and lubricated his grip. He slipped to the end of the metal.

"Last chance."

Tireman flung his body as far as he could away from the heat. He let go, dropped, and fell across the top of a flaming Ford. He slid to the ground, rolled across the flames on his back, and crawled on all fours away from the heat. Hot glass mashed into his palms and knees. Voices and shrieks grew closer as he hid behind a stack of tires at the edge of the body shop. He tried to catch his breath and make sense of what he'd done.

It wasn't vandalism. The auto shop where the billboard resided belonged to him and his brother, but their lawyer had told them that the sign was not theirs. It sat in front of their business like a wart on the land reminding Tireman that someone could take from him all that he'd worked for.

Tireman was caught between his desire to be good and his demand for justice. He'd come to America for the dream, and his dream was now tarnished. He'd acted out of anger and frustration. He had no thought of long-term consequences. Nor did he realize he had just become the murderer of the homeless man passed out in the back seat of the flaming blue Chrysler, not five feet away from him.

2

Boots King was fired up and back in action. He got the call at 5:11 a.m., pulled on his signature snakeskin boots, jumped into his black diesel 4x4 and drove north to Austin from San Antonio. He'd worked for Nixon Outdoor Advertising for almost three years, and he was on call twenty-four seven. He arrived on South Congress about an hour later as the sun came up, hid his truck a few blocks away behind Weird Pizza, and walked toward the smoke. The yard at Estevez Tire and Auto Shop was a smoldering hot mess. The billboard was gone except for remnants of metal halogen lights and nubs of creosote poles. Several car carcasses were steaming and dripping water. A fire truck stood guard in case of flare up, and a uniformed Estevez employee helped firefighters hold people back from the sidewalk.

Boots chuckled to himself and whistled out loud as he looked at what was left of the giant billboard.

"How in the hell did someone burn that down?" Boots asked.

This was Boots' favorite part, the chaotic aftermath, second only to the rush he got when he conned the innocent and unsuspecting into signing the leases in the first place. In his years working for Nixon Outdoor Advertising, he'd caused more chaos and distress among small business operators and naive landowners than ten other ex-cons combined. This was a new one, even for Boots. No one had ever gone so far as to burn down one of the billboards.

Prior to working for Nixon's sign company, Boots had been a landman in West Texas conning small-town folks into executing oil and gas leases for a fraction of their worth. He had a knack. If he couldn't get the men to agree, he'd work on their wives. Women were his specialty. His old man had taught him to go for the women and they'd work on their men. It was sage advice from the best con man in the business, until Boots had surpassed even his father's expertise. He took pride in his ability to soften 'em up, sign 'em up, and watch 'em squirm trying to extricate themselves from the bad deals they'd struck with him and the people he worked for. He was a master.

King wasn't his real name of course. He'd gone through so many since the old man died he'd forgotten half of them. King was his favorite, and Boots just stuck from years of identification with the footwear.

After each sales job, Boots could no longer be contacted. He'd used aliases on most documents, and he changed phone numbers often. Nixon Outdoor Advertising would tell anyone who called that no one named King worked there.

"Could we be of service?" the receptionist would say.

Nixon wanted Boots to stay in the shadows just as he was today, watching and listening, but not showing his rugged face, his noticeable footwear, or transportation.

Boots eavesdropped on the conversation in the crowd and tried to get close enough to the fire truck to pick up on the official buzz.

A redheaded reporter in a short skirt with KNEW-9 on the microphone interviewed several onlookers. As soon as she was off camera, she threw on a blanket to insulate her scantily clad body against the winter chill.

4

A policeman interviewed neighboring business owners as they arrived for work and unlocked their doors. Boots saw a cop leave the Congress Bake Shop, two doors down from Estevez Tire and Auto Shop. Boots strolled in and smiled at the pretty woman behind the counter who was putting on a tie-dyed apron.

"I'll take a cup of coffee when you get one brewed," he said, pushing his sunglasses up onto his wavy hair and giving her the full benefit of his sparkling blue peepers.

"Comin' right up." The shopkeeper blushed and avoided eye contact, focusing on the coffee preparations.

"What happened over there?" Boots asked.

"Cop said someone burned down the sign during the night. Don't know who yet. Wanted to know if we'd seen anything," she said as she measured the coffee and switched on the urn.

"Why would anyone burn down a sign?" he asked.

Boots picked up a pair of tongs and served himself a fried pie.

"They've been fighting over that billboard for a year," she said. "It's huge. Was huge, that is. Trashes up the place, and from what I hear, they tricked the Estevez brothers into signing the lease in the first place."

"Really?"

"I don't know. If it had been me, I'd have burned it too. Don't know if they did it though. Innocent until proven guilty, and all that." She handed him the steaming coffee and wiped her hands on her apron.

He laid a ten spot on the counter.

She rang up the sale, gave him his change, and said, "Stay as long as you like, I've got to set up the rest."

He dropped the change into the tip cup and gestured at her with the pastry. "Thanks."

Outside, he took one bite of the pie and tossed the rest into the grass by the building. He lit a cigarette and took a deep drag and a scalding swallow of coffee. He speed dialed a number on his smartphone.

"Hey, it's Boots King. I need to talk to Old Man Nixon."

He listened.

"I'm on South Congress. It's Estevez. Cops can't prove it yet, but they did it. I'm sure of it. If we didn't have the case made already, this insures it." He laughed, taking a drag on the cig and slapping the phone against his thigh.

3

"Here comes another one," Merit Bridges groaned. She reached over John's naked body and grabbed her cell phone off the charger. The clock behind it glowed indigo: 4:11 a.m. Her brain switched on, and she thanked God that it was not her son's Jimmy Vaughan guitar riff ringtone.

She tried to register the number as she cleared last night's wine fog, pushed the talk button, and spoke into the speaker, "This better be important."

"Merit, it's Manuel Estevez, my brother did something really bad. We need your help."

"Manny, hold on," Merit said. She climbed out of bed, hit the mute button, and took the phone into the bathroom. She pulled up her Longhorn t-shirt, sat down on the toilet, willed herself awake, and re-activated the call. "Ok, what is it?"

"Tireman burned down the sign at the South Congress shop and a bunch of cars blew up under it. The police and fire department are here and they're asking questions."

"Was anyone hurt?"

"No."

"Do they know he did it?"

"Not yet."

"Is he there with you?"

"Yes."

"Did anyone see him do it?"

"I don't think so."

"Have they interviewed him yet?"

"No."

"I need to talk with him before the police do."

"I'll send him to the junkyard office on Airport."

"I'll meet him there in twenty minutes. You stay and deal with the police. Don't tell them anything yet, but don't lie to them. Meet us at the junkyard when you get the situation under control."

"Okay."

"And, most of all, don't talk to the press."

Merit went into the closet and wiggled into a pair of faded jeans and a Rice Owl sweatshirt. She spoke over her shoulder to John. "I've got to go help a client with a problem. I'll call you later."

Merit rooted around for shoes in the closet. She could not see John take a surreptitious peek at her last call number.

"Want me to go with you? I don't have to be at the station until later."

"Yeah, right, let me take my twenty-eight-year-old boyfriend along at six in the morning," Merit said as she slid her thirty-eight-year-old perfectly manicured feet into a pair of leather flats.

"Okay, good point. Later."

John appeared to be asleep before Merit was out the door and in the garage. Even if it was in vogue to do the cougar thing, it wasn't good for business for a woman to be seen dating a younger man. Demi Moore might get away with it, but Merit was no movie star.

Merit could see her breath in the cold garage. She slid into her SUV, hit the garage door opener and waited for the panel to rise. As she pushed the button to start the BMW, she organized her thoughts.

Merit had been the business attorney for the Estevez brothers for more than ten years. Her practice was rooted in real estate with a twist. She handled all things related to land, on or under; real estate, development, buildings, oil and gas, and civil litigation where contracts were involved. Manny Estevez had been referred to her when he purchased his first business in Austin.

Manuel and Tarantella Estevez had emigrated from Mexico, speaking Spanish thanks to their father and Italian thanks to their mother; but no English, thanks to both of them. Manny had arrived first and set up one shop, then another and another. He established a junkyard on Old Airport Boulevard where wrecked cars were stockpiled for use as parts supply. Tireman moved to Austin five years later and acquired his nickname because no one could pronounce Tarantella, and because he sold more tires than any other shop in town. He shared his brother's work ethic, but never quite attained Manny's command of the language and business savvy. He made up for that with his knowledge of cars. He could tell just by the sound what was wrong with an engine, and usually had it fixed in less time than most repair shops. Manny bought expensive diagnostic equipment, but used it mostly to prove that Tireman was right.

Merit had been trying to work out a peaceful solution to the sign problem for months. Why would anyone sign a contract without a lawyer? After the issue with Nixon on the sign, she'd put the Estevez brothers on retainer. She didn't want them to have any excuse not to call her regardless of how small an issue might seem. If Manny had just consulted her before he'd executed Nixon's billboard lease, none of this would have happened, and she wouldn't be driving across town at this hour to fix what should never have been broken.

4

Merit left Tarrytown and cut across midtown between the Capitol and the forty acres comprising the University of Texas campus. She turned onto I-35 north then exited east on Old Airport Boulevard into a scruffy part of town. The metal gates to the junkyard were wrapped with a thick chain and padlocked. Until now, she'd only been there in the daytime when the double gates were wide open. Now, in the semi-dark, she wasn't quite sure how to access the place. She pulled up to the fence, blinked her brights at the makeshift office, and waited. A short male figure came out of the shack's side door and shielded his eyes with his arm. He wore a khaki work uniform with Tireman printed on the breast pocket. He signaled for her to pull around back where she tucked her vehicle amongst the wrecked cars.

She cut between the mangled metal vehicles and went into the office. Tireman moved the growling mutt that guarded the place from an old frayed car seat and Merit sat down. The dog settled and nuzzled Merit's leg.

Tireman put on a pot of coffee while Merit interrogated him. One of his hands was wrapped with a dirty rag, the other was red and scraped. His dark brown skin was covered in soot and oil.

"Why did you burn the sign?"

"Yesterday the man came with papers."

"I told you to expect a process server. They refused to let me accept service just to intimidate you."

"Misses Bridges, lo siento, I cannot take it anymore. If the sign is gone, there is no more fighting."

"You know it's illegal to destroy someone else's property. This is going to make it worse."

"It is my property. I work hard for it, and they want to take it for nada."

"I've explained before. It's your land, but their sign. We have to let the judge decide if the lease is going to hold up. You can't take matters into your own hands and expect a good outcome."

"It's not right what they do."

"In Texas, a lease is like a sale of part of your property. They own that lease right."

"We fight for months."

"I know, but illegal things like burning the sign will just make it last longer."

The dog's ears perked up as a car pulled into the yard. Its tires crunched gravel and its headlights splashed light along the office walls. Tireman peeked out the broken blinds.

"Police?"

"No, is Manny. Es bueno."

Manny walked in and pulled an oily rag from his back pocket, on which he wiped his hands before shaking with Merit.

"Merit, are the police going to arrest him?" Manny asked.

"He should turn himself in. I'll get a criminal lawyer who can take him down to the police station tomorrow. Did they put out the fire?"

"Yes. I left one of the mechanics to guard the store. Tarantella burned the sign and a few cars, but not the shop," Manny said.

"I'm not going to police," Tireman said. "And, you cannot tell anyone because you are lawyer."

"If they catch you, and arrest you, it will be worse," Merit said.

"Dios mío," Manny said.

"Did anyone see you set the fire?" Merit asked.

"No sé." Tireman shrugged. "I climbed up the pole and poured gasoline on the billboard. I thought it would fall from the top down, but the fire spread where I spill gas. The sign fell on the cars," he said.

"You could have been killed, or even killed someone else. Hermano, why didn't you come to me?" Manny said.

Tireman lowered his eyes.

"I'm concerned about the insurance coverage on the cars if they determine it was not accidental and connect you to the incident," Merit said. "But, that's the least of our problems. Nixon is going to go after you on this. They will use every mistake you make to their advantage."

"What do I tell the insurance company?" Manny asked.

"Tell them you are pulling together the loss information and you'll get back with them. If they press you, refer them to me."

The three continued to strategize how best to protect Tireman. When Merit was satisfied that she had the whole story, she gave her final advice.

"If you won't go in, at least give me permission to speak with a criminal attorney tomorrow and see if he has any ideas about how to proceed," Merit said.

Tireman froze.

"Go ahead and do it," Manny said.

Tireman reluctantly nodded his head in agreement.

5

Merit ran home for a quick change into a navy Tom Ford business suit with a pencil skirt. From the wet towels on the bathroom floor, it appeared that John had showered. His clothes from the night before were missing off the bedroom chair. She felt a little butterfly in her stomach thinking of him. So cute, so sexy, so damn much fun in bed. So messy.

"Oh well, I'm not going to marry him, just have a little fling."

She put fresh water and a scoop of kibble into bowls for Pepper, her teenage son's Cairn terrier.

"Guard the house," Merit said. She patted Pepper on the head. The twenty-pound fur ball rolled over and Merit rubbed her tummy. When Pepper appeared satisfied, she flipped over onto her feet, and dug into her breakfast bowl.

Merit dumped the last of her tea in the sink and pulled on her coat. She grabbed her briefcase and purse, and scooted out the kitchen door to the garage for the second time that day.

As she drove to the office, Merit contemplated the predicament that Manny had gotten himself into. Worse than the lease, Tireman's burning the sign. Merit had gone to law school for just this reason. Some misplaced notion of preserving order and helping the underdog. She had plenty of corporate clients as well, but did not defend criminals, wife beaters, drug addicts, or cheaters. She hated the cheaters the most. There were plenty of businesses making lots of money without swindling anyone. She was no goody-two-shoes, as her Auntie called her, but Merit had her own gauge of what was just and unjust.

Merit arrived at her downtown Austin office before anyone else was there. This seldom happened as her office manager Betty, an early riser, usually had the coffee on before anyone else hit the parking garage. She went up to the third floor and unlocked the glass doors labeled "Law Office of Merit Bridges."

As she stashed her purse in the bottom drawer of the credenza, Merit's investigator entered the inner office with a quick knock. She watched him stretch his long frame into one of two leather guest chairs in front of her desk. He had a winning smile and eyelashes that women envied because they curled into a tight roll without the use of an eyelash curler.

"Good Morning, Ag," Merit said.

Albert "Ag" Malone had been Merit's investigator since she'd moved back to Austin from Houston and hung out her shingle. Although Merit was a University of Texas Law grad, Ag was willing to work for her because she paid well, was smart, and she made him laugh. Besides, almost every attorney in town was a UT law grad. If he was going to live in Austin, he had to work for someone. He acquired his nickname when he graduated from Texas A&M, and although he lived in a burnt orange town, he continued to wear maroon, drive a maroon pickup truck, and hold season tickets to the Aggie home games in nearby College Station. It was heartbreaking for him when

A&M went to the SEC in 2012 and ended the old rivalry games with UT forever.

"You rang?" Ag asked.

"Yeah, thanks for coming in. Tireman burned down the Nixon sign at his South Congress shop last night, and I need you to start doing damage control," Merit said.

"Are you talking about that huge forty-five-foot tall advertiser?"

"Exactly."

Ag rolled his eyes and chuckled.

"Go over and talk to Tireman. Speak to the local businesses and see if you can find out who might have seen him. Be discreet, as always. Check with your sources at the police station and see if they have any evidence connecting him to the fire."

"Okay, do you want to fill me in on why he would burn it in the first place?"

"Yeah, I was going to bring you in on this for possible trial prep, but I thought we had more time. About five years ago, Manny Estevez executed a crappy lease with some sleazy leasing agent named Boots King. It gave Manny a few thousand dollars a year, and it didn't interfere with the use of the store. I think he got the first month's ad free for the shop."

"Sounds good," Ag said.

"Yeah, but he didn't let me read the document because it was a fill-in the blank form. You know the kind that looks like a receipt book and makes a carbon copy? He thought it was a simple yearly lease. He assumed he could always terminate if he decided he didn't want to keep the sign there in the future."

They could hear Betty in the hallway, waking up the office by getting the lights on and machines running.

Betty stuck her head in the door. "First mistake, not having an attorney read everything."

"Morning, Betty," Merit and Ag sang in unison.

"Mornin'. Saw it on the news. Worse than a Texas shit storm," Betty said as she moved on down the hallway. "Coffee's brewing," she yelled over her shoulder.

Merit turned back to Ag. "So Manny forgets the sign and the lease automatically renews."

"How do you forget about a billboard?"

"Exactly. Last year, Manny transferred the South Congress shop to a corporation he and Tireman owned, so they could pull out half a million through a bank loan. They wanted the money for new equipment. The re-structure triggered a hidden boilerplate clause in the sign lease and everything blew up."

Betty, her gray hair plastered in an Ann Richards' style dome with Aqua Net, placed steaming mugs in front of them. "That Nixon is lower than a snake's belly in a wagon rut!" she said over her shoulder as she left the room.

"Did you handle the loan?" Ag asked.

"Yes, but the lease was not on my radar," Merit said.

"What difference does the lease make to the loan or the sale?" Ag asked.

"I'm getting to that," Merit said. "A few months after the deed was filed to transfer the property from Manny to the new corporation, Nixon's attorney sends Manny a certified letter stating that they want to exercise their option to purchase the property. They asserted that Manny was in breach of contract because he didn't notify Nixon in advance of the sale."

"How did they get an option?"

"In the tiny print on the back of the lease was a first right of refusal to buy the land under the sign in the event it was sold during the term of the lease or after."

"You're kidding."

"No, I'm not."

"Isn't that fraud?" Ag asked.

"It is in my book, but Nixon disagrees. They've filed suit to take the land, and Manny is in way over his head, but trying to stay within legal limits."

"But not Tireman?"

"Tireman only sees the law of the street, and in his mind the land is his, he worked hard for it, and he can do anything he wants with anything placed on it."

"So he burned it down."

"Exactly. Nixon wants the land for the price the brothers used in the deal, but it would have been four times that to an outside buyer. Nixon is trying to enforce the option at half a million and steal the land."

"What a mess. What do you want me to do after I talk to Tireman?" Ag asked.

"I want you to find out about this leasing agent so we can look further into the fraud angle. The witness signature says 'Boots King'. We're going to need to take his deposition eventually. Ask Manny what he remembers about him after you talk to Tireman."

"Why do you need him if he was acting as agent for Nixon?" Ag asked.

"If we are going to prove fraud, we need to depose him about what he said to Manny. Otherwise, the court might find it hearsay," Merit said.

Betty popped her head in the door. "Appointment's here. You've got a full calendar already without this sign problem."

"Yes ma'am," Merit said.

Ag stood up. "You want this written or verbal?"

"Let's start with a verbal report and see where we go from there. Don't put anything in writing about Tireman until I see what he decides about going to the cops."

"Ok, I'll get something for you by tomorrow. Gig 'em." Ag gave a thumbs up and started for the door.

"Hook 'em," Merit said and displayed the horns with her right hand.

Ag gave her a dirty look then winked. They both laughed.

After her next client, Merit clicked on the flat screen TV on her credenza and surfed over to KNEW. John was reporting the weather and looking cute in his weatherman way. His professionally styled black hair and straightened teeth were the perfect image for KNEW. Merit muted the volume and worked while she kept an eye out for the fire story. It came on after a Matt's El Rancho commercial and she unmuted the sound.

"SoCo, a local homeless transvestite, was killed in a fire last night at the Estevez Tire and Auto Shop on South Congress. The police did not know until this morning that the man was sleeping in the back of one of the cars. His charred remains were discovered once the fire was cooled enough to examine the vehicles."

"Oh shit!" Merit said.

Betty popped her head in the door. "You got that right."

The report continued. "The fire department reports possible arson, but a suspect or suspects have yet to be identified. We go to Redmond Thallon who has been at the scene since early this morning. Red?"

The short-skirted reporter appeared with a microphone in her slender hand. While she spoke, the station cut to video from the night before. The smoldering sign, burned out cars, and attendant fire trucks appeared on the screen.

"Local residents and business owners mourn the death of SoCo, who has been a longtime colorful character in Keeping Austin Weird. Several vehicles were burned and the advertising sign, which appears to be the target, was toppled and destroyed."

The video stream changed to a live view of South Congress with traffic moving along behind the reporter.

"It appears that the target could have been the message on the sign, Nixon Outdoor Advertising commented. Recently, the sign had housed an advertisement for PETA and showed a message against overcrowded animal farming."

"Hogwash," Betty said.

"Get Tireman. No, get Manny on the phone please," Merit said. "And, let Ag know he's walking into a firestorm."

"On it," Betty said

"Spin doctors. Nixon knows exactly why the sign was burned," Merit said.

Ag walked from Merit's office over to the Austin Police Department. He put his 9MM into the lockbox marked four, pocketed the key, and went through the metal detectors. He was oblivious to the whispers of the female clerks behind the desk as he walked in. He'd never thought of himself as handsome. His family put more stock in hard work and personal cleanliness, being next to Godliness, of course.

"Is Detective Chaplain in?"

"May I tell him who's askin'?" one of the clerks said.

"Ag Malone."

Chaplain came around the corner from his office and motioned toward the coffee pot. He was tall and slim and had crinkles around his eyes. Ag didn't know if they were from smiling or too much Texas sun.

"What brings you here, Ag?"

"Hey, Chaplain. APD picked up an arson call last night on South Congress. Now appears that tranny who lived down there was killed in the fire. Just wondering if you'd gotten wind of it."

"I heard a little something about that. What's your interest?"

"Just sniffin' around."

Chaplain gave Ag the stink eye and said, "If I did know who did it I couldn't tell you, but we haven't sorted that one out yet. Is there something you want to tell me? Which ambulance chaser are you working for this week?"

"Same ol', same ol'," Ag said.

"Check back with me in a few days," Chaplain said.

"If I did come across the perpetrator and he wanted to surrender himself, could I count on you to give him a fair shake?"

"As always. But, this is manslaughter."

"If I did know who it was, it would have been an accident and SoCo would have been trespassing to sleep in the car."

"Is that so?"

"I'll talk to you before the end of the week," Ag said.

"Hmm," Chaplain said into his coffee cup. "You do that."

Merit sat in her office before a stack of books on the conference table in the dual-purpose conference room and law library. She watched her paralegal Valentine Berry Louis climb up a ladder to the books on the highest shelf. He acquired the desired tome, climbed down and straightened his bow tie and purple velvet vest over his khakis, all the while looking as graceful as a ballerina. Val was Merit's paralegal, part time law student at St. Mary's Law School in San Antonio, and expert on all things fashion related.

Val opened the copy of Weintraub on Contracts and perched on the side of the conference table. He swung his foot clad in a vintage Calvin Klein loafer back and forth to the rhythm of Willie Nelson playing through the sound system. He hummed along.

"Willie's version of that song is the best," Merit said.

Val sang a few lines changing the feminine to masculine in the verses.

"Nice voice," Merit said, remembering that Val sang with Conspirare, the Austin choral group.

"Thanks, Merit."

"Find anything?"

"I'm checking the basics before I go further. I just finished first year Contracts last semester."

"Okay, let's start there," Merit said. "The elements of a contract are offer, acceptance, and consideration. Clearly, the Estevez lease had all three. Nixon had offered the sign, Estevez had accepted the arrangement, and lastly, been paid a consideration for the deal."

"Right," Val said.

"Next," Merit said, "there had to be a term certain. The lease shows a three-year renewable lease."

"Got it," Val said. "So where does the problem come in?"

"There was no meeting of the minds between Estevez and Nixon as to their intention regarding part of the contract."

"So they had to agree on what they planned to do with the lease in all aspects."

"Exactly. Next, the option problem is twofold; whether the clause was intentionally hidden, and whether this Boots King character was deceitful," Merit said.

"In Texas, aren't we responsible for anything we sign?"

"Yes and no. In Texas, any contracts surrounding land have to be in writing. The four corners doctrine says that a contract's terms have to be within the four corners of the document."

"We have that," Val said.

"Yes, but we also have an option that's in the small print. There's no doubt that the lease is valid, but we need to attack the option clause as invalid."

"How do we do that?"

"That's what I want you to research."

"Okay."

"First take a look at option clauses in general. Next, fraudulent inducement. I want to know the consequences because the leasing agent misled Manny Estevez," Merit said.

"On it, Boo," Val said.

Betty called around the corner. "Telephone. You'll want to take it."

Merit looked at Val with amusement. "How does she always know which ones I'll want to take?"

Val laughed.

"Be sure and check the pocket parts in the back of the books to see if there were any changes, and run all the cases through LEXIS to make sure they haven't been appealed," Merit said on her way out the door.

"I do know a few things, girlfriend," Val said and snapped his fingers three times in a Z.

Merit met Ag for lunch at Opal Divine's next to St. Edward's University. They dined on polenta planks in gorgonzola and black angus beef burgers while bringing each other up to speed on the research to date.

"May I have a to go box?" Merit asked the waiter.

"Pantywaist," Ag said.

"How can you eat all that and not take a nap?" Merit asked.

"It's good," Ag said.

Merit laughed.

After they paid the check, they grabbed their gear from their vehicles and walked down South Congress to Estevez Tire and Auto Shop. Merit snapped pics with her Nikon from a few blocks out to get some perspective, then increased the number of shots as they walked closer to the remains of the fire. Ag took his own photos with his smartphone camera.

"Is that the car the body was found in?" Merit asked.

Ag flipped open the police report and looked at a diagram.

"Looks like it."

"What a mess," Merit said.

They got as close as they could on each side of the yellow tape surrounding the crime scene. When they were satisfied they had fully documented the scene, they walked over to the office and checked in with Manny.

"How's Tireman holding up?" Merit asked.

"He's not doing well. He's staying around the junk yard for the time being," Manny said. "He feels very guilty about SoCo, the homeless man. We knew him."

"He's going to have to face the music eventually," Merit said.

Later that day, Merit refreshed her memory by reading Val's memo on fraudulent inducement. She plugged the most promising cite into the LEXIS search engine and a catalogue of references appeared on-screen as Betty popped her head in the door. "How goes it?" Betty asked.

"I need some ammo for court that will let me get around the merger clause that makes the contract the entire agreement of the parties," Merit said.

"That is a problem," Betty said.

"I want to bring in evidence with regard to the verbal statements made by the leasing agent on behalf of Nixon. The parol evidence rule usually bars evidence outside the four corners of the document," Merit said as she scanned the various cases and cross-references.

"Bingo."

"Pay-dirt?" Betty asked.

"Yep, a Texas Supreme Court case, Italian Cowboy Partners vs. Prudential Insurance. The case allowed evidence outside of the document as proof of fraud."

"I'm your lucky charm," Betty said.

"Yes, you are," Merit said and made notes in an email for Val to copy the case and others referenced therein. "Next problem, I have to prove that Manny relied on the lies."

"How do you plan to do that?" Betty said.

"There are pros and cons to our position," Merit said. "This is going to be a tough fight," Merit said.

"Aren't they all, darlin'," Betty said and pointed to a stack of files on the corner of Merit's desk. "Please sign all that before you go. See you tomorrow."

"How many trees did you kill to create all that paperwork?" Merit said.

"I know. I'm scanning as much as I can, but sometimes there's no substitute for paper. Don't worry, we shred and recycle every scrap," Betty said.

Merit signed, as instructed, then returned to her computer and typed Boots King into a general search engine and found nothing. She went into her security subscription service and tried again. She found a landman named King with various a/k/a's in West Texas and the Panhandle, mostly Midland and Pampa. The report indicated that Boots had two arrests, one for arson and one for assault. He apparently was incarcerated at one point, but it didn't show which prison or how long.

"Nice guy," Merit said.

The trail grew cold, so Merit switched over to the American Association of Professional Landmen website. She found that a Boots King was kicked out of the AAPL and his license jerked for inappropriate practices about ten years back. No further details. Nothing showed up on the Texas APL website.

Merit picked up the phone and dialed a landman in Midland whom she'd known since law school. He was the husband of a classmate, and they had stayed friends.

"Hi Blake. This is Merit. How are you two doing?"

"Fine, Merit. Can't complain. How are you and that handsome son of yours?"

"We're up to the same no good as last time we spoke. Ace is still at school in Houston. I miss him," Merit said.

"I bet. What can I do for you?"

"I have a client that has crossed paths with a shady looking landman. I was hoping you could help me out with that."

"Sure. What's the name?"

"Boots King."

"Sounds vaguely familiar. Let me check the database," said Blake.

"Thanks."

Merit put away pens and post-its while Blake searched.

"Okay. Here's something. Looks like he was adding an overriding royalty interest to leases in an alias of his without disclosing to the lessor or lessee."

"I guess that's against the rules?"

"The alias is suspect, but it's a rule violation only if he didn't disclose the ORRI, and apparently he didn't. There were a few other warnings about completing his continuing education, but nothing further. AAPL jerked his credentials, but he can still work without creds. I'm surprised he hasn't changed his name again. Looks like he has a lot of aliases."

"Maybe he had to keep his name to receive the override payments," Merit said.

"Good point. I can check the online database for Midland County, but I'll probably need to go down to the clerk's office to see if he's still in the chain of title. If so, we can contact the producer and possibly get the address where they send his checks from their division order department."

"Put me on the clock and run it out for me when you have time. When you email the runsheet, please send a copy to Ag as well."

"Will do."

"Progress?" she asked the four walls.

6

The next morning, Merit entered her office building in a huff. She made her way down the hallway and into her office reception area, juggling her purse, briefcase, bag of files, coat, and umbrella like a circus clown.

"Good morning," Mai, the UT intern and part time receptionist said cheerily. She offered up two pink slips with messages written on them. Mai looked like an orchid with her pale skin and lavender lipstick. Merit read "Biology" upside down on Mai's book.

"Mornin'," Merit tucked the messages into the melee and kept moving between the sofa and guest chairs down the hall to her office.

"I sent the other calls to voicemail," Mai said.

"Thanks."

Merit blew past Val's open door with a grumbled greeting and went into her office without commenting on his ensemble for the day, which she seldom missed.

"Good morning. I think," Val said.

Merit dumped her baggage on her desk and plopped down in her chair.

"This is not going to be a great day."

29

Betty, hearing the fussy arrival, and observing a beseeching look from Val, brought in a cup of tea with milk for Merit and a cup of black coffee for herself. She gently closed the door and sat in one of the guest chairs. She balanced a steno pad on her lap and sipped her steaming Joe. Betty had been with Merit for over ten years and she knew that only two things upset her this much, her son, Ace, and men in general. Betty had opened Merit's first office with her after she'd left the big law firm to go out on her own. The two had been partners since then through a few tough years and eventual prosperity when big oil propped up the Texas economy after the Bush administration gave producers free reign again. Merit was a fierce competitor, and usually found the next step where her work was concerned but when it came to men, she went into chaos. Ever since her husband's death, she had lost her footing during personal crises. She reverted to some dark time where she was a small child without a clear path.

Merit slapped folders around the desk. She closed the desk drawer on her finger and yelped. "Ouch."

"Merit Lady Echo Bridges, slow down," Betty said. Betty used Merit's entire name when she wanted to get her attention. Lady and Echo were Merit's beloved maternal and paternal grandmothers, long deceased. After the admonishment, Betty sat quietly, and waited until Merit was ready to reveal the problem.

"Right, right," Merit said. She wiggled her fingers and toes and appeared to ground into her body. She took a sip of her tea and looked a little more stable.

Betty drank, waited patiently, and admired the photography on the walls. If Merit ever decided to leave the practice of law, she could make a fine living as a photographer. There were four black and white photos of Texas bridges and two in color of Austin bridges. The first color pic was of the South Congress Bridge over the Colorado with the bats caught in mid-air flying out from under it. The second was of the 360 Bridge over Lake Austin at sunset. Behind Merit's desk was an oil painting by a local artist of the railroad bridge over Lady Bird Lake.

The office suited Merit. She had re-decorated it right after her husband died. Betty had hoped it would give her a fresh start, a way to rise from the tragedy. Merit was not the type to brood for long, and Betty worried that she might have buried more than she had grieved. These outbursts from time to time told her she was right. Merit's emotions were like a balloon trapped under a board, they bulged out in the weakest spot whenever an opportunity presented itself. Fortunately, that wasn't often.

"Take a breath," Betty said.

Merit looked at Betty and her eyes focused.

"You're safe, the world is in order," Betty said.

"It's Ace. He hasn't been to his tutor, Mary, in over two weeks. She called me last night. I finally reached him this morning and he said the tutor wasn't helping him."

"I understand, love," Betty soothed.

"He's skipping classes again, and his sleep patterns are off so he stays up half the night and can't get to class in the morning."

"It's not Ace, it's the dyslexia. He's a good son. You know that. It's happened before. Did you talk to him?" Betty asked.

"He dodged my call this morning. I left him a message."

Betty knew Merit had struggled with the idea of sending Ace away for his last two years of high school, especially so soon after his father had died. There was no local school qualified to finish his reading remediation and help him with his disability. Now he was a hundred miles away in Houston, and it might as well have been a thousand since she couldn't reach him and protect him and maybe even give him a little scolding when needed. Like right now.

"Maybe he was in class. I bet he's fixin' to call you. He's probably just confused again," Betty said.

"That's why he has a tutor, to help him keep everything in line," Merit said.

"I know. I know. Take it easy," Betty said.

Ace had been diagnosed with dyslexia in fourth grade and had been in various Montessori schools and then Rawson Saunders School for Dyslexic Students through the middle years. He'd had tutors each year, gone to summer camp for dyslexics in Durango, Colorado, and participated in Reading for the Blind and Dyslexic. Merit had found every resource she could that would give him a leg up, but from time to time he still stumbled. Even at sixteen years old, he was just a kid.

The phone rang, and since no one in the outer office answered it, Betty picked it up on Merit's desk. "Law Office of Merit Bridges. May I help you?"

She listened.

"Fine. Here she is," Betty said.

Betty handed the receiver to Merit. "Speak of the Angel."

"Ace, what's going on?" Merit asked.

"Mom, I'm stuck. I can't do it. I'm confused and school is too hard, and I'm behind in all my classes," Ace said.

Merit had made sure that Ace received everything he needed to support his learning disability. He had a CD, which corresponded with each of his textbooks, an Apple laptop with an external CD drive, Dragon Software and the latest iPhone.

"I know Ace. It is hard. It's always been hard, but you can do it."

Merit could hear a fellow student's voice in the background and Ace's response.

"Get out of here."

A door slammed shut.

"What was that?" Merit asked.

"My asshole roommate."

"Hey. I thought you liked Eddie."

"It's nothin' Mom. I need to play the game."

"Ok, Sweet Pea. Settle down. I'll start. Who is that English actress who played Elizabeth Bennett?"

"Keira Knightley?"

"That's it, look at her. She was so dyslexic she could barely function. Now, she's one of the biggest stars in the world."

"Ok, I've got one. Whoopi Goldberg," Ace said.

"She's very funny. Smart too," Merit said. "My turn, Buckminster Fuller. Geodesic domes, synergy, very smart."

"Right. How about Einstein, genius."

"Let's see. Suzanne Somers. Dumb blonde smart."

"Charles Schwab, investment guru."

"Vincent Van Gogh!"

"Patrick Dempsey!"

"Eddie Izzard!!"

"Agatha Christie!!!"

"Mark Twain!!!"

They broke the tension with laughter.

"See, you're in very good company," Merit said. "Free thinkers every one, and all dyslexic."

"I'm sorry Mom. I should have called you sooner."

"Anytime. Call me anytime. You'll find your way Sweet Pea. Just don't give up."

"I miss Dad."

"Me too."

"Thanks, Mom. I feel better."

"I'll see you over parent's weekend. It's coming up soon."

"Okay. I guess I better call Mary," Ace said.

"Yes, and be sure to apologize for missing your other meetings."

"I will, and I'm sorry I wasted the money. I know you have to pay her anyway."

"Don't worry about that. Just get yourself back on track with her and get some sleep."

"Okay."

"And, don't forget to have some fun."

Ace let out a childish giggle.

"And eat your vegetables."

"Aw Mom."

7

M erit and Ag sat in her office at the end of a long day. She poured a second glass of Malbec for herself, and gestured with the wine bottle toward Ag's frosty 512 IPA.

"Want another?"

"No thanks. I'm driving," Ag said.

"I remember when my father would drive around town drinking a beer with a cooler in the back seat," Merit said.

"The good old days that weren't so safe," Ag said.

"Before MADD."

"Right."

"Have you gotten a lead on this Boots King character, or whatever name he's using at the moment?" Merit asked.

"His old driver's license is the only picture we could find of him."

"That's it? How old is he?"

Ag looked toward the ceiling as he did the math.

"About forty-five."

"Hard to imagine what he'd look like now. If Manny's description is correct, he's aged well," Merit said looking at a file on her desk.

"Right, I also checked further into his criminal record after I got your email. He doesn't seem to have gotten into any trouble after the assault arrest five years ago. At least nothing showed up in the data banks."

"Well, let's subpoena him for a deposition anyway. Maybe the sheriff's office will get lucky and serve him," Merit said.

"Doubtful," Ag said.

"Maybe he's gone straight," Merit said.

"You've heard the one about the scorpion hitching a ride across the pond on the back of the turtle?"

"Enlighten me," Merit said.

"The scorpion promised the turtle if he'd give him a ride he wouldn't sting him."

"And?"

"After he stung the turtle, the scorpion said, 'Well, you knew I was a scorpion,'" Ag said.

"Your point?"

"These guys don't change much."

"I got the report from Blake on the unauthorized overrides in Midland County. Looks like King sold them for a tidy profit to the very client he was working for when he snagged them," Merit said.

"Told you. A con man is always a con man," Ag said.

"Well, that leaves us with no way to trace him. He could be thousands of miles away right now."

"It might be best if he is," Ag said on his way out the door.

Merit logged into the Travis County property records online research site. She typed in Manuel Estevez and was rewarded with a list of the properties he owned in the county. She found the chain of title covering the South Congress property where the sign was located, and began to trace it forward from the date of purchase to present date. To do so she had to zigzag back and forth from

Grantor to Grantee, which included the sale to the new corporation Manny had formed with Tireman. In conjunction, she found the mortgage to the bank for the equipment purchase that had caused the problem with Nixon.

She searched further and found a few liens, which were subsequently released and a lis pendens notifying the public of a mechanic's lien suit that she already knew about and expected to settle soon. Most recent in the records was an affidavit filed by Nixon's attorneys notifying the public of the lease.

"Those bastards."

The affidavit was signed by Sonny Nixon and asserted the property description, the date of the lease, and the existence of the option clause contained therein. The lease copy was not attached.

"Wonder why," Merit said.

It was a clear cloud on Manny's title and anyone finding it would be on notice of the issues affecting the property. Merit noted that it was filed of record the day before Nixon filed the lawsuit against Manny. It was an underhanded tactic to give the appearance of transparency. Merit would need to point out the dates and order of events to make it clear to the judge that it was a ploy. If the lease had been on the up and up, they would have filed the affidavit immediately after the lease was signed and attached a copy of it. It was the usual procedure to put everyone on notice, especially the title company that closed on the loan for Manny. Waiting until the property was already conveyed allowed Nixon to sweep in after the fact. The filing strategy was obviously designed to hide the existence of the option clause in the lease in order to take the land for less than fair market value.

"Two can play that game," Merit said.

8

Boots pulled off the highway on his way back to San Antonio from Austin. His big black 4x4 sent a spray of gravel from the dually truck tires onto the cars behind him, chipping several windshields. Horns sounded as he scoped the property for signage, and seeing none, entered the I-35 Self Storage facility in Schertz, Texas.

"The owner in?"

The petite blonde clerk behind the counter answered, "He's upstairs in the residence. May I help you? We have a special on ten by twenties going until the end of the month."

"No, thanks." Boots gave her his second best smile as he pushed his shades on top of his head. "I need to see the owner or the manager."

"May I tell him what this is about?" the clerk responded while picking up the phone and pressing the intercom button.

"I want to put an advertising sign on the corner of your property over there. It's good money." Boots jerked his thumb over his shoulder.

"What's your name?" she smiled as she placed her hand over the mouthpiece.

"Boots King."

"Mr. Boots King here to see you Mr. Packing."

Boots waited in a small office beside the reception area. The sign said climate controlled, but it felt hot to him, even in winter. He browsed the various boxes, rolls of tape, locks and bubble paper as he waited for the manager.

When he was finally allowed into the inner office, Boots gave Mr. Packing his usual spiel about how much benefit the sign would bring to his business. Mr. Packing, an ex-military man with a buzz haircut listened politely. Boots went on about how other clients all around the area were getting in on the outdoor advertising craze. Mr. Packing didn't seem to be impressed, so Boots sweetened the pot.

"We can give you the first three months advertising for the storage facility on the sign. You'll be the first on the billboard. You'll be getting paid for the sign rental, and getting the free advertising," Boot said.

"What's the catch?" Mr. Packing asked.

"No catch," Boots said. "You'll have to go the full lease term on the sign, then after that you can cancel with a month's notice in writing. If you don't cancel, we just mail you another check for the next year."

"I could use some attention for the place. People drive by it so quickly, they don't fully register that we're here," Mr. Packing said.

"Outdoor advertising works," Boots said, pulling the lease pad from his pocket. "See, it's just a short lease between us. No big deal."

"Seems simple enough. How about four months free advertising on the sign," Mr. Packing said as he looked at the lease and took the pen from Boots. He did not turn the lease over to look at the boilerplate listed in small print on the back page. He did not read the option to purchase clause or the penalty for conveyance. He scanned the first page, read the start and end date and filled in the business address.

"You drive a hard bargain," Boots said. He marked out the three and put a four in the appropriate place. They both initialed the change.

"I'm still not sure," Mr. Packing said.

"Okay. I've had some nibbles from A-1 Storage down the road."

"No. I think it's a good idea, I just want to sleep on it."

"I really need to close this out today," Boots said.

"Right. I'm sure it will be fine. I really need the exposure," Mr. Packing said.

Boots pointed to a line below the admonition to consult an attorney. "Sign right there."

"It says to see a lawyer," Mr. Packing said.

"You don't need to pay a lawyer to read plain English. Unless you feel like you don't understand the lease," Boots said.

Mr. Packing paused and measured his ego.

"Right. Waste of money," Mr. Packing said.

Boots returned to his black dually and headed to San Antonio from Schertz. He turned up the stereo when Waylon Jennings and Merle Haggard started singing "Workin' Man Blues". He watched the billboards all along the drive. One sign touted a new brand of tequila, the next computer repair, the next burgers and fries. An empty one said, "DOES ADVERTISING WORK? JUST DID!"

About half of the signs had "NIXON" in red, white and blue letters along the bottom.

"Patriotic, that's me," Boots laughed out loud.

City governments had been limiting signage increasingly over the years. Now, with few opportunities left in the city, sign companies like Nixon had started leasing up along major highways in the counties. The plan was, as new cities pushed their boundaries outward and incorporated more land, the billboards would be grandfathered in. The signs would continue to exist in the new towns, and competitors could not come in because of new city ordinances. The signs that did exist would be more valuable and rent for more per ad. Scarcity driving prices, worked every time.

Boots phone rang showing Old Man Nixon's number.

"Just nailed another one for ya," Boots said.

"Great. I've got something else for you to do. Are you in Austin?"

"Can be in twenty minutes."

"I don't want to discuss it over the phone."

"Turning around now," Boots said.

He smiled all the way back to the Austin city limits sign.

9

Merit and Manny Estevez entered the offices of Rooter & Brown on the top floor of the Austin Bank Building. Merit gave her card to the receptionist behind the counter, and announced her appointment with Richard Rooter. Merit had brought Ag and Val along to take notes and for moral support since she was sure intimidation tactics by Rooter were on the agenda. Elevator music played quietly over the speaker system.

Val sat between Merit and Ag in a Queen Anne chair and examined the ornate arm. Manny stood in the corner and did a mini pace in a three-step circle.

"It's a copy," Val said and pointed at the joint in the wood.

Ag looked at the chair and grunted, "Hmph."

"That breakfront might be an original." Val pointed to a large antique looking piece in the corner filled with impressive legal books and awards given to the firm. Law Firm of the Year; Top Donor—Special Olympics; Sponsor—Salsa Festival; University of Texas School of Law—Moot Court Judge; just to name a few. The display was enclosed behind ornate doors with beveled glass. Metal skeleton keys were inserted in the locks. Large crimson tassels hung from each key and gently swayed when the heater blew from the register above.

Ag looked at the antique piece. "Why lock the doors if you leave the keys in?"

Val rolled his eyes. "Neanderthal."

Manny turned to Merit.

"I need to talk to you about Tireman," Manny said.

Ag and Val sobered at the reference to Manny's brother.

Merit pointed to a camera in the corner of the room and put her fingers against her lips.

Manny nodded and they sat in silence waiting for the receptionist to escort them into the inner sanctum.

Nixon Outdoor Advertising had long been represented by veteran attorney Richard Walker Rooter a/k/a Scooter, Roto Rooter, and Richy Rooter around Austin. He'd picked up the nicknames at Austin High School. The only one of those names spoken to his face was his childhood moniker, Scooter, and he didn't like that much either. He'd heard of the others, but dismissed them as jealous attempts to belittle him in light of his self-defined magnificent legal career, post Harvard Law School. His tactics were well known, and more than one junior attorney quaked at the sight of him in court. Merit had a run-in with Rooter when she had first arrived in Austin, and she was not looking forward to seeing him again today.

Rooter's saving grace was his love of his only son, who was relegated to a wheelchair due to a childhood disease of unpublicized origin. Though Merit had never seen the boy, she heard rumors that Rooter doted on his son and gave him everything. Rooter's anger at the injustice of his only son's handicap poured into the world in the form of legal vengeance at every opportunity. Merit knew winning was his only game, and he usually came out on top.

By contrast, while Rooter protected his son from the public eye, Old Man Nixon had started playing golf about four years ago and pushed his only son, Sonny, into the forefront of the company's business. Sonny Nixon was a confused soul who was the only heir. He had no real power, as Old Man Nixon could not let go and micromanaged him at every opportunity.

Rooter and Old Man Nixon were of the same mind when it came to business, every man for himself, unless you were on their team; then it was everything for their side. Sonny just tried to keep up.

Old Man Nixon had gone so far as to sue the doctor who had circumcised Sonny. Apparently, there had been a surgical mishap causing a slight deformity. Old Man Nixon's major argument in the suit was that a father wanted his son's penis to be like his. Sonny still suffered when cruel whispers and jokes perpetuated the public knowledge of his secret.

Sonny had attended Texas Tech in Lubbock, near their ancestral home of La Mesa, after Old Man Nixon had been unable to buy his son a spot at the University of Texas. Sonny was not stupid; he just lacked his father's edgy street smarts and Rooter's self-confidence. If he'd ever been allowed outside his father's shadow, he might have had a fine career as a photographer. After Old Man Nixon dismissed his dream as a hobby, Sonny gave it up in college.

Richard Rooter had drafted the original lease for Nixon Outdoor Advertising that landowners signed to allow billboards on their property. The original document was several pages long with many boilerplate clauses and capitalized warnings. Old Man Nixon and Rooter had conspired to tailor the document to a one page, fill-in the blank form, on paper with multiple copies that printed through the paper if pressed hard with a pen. The plan was to discourage landowners from consulting an attorney or reading the boilerplate. The strategy had worked, and in over ten years, less than ten percent contacted legal counsel when presented with the lease form. It seemed so innocuous and harmless. Fill in a year or so, get paid, end the lease at will. After the lease was over, Nixon went away. Except, they didn't.

Richard Rooter's receptionist escorted Merit and her entourage into the large conference room with a huge window overlooking Lady Bird Lake. She asked if they'd care for a beverage. All declined.

Rooter entered the room with an associate in tow behind Sonny Nixon. All three sported starched white button-down shirts with cuff links and red striped ties. The associate had on loafers, but the other two wore wingtips.

Merit was glad she'd worn her best suit, and was never disappointed in Val's attire. It often amazed her that he could look better in vintage than she did from Neiman Marcus. Ag and Manny were in jeans and starched shirts, white for Manny and maroon for Ag.

After introductions all around, Rooter took charge of the room.

"You called this meeting." Rooter looked at Merit.

"Yes, my client has asked me to explain to you the nature of the transfer of interests on the South Congress property in an attempt to settle the dispute without going to trial. He was surprised to receive your letter notifying him of your intention to exercise a right he didn't know he had given in the lease."

"Hmm," Rooter said.

"I assume you received the package I messengered over earlier," Merit said.

"Yes, we received it," Rooter said.

"Then you now are aware that the transfer of ownership on the land was to Mr. Estevez' brother, and not to a third party purchaser. The transaction was in the family and it was never their intent to sell it. Your option clause, if it is valid, should not apply to this situation," Merit said.

"The lease is valid, including the first right of refusal on any sale. And, as you are surely aware, a corporation is a third party under the law regardless of who owns it," Rooter said.

Merit made eye contact with Ag.

"Technically, yes," Merit said. "We can set aside for now whether the lease is unconscionable. The spirit of the clause allows your client a first right of refusal in the event of sale to an arm's length third party. That party would purchase the land at fair market value."

"Well, technically is correct. Mr. Nixon had the right to notification prior to the conveyance to make sure his rights were protected, and he was not given that opportunity," Rooter said.

Merit felt her armpits prickle which threw her into alert mode. "We've given you that information now. It was in the messengered package. It shows clearly that the brothers own the corporation that the land was conveyed into, and no other shareholders exist. In addition, we sent you a copy of the bank loan documentation, which was the entire reason for the transaction."

"That's all well and good," Rooter said, "but my client is going to enforce his rights under the contract, regardless."

"It sounds as if you planned this all along," Ag said.

Merit shot Ag a warning look.

Val looked at them both and backed into his seat as far as his velvet pants would take him. He lowered his eyes and scribbled on the legal pad before him.

"I'm sure we can work something out that everyone can be happy with," Merit said.

"Only if your client is ready to move off the land or give us a permanent sign under a new lease," Sonny said.

"That's not going to happen," Manny said.

Merit gave him a sturdy look. She hoped he would get the hint and let her do the talking.

"We'll see what the court says," Rooter said.

"I notice you filed the affidavit in the property records the day you filed the lawsuit," Merit said. "If the lease had been on the up and up, you'd have filed the affidavit immediately after the lease was signed, putting everyone on notice, especially the title company."

"It was our choice when and if to file it," Rooter said.

"Handy timing," Merit said.

"Could have, should have, would have," Rooter said.

Manny, who had been clinching and un-clinching his fist, stood up and said, "I knew men like you in Mexico. It's why I left to come here. You are thieves and liars. My brother was right."

"It's just business," Rooter said as he flashed power in his eyes for an instant before resuming his poker face.

Merit reached for Manny's arm, but he was already heading toward the door.

"Looks like this meeting is over, Scooter Rooter," Merit said.

10

Merit waited outside camera range on the weather set at KNEW-9, Austin's premiere television station. John Brewing was on camera showing the latest cold front, threatening thundersleet by nightfall, moving across the panhandle and settling into central Texas. Typical February weather. Cold today, mild tomorrow.

When she looked at John's boyish smile she had a visceral response. His hair looked tousled, but Merit knew it took a stylist thirty minutes to make it appear that natural. She winked at him and pointed to a chair off camera. She sat while she waited, checking her email.

The phone vibrated one short burst in her hand, indicating a text message. She tapped the screen and an emoticon appeared. It was an animated cow skull, decayed and bony wearing black sunglasses.

Merit chuckled at the unusual valentine.

The sunglasses disappeared and blood poured out of one eye. "I can see you, but you can't see me!" flashed on the screen then the bony head flared into flames. Her armpits prickled in alarm. She took in a sharp breath.

The first time her armpits had prickled, she was about thirteen years old. She was walking home from school and felt someone behind her. Instead of cutting through the park, which took her away from people, she ran into the street and got the attention of Mr. Johnson from down the block. She looked back to see three men lurking at the edge of the trees. It was never confirmed whether she had avoided danger or just been a frightened schoolgirl, but she knew. She knew and she never ignored the prickle again.

Later, her father told her that her paternal grandmother had the same physical warning sign. Grandma was not a saintly woman with information from angels up above, she was horseradish and sauerkraut all rolled into a short little spitfire who never backed down. Merit always thought of her Grandma when she was close to Betty or when she got the prickly danger warning.

She tried to re-start the emoticon, but it was gone. It wasn't close enough to Halloween for such a joke, and she didn't think it was funny. She touched the screen to try for more information, but no luck. She made a mental note to have Ag check it out.

John wrapped the weather report with the seven-day forecast. He took off his microphone and came over to her with a big lopsided grin. He tried to kiss her, but she turned her cheek toward him and gave him a friendly hug.

"Not here," she said. "Later you can show me your Doppler."

"I've got you on my radar already," he said, and looked down to a bulge in his trousers.

"I just have to run by the office on our way. Hold that thought."

"You hold it." He grinned.

Merit rolled off John and reached over the side of the bed and grabbed a pillow from the floor. She pulled it under her head with a huge sigh. "Nice one, big boy. Want something to drink?"

John pulled the covers over his muscular legs and grabbed for her. He just missed her as she left the bed. "Yeah, thanks."

"I hope you're not asleep," Merit called from the kitchen. "I've got plans for you."

"Get in here, then," John laughed.

She entered the bedroom naked, with two glasses of wine in her hands. She saw him drop something on the nightstand and roll over toward her.

"What are you up to?" Merit asked.

"No good. Come here," he said.

After another round of mattress gymnastics, Merit and John stood in her kitchen over a large skillet, drinking wine. Merit wore John's shirt and he was in his boxers with an apron hung over his bare chest and tied around his waist.

"This is my grandmother's Greek salad. She was Polish, but what the hell. I've put it in an omelet. It's Ace's favorite," Merit said.

"How do you put a salad in an omelet?" John asked.

"Well, not all of it. First I chop up a little bacon and while that browns in the skillet, I whip up three whole eggs and two egg whites, like this," Merit said whisking the eggs in a glass bowl.

"That's a lot of eggs."

"Well, are you hungry or not?"

"Guilty as charged, Counselor," John said.

"Next, I put all sorts of Greek herbs in the egg mix, and pour it over the bacon. Like so," Merit said.

"Mmm smells good."

Merit grabbed her Nikon off the top of the refrigerator where she had placed it out of harms way and snapped a picture of John with his messy hair and just satisfied smile.

"You're not going to show that to anyone are you?"

"Nope. Just for me. Now cook."

"Taskmaster," John said.

"Next, we sprinkle the egg mixture with cubes of feta cheese, like this, and pile the spinach high on top."

John put a mound of green leaves on top of the skillet mixture.

"I pour in the gooey stuff and work it around the edges as the spinach wilts and let it all get nice and mushy. When the egg starts to congeal, I pop the skillet under the broiler for a couple of minutes," Merit said opening the oven and sliding the skillet onto the top shelf.

John got a couple of plates out of the cabinet and set napkins and flatware on the island bar.

Merit removed the browned and bubbling omelet from the oven, cut it down the middle with a spatula, folded each half over and slid it onto the plates. The aroma of the crisped bacon was intoxicating. She topped each plate with a few slices of avocado. They sat and dug in.

"Food is always better after sex," John said.

"Mmm hmm," Merit said with her mouth full.

"What's new on your case? Was that the fire you went out for?"

"Can't say," Merit said.

"I know the Estevez brothers are your clients," John said.

"You know I won't talk about that. Anyway, you saw it all on KNEW," Merit laughed.

"Smart ass," John said and rubbed his napkin across her lips then kissed her.

11

Rooter nodded at Sonny Nixon and hit the intercom button on the credenza phone. "We're ready."

Boots King tapped once on the conference room door as he entered. He sat at the opposite end of the table from Rooter and Sonny. He didn't bother to remove his shades or offer his charming smile.

Sonny looked like a child sitting in an oversized chair with his anemic stature.

"It didn't go well with Estevez and his lawyer. There's going to be a fight," Sonny said.

"Expected as much," Boots said. He looked at Rooter when he spoke and turned his side to Sonny.

"I want you to lay off the new leasing for a while and focus only on the Estevez brothers. Keep an eye on the bitch lawyer, too. Hire some help if you need it," Rooter instructed.

"Yes," Sonny said, blowing the cedar fever out of his nose on a monogrammed hanky. "I'll clear it with Dad and the others."

"Others, what others?" Boots asked.

"Don't worry about that," Rooter said. "It's just a few other sign companies. They're keeping up with the case."

"I've got a few leases almost wrapped," Boots said.

"Okay, finish those up and then let's focus on this case," Rooter said.

"I'm on it," Boots responded as he scraped his chair across the wooden floor and stood. "Anything else?"

"Dad said to tell you to be invisible," Sonny said.

"Yes," Rooter said. "You cannot be found to testify under any circumstances. It's not enough for you to be silent. Old Man Nixon doesn't want you in the picture at all."

"No worries. I won't be seen. I prefer it," Boots said.

"Another thing. That investigator of hers is smart. Folks call him Ag. He's worked around town for years and is not to be underestimated. Merit either," Rooter said.

"Yeah, I've caught wind of him before. No problem," Boots said.

Boots drove around Austin thinking of his next move. He wasn't afraid of a lady lawyer and a private dick, but knew he had to be careful not to blow the job with Nixon. It paid well, and he had a lot of latitude, so long as he didn't get caught going outside the boundaries. Not many companies were willing to work with someone with a record and so many aliases. Nixon considered it an asset, as did Boots. His primary worry was the police. He had jumped bail a few years back and did not plan on surfacing again. He had always been able to move in the shadows, but this job was requiring his presence and he had to watch out for a cop named Chaplain and the rest of APD. Getting arrested was not in his game plan.

He needed more ammo for Rooter to use in court. It would also keep Old Man Nixon happy to know that he was making progress. Sonny was just a front for the company. He needed some dirt to make himself appear more valuable. Doing research was a skill he'd developed during his days as a landman in West Texas, and he had a lot of contacts to help when he threw Nixon's money around. He'd dug up some shady history on Tarantella Estevez through a private investigator in Mexico City, but couldn't find much on Manuel Estevez. Boots pondered his next move.

"Who were these other sign companies?" he wondered.

He didn't need any more bosses telling him how to do his job or tracking his movements. He liked it nice and cozy.

"Just pay the money and I'll keep the mischief going. Maybe have a little fun for myself."

It had been a while since he'd really sunk his teeth into something. He felt the tension build inside him just thinking about it. This was going to be a good run. He could feel it.

12

B oots checked the office for an attendant at Estevez' junkyard on Old Airport Boulevard. Seeing no one at the desk, he slipped between the long rows of cars in the salvage lot. He spotted a shaggy dog running after a boy about seven years old. The sun hit the windshield of an old pickup and shot a beam of light into Boots' eyes as the shadow of a second boy ran by calling out.

"Emmi, wait for me."

Even by Boots' estimation, Manny's kid was a cute little bastard running around his Daddy's junkyard, playing with his mutt, and vying for the attention of the customers. Searchers came from all over Austin seeking the perfect replacement hubcap, carburetor, or grill from the rows of parked junkers long ago abandoned by their former owners. A wrecked '77 Chevy provided the perfect hiding place for Emmi and his dog.

Boots watched Emmi and Miguel pop out of a trunk or window at an unsuspecting shopper and scare the bejesus out of them. He tired of their game and moved on down a row of crumpled metal.

Boots looked through his shades as he searched the rows for Tireman. Maybe he could have some fun carrying out Nixon's instructions to create some trouble. He slipped down one long row after another and heard men's voices in the back of the lot.

He sneaked toward the customers who were scavenging parts off an old Cadillac, but neither guy was Tireman. Boots crept away unseen.

As Boots moved down another long row, he was startled by a loud *pop*!

Boots jumped and went for his pocket as a firecracker went off behind him. He had never become accustomed to any sound that was akin to gunfire. It was distracting and made him nervous. Emmi was popping singles with a sparkler on a yellow VW with the fenders missing. Boots cursed under his breath and jumped behind a rusted out eighteen-wheeler. He lit a cigarette and puffed while he watched Emmi, kept an eye on the mutt, and looked for Tireman.

Miguel held up a lighter for Emmi to see. A customer worked his way down the aisle and Boots saw him hide the lighter in his pocket. The junkyard had a huge fence around it and the boys roamed free in the chain-linked perimeter as if at an amusement park. They climbed, jumped, and flew.

"I'm Batman," Miguel said. "Pow, bam!"

"I'm Superman," Emmi said swirling a towel around his arms like a cape and jumping off a car. Emmi landed right in front of Boots.

Too late for Boots to hide, Emmi had spotted him. The last thing Boots needed was for someone to be able to identify him as he appeared now. As far as he knew, there were no current photos of him floating around.

Miguel ran toward the office at the sound of his mother's voice.

Emmi kept his distance from Boots and held onto the dog's collar as he growled and pulled.

Boots readied the point of his boot in case the mutt broke free.

"Don't worry, he won't bite," Emmi told Boots, releasing the dog and picking up a sheet of Black Cat Firecrackers from the hood of the car.

"What kind of mutt is that?"

"His name is Taco. He's mixed meat," Emmi giggled.

"Where's Tireman?"

"He's not here."

"Is he really not here, or are you supposed to tell people that?"

Emmi's eyes jumped around as his mind searched for the right answer. "Maybe someone is in the office."

"Is that right?"

"I dunno." Emmi lit another single. Pop! Boots was mesmerized watching the sparkler. Taco yelped and shot off down an aisle of refurbished tires.

Emmi laughed when Boots jumped, and popped a few more. He placed one on the shock absorber of the VW and put the sparkler to it. This time, no pop. The firecracker smoldered but didn't catch fire.

Emmi lit it again, then stepped back and waited for it to blow. Nothing happened. The sparkler went out and Emmi threw the burnt wire into the Chevy. He stood for a while looking at the firecracker. It began to emit a tiny curl of smoke. He waited and looked up at Boots with a question mark in his eyes.

Boots took a long drag on his cigarette and let out three interlocking smoke rings. Emmi watched the rings dissipate overhead. He looked down at the firecracker, now emitting a small tornado of gray smoke.

Boots took another drag on his cigarette until the burning ember glowed red and gestured toward the firecracker. He raised his cigarette to his lips and exaggerated a puff.

Emmi laughed, picked up the firecracker, and put it to his lips like Boots' cigarette. He pulled a long train of air through the cylinder. Nothing happened. He puffed harder. The cracker ignited and exploded. His right eye turned dark and then red as he screamed and fell against the VW. His eyes went shocky. The skin on his right hand was black. He slumped down the side of the VW, hit his head on the rocky ground, and passed out.

Boots heard heavy footsteps coming toward them. Tireman and Taco came running around the end of the row.

"Emmi, Emmi!"

Boots retreated down a row of cars, looked back over his shoulder unseen by Tireman, and mumbled under his breath, "That'll teach you to burn down private property, wetback. Go back to Mexico where you belong."

13

Merit escorted Tireman through the door of the Travis County Courthouse. Limestone pillars supported the rock and metal giant lined with pictures of Texas heroes. Sam Houston and Stephen F. Austin were framed and hung, as if guarding the east wing.

Merit and Tireman both cleared the metal detector. Merit snagged her briefcase off the conveyor belt and they walked down the stone corridor toward the elevator.

"How is Emmi?" Merit asked.

"He still in hospital. Manny wife is staying with him."

"Sorry we have to do this today, but there is so much attention on your family now. When APD found SoCo's body in the car, the spotlight on you increased. Ag thinks they might pick you up any minute."

"I still don't know how they thought it was me," Tireman said.

"I don't either, but there is a warrant out for your arrest. Nixon may have had something to do with that. You can't hide at the junkyard forever," Merit said.

"I know, let's get over with it."

"Okay. Remember, let me do the talking," Merit said as she pushed the up button to call the elevator.

"Sí," said Tireman.

"They are going to take you into custody after the meeting just like we discussed. I'll be at the hearing later and will get you out on bail if I can. Remember, they have no hard proof, so don't talk to anyone. Ag thinks it's all circumstantial."

Tireman looked frightened as if he would run if the elevator didn't appear soon.

A small group of reporters wandered into Courtroom Number Three, obsessed with the latest scandal involving the Austin City Council.

"They're not concerned with us. No one knows we're here. We're going upstairs to the prosecutor's office," Merit said.

At that moment, John Brewing came around the corner and caught site of Merit and Tireman.

Merit gave him a look that said "Not now," and entered the elevator.

"What's he doing here?" she said to Tireman without really expecting a response.

After turning Tireman over to the prosecutor, and the setting of a bail hearing for that afternoon, Merit went downstairs, exited the elevator on the first floor of the Courthouse, and ran straight into the KNEW-9 microphone of John Brewing. His cameraman was filming, and he was the only reporter on scene.

"Ms. Bridges. I understand that your client, Tarantella Estevez, has turned himself in for the arson and involuntary manslaughter on South Congress. Did he do it?"

Merit looked into the camera and fought to compose herself. "You know I can't answer that. My client will cooperate fully with the authorities to clear up any misunderstandings."

"Are you saying he didn't burn the sign?"

"No further comment."

"Is he going to get bail? Does he have a defense?"

"No comment."

Merit walked toward the exit.

John made a slashing motion across his throat at the camera, handed off the microphone to the cameraman, and followed Merit. "Come on Merit, give me a break."

She swirled around and faced him. "You bastard."

"I'm sorry."

"I thought I could trust you. That you cared for me."

"You can. I do care for you. You know I've wanted to go from the weather desk to news, and I had to get the scoop when your client burned the sign. It's the break I've been waiting for. I don't know what else to say." John avoided eye contact.

"You have no idea whether he burned the sign or not, and if you broadcast otherwise, I'll sue you," Merit said.

"Don't be that way. What did you expect?" John asked.

Merit gave him a cold stare. "I expected some loyalty from the man I've been fucking for three months."

"Give me a break. It was for grins. We had a good time."

"Well, we won't anymore," she said.

Right, but with some level of loyalty. Was this the way it was always going to be with every man she trusted, she thought.

"Come on Merit. You'd do the same," John said.

"No, I wouldn't. How'd you know I was here anyway? This was a secret meeting."

John moved away down the hall.

Another betrayal.

14

Merit and Betty sat in the break room at the firm drinking big ass iced teas and eating Betty's homemade lemon squares with chocolate drizzle.

"What did you expect of a twenty-eight-year-old social climber?"

"I knew it wasn't permanent, but I thought we were friends."

"I know, sometimes you can't win for losing," Betty said.

"I wasn't expecting a marriage proposal, but I thought we had a mutual respect of sorts. What a bastard."

"You set up the betrayal before it ever happens," Betty said. "Choose a trustworthy man to begin with and you'll get trust and loyalty."

"I don't see many good men around these days," Merit said.

"I know." Betty patted Merit on the arm. "My husband Randy, God rest his soul, might have been the last good one alive."

Merit met her eyes and they both grinned then laughed.

"Seriously, sugar, there are lots of good men out there. Mature men with big hearts."

"You mean like my dead husband?" Merit asked.

"Not all men leave. Tony was sick. He wasn't thinking straight. You know that," Betty said.

"I know, but it still doesn't mean John wasn't a jerk. And Tony did abandon Ace and me. Sometimes I feel so alone," Merit said.

Betty patted her hand.

"You're right. John's got more nerve than Carter's got liver pills. As for Tony, I won't speak against the dead. I'm sure he did what he thought he had to do."

"Yeah, if he thought at all," Merit said.

Betty patted her hand harder.

"I know. I know," Betty said. "Men are hard to understand sometimes. When I was a kid we were so poor that Daddy used to pay us kids ten cents to skip supper. After we'd fallen asleep, he'd sneak into our bedroom and steal back the coins. In the morning we'd wake up and start hollering that our money was missing, so he'd whip us for losing it and make us go without breakfast."

Merit laughed.

"See, it could be worse. You want the last lemon square?" Betty asked.

"Yeah, I can't have any wine until after court. Sugar will have to do for now. I still don't know how John found out I was going to the DA's office with Tireman," Merit said.

"I could shoot him deader than road kill armadillo," Betty said.

"Would you do that for me?" Merit laughed.

"Was attorney client privilege breached?" Betty asked.

"I was thinking about that. I don't think so. There are only old files and case research on my desk at home, all my client files are here. Maybe he heard me talking on the phone, but I can't imagine when."

"What's the latest with the lawsuit?"

"Looks like we're headed for a huge expensive fight."

"You need some rest before you take on the cases next week."

"Yeah. I could use some sleep."

"Just take a short break and spend your time on your son. That will keep your mind off bad men. How's Ace doing?"

"He's beautiful," Merit smiled. "It takes a village, but he's back on track."

Betty smiled.

"For now," Merit said.

15

ater that afternoon, Tireman was arraigned. Merit arrived at the courthouse early to avoid the press, but they were already there. The courtroom was filled with reporters now that the word was out that the man who had killed SoCo was in custody. The arraignment was public, and Merit therefore could not keep the proceeding quiet as she had the morning meeting with the DA. Four local TV news stations, plus the *Austin American-Statesman* and *Austin Business Journal* had representatives with microphones, cameras, recorders, and various other media circus-creating elements.

The judge took the bench looking like a crow with his black robe and pointed nose.

"The People versus Tarantella Estevez," the court clerk called.

Merit handled the not-guilty plea, expecting they would change it later if a plea agreement was worked out. For now, she needed some leverage to keep Tireman out of jail, and from what she could see the prosecutor had no hard evidence against him. She'd brought in Kim Wan Thibodeaux to help out with the criminal proceeding because he was well versed in criminal law and a good litigator in general.

Kim Wan was a mulatto with a Chinese mother and a Black Cajun father. He had dermatosis papulosa nigra, which caused an appearance of freckles on his face like Morgan Freeman. Rather than making him look ugly, he appeared strangely exotic. He'd graduated from Tulane in Louisiana, but had also passed the Texas bar exam and become licensed in the Lone Star State. He had settled in Austin when his spouse started graduate school. His wife did some type of research at the University of Texas that no one talked about. Probably big grants involved. Merit planned for Kim Wan to weigh in heavily on the criminal case as Tireman became more comfortable with him.

The bailiff brought Tireman to the defense table in handcuffs. The prosecutor stepped up, after a nod from the bench, and addressed the judge.

"Your honor. We request no bail in this case."

"No bail?" Merit asked. "Your honor, Mr. Estevez is part owner of a business on South Congress, and his family and brother are here. There is no reason not to set a reasonable bail or even release him on a personal bond."

"Your honor, there is a question about the green card status of this defendant. Also he has known ties to a gang in Mexico called Banda de Mexicanos. If he returns to Mexico, we will not be able to find him and therefore bring him to justice," the prosecutor said.

Tireman turned around to look at Manny sitting in the first row behind him. They exchanged a knowing look not lost on Merit.

"Your honor, this is not a violent crime, and we presented Mr. Estevez' papers to the prosecutor when he turned himself in. There is no hard evidence against him. It is unconscionable that he is here at all," Merit said.

Rooter, seated in the rear of the courtroom, exchanged glances with the prosecutor.

"We do have evidence, your honor, which will be given at trial. We need to make sure Mr. Estevez shows up in order to present," said the prosecutor.

"May I have a moment to confer with co-counsel?" Merit asked.

"One minute," the judge said.

Merit turned to Kim Wan and whispered. "Do we have any other course of action?"

"This is usually all we have to do. It's up to the judge if he wants to grant bail," Kim Wan said.

Merit turned back to the judge.

"Mr. Estevez' brother has become an American citizen and my client is in the process of qualifying for citizenship, Your Honor," Merit said.

"That's not enough, Ms. Bridges. Bring in the green card and we'll talk again. For now, bail is denied. The defendant is remanded. Dismissed," said the judge.

"This is outrageous," Merit said

Kim Wan appeared stunned.

Tireman looked at Merit with questioning eyes. After the Judge left the bench, Manny patted Tireman on the shoulder from behind the railing.

"Hang in there Hermano," Manny said.

"I can take care of myself. Just get me out of here," Tireman said.

"We'll get to the bottom of the green card issue and continue to seek bail. Try to stay calm," Merit said.

"Okay," Tireman said, as he let out a deep breath.

Outside the courtroom, cameras were set up and a podium was arranged for a joint press conference with the City of Austin, Sonny Nixon, and Rooter.

The mayor was speaking when Merit exited the building.

Merit walked by without a comment. *Apparently Sonny and Rooter have been working on their image with the city*, Merit thought.

"The signs around town will be upgraded with metal poles and new framing. We are working with Nixon Outdoor Advertising and the other major sign companies to beautify the city, while still honoring the property rights of these companies and landowners," the mayor said.

Next, Sonny stepped up to the microphone. "It's unfortunate that vigilantes have taken matters into their own hands, but we will continue to work with the City to improve relations for all involved," Sonny said.

Merit fumed inside. "What a crock." Tireman was about as politically active as a stoner.

Rooter and Sonny left the press conference and walked back to Rooter's office. Boots waited in the shadows, watching until they'd cleared the crowd, then joined them.

"Nice spin, making it look as though environmentalists burned the sign," said Boots.

"No need to call attention to the lease issue," Sonny said.

"The company donation to the mayor's last campaign didn't hurt either," Rooter said.

"Nice move," Boots said.

"All very legitimate. I knew it would work," Rooter said. The City will make you do some cosmetic work on the older billboards, and we'll be grandfathered on all the existing signs," said Rooter.

"Big business," Sonny said.

"Yeah, they'll never get us out of here now, and Estevez looks like a maniac," Rooter said.

Boots chuckled. "An illegal wetback maniac with a can of gasoline," he said.

16

Merit frowned up at Ag. He stood on a ladder installing a camera over the front door of the office. "I don't know that all this is necessary. Isn't it a bit much?"

Ag looked down at her and jerked his head toward Betty's office. "It's her idea, and she has the checkbook, but I think she's right."

"We have security in the building already," Merit said.

"Sure, a flimsy lock, a sleepy guard, and one security camera per floor," Ag said.

"We don't even know if the firecracker incident with Emmi was related to the case," Merit said.

"What about the burning skeleton and the phone hang-ups?"

"We don't know who that was either," Merit said.

"Remember Susan Browning?"

Merit frowned.

Susan Browning was a family law practitioner in Austin in the late eighties. She had been representing the wife in a messy divorce when the husband went off the deep end. He shot her while she was working late in her office one night after he'd lost at a hearing. Browning didn't make it and Austin lawyers never forgot.

Merit looked at Betty. "Is all this your doing?"

"You better believe it. Your client list has enough dangerous scenarios to warrant protection from any number of them," Betty said.

"So you think adding cameras will protect me?" Merit asked.

"Yes, and you need to get a gun. Ag will take you," Betty said.

"A gun! Why would I get a gun? You know how I feel about handguns," Merit said.

"Everyone in the DA's office is licensed to carry. What do you think makes you safer than them?" Betty asked.

Ag looked down from the ladder at Val who was handing him tools and camera parts.

"Who's going to win this one?" Ag asked.

"I'll bet my paycheck on Betty," Val said.

Betty smoothed the nape of her neck, patted her stiff gray dome, and put her hands on her hips.

Merit knew that move. It was going to be a standoff.

"This is Texas, we have handguns and the death penalty, and you're not going to change that," Betty said.

Ag dragged Merit into McBride's Guns on Lamar Boulevard. The place was busy with shooting enthusiasts looking at everything from antique Winchesters to modern day hunting rifles. One wall housed fishing equipment, and the center aisles displayed all manner of holsters, security devices, and accessories. A couple of what appeared to be grandparents looked at a Daisy Red Rider BB gun.

Ag held up his hand to signal a salesman and pointed toward a glass case filled with handguns. Merit approached the display with mixed emotions. This seemed a huge line to cross in her mind. Could she really shoot someone? Maybe she could just point it at them and tell them to leave her alone. Hopefully.

There was a news article almost every day about an accident with a handgun. There was a story just last week about a professor in Idaho who had shot himself in the foot on campus. He'd been carrying his pistol loose in his pocket. There was a big brew going about whether concealed carry should be allowed on college campuses. Several states, including Texas, had recently modified their laws. Merit wondered if she could walk through the University of Texas campus and tell which students had guns and which ones did not. After Whitman, the tower sniper in 1966, there were probably plenty of opinions about that. Of course, Whitman didn't try to hide a gun in his pocket; he had a full sized rifle in a case.

"Merit, meet Max. Best gun salesman since the wild west," Ag said.

Max had a weathered face and scarred hands as if he'd been working barbed wire fences his whole life.

"Hi Merit. Don't listen to him," Max said. "What can I show ya'?"

"Pick one," Ag said.

Merit looked at the rows and rows of pistols in glass cases. She wondered if this was where Tony had bought his gun.

Max laid out a pad on the glass top and started to set out guns of various sizes and metals.

"I don't have any idea what to buy," Merit said.

"Just put your hands on a few. Make sure it will fit in your purse or briefcase. It won't do you any good in a drawer," Ag said.

"You sound like Betty," Merit said.

Merit uneasily picked up a Glock Seventeen and the weight of it made her immediately put it back down.

"Have you ever shot a pistol?" Max asked.

"My dad taught me how to use a deer rifle when I was about twelve, not much since high school," Merit said.

She picked up an elegant looking piece with a carved wooden butt and blue metal barrel.

"This looks like jewelry," she said.

"That's a Browning nine millimeter. It fits you," Max said.

"It feels so heavy," Merit said.

"Just take your time and see what seems right," Ag said.

"Maybe you'd like to see something a little smaller," Max said. He put the nine-millimeter guns to the side and laid out two smaller guns, both black.

Ag picked up one and handed it to Merit. "This is a Ruger .380."

"That feels a bit more manageable," Merit said.

Max picked up the other gun, "This is a Keltec .380. A little more economical pricewise than the Ruger, but still very accurate."

Merit put the Keltec in her left hand with the Ruger in her right, and held the two guns up in front of her. She saw herself in the mirror behind the counter and put both down on the pad. Merit looked as if she would bolt for the exit. She was terrified to take the step into gun ownership. It seemed to make some kind of social statement about her beliefs, even if private to her and close friends. She wasn't sure if the feeling of security outweighed the thought of owning a handgun.

"Just look at this as if you're buying a blender. Get the best quality that feels right for you and then learn how to use it later," Ag said.

"Okay, okay. I'll take this one." Merit settled on the Ruger .380.

"Let me get a new one from the back. Meanwhile, there's some paperwork you'll need to fill out," Max said.

"She'll need an extra clip and two boxes of ammo; regular cartridges for practice and hollow points for keeping in the pistol. Does it come with a trigger lock?" Ag said.

"Yes, and you can pick out a case on aisle three, free with purchase," Max said.

"Do I need all that?" Merit asked.

"Yes, and you'll need some ear protection to use during target practice and in your class," Ag said.

Merit read the tag on a black alligator handbag with a false bottom. It had a slot inside where she could slide her hand and hold the gun that would be stored out of sight. The tag showed a woman shooting through the purse at a mugger in a ski mask.

"Who would buy this?" Merit asked.

"You'd be surprised," Ag said. He laughed to himself, garnering a puzzled look from Merit.

Merit filled out a form and gave it to Max with her driver's license and credit card.

"What else do you need, and when may I pick up the gun?" Merit asked.

"You can take it with you. There's no waiting period to buy a firearm in Texas, and there's no state firearms registry for handguns or long arms. Just need your ID. We carry a Federal Firearms License, FFL for short," Max said.

"So it's that easy," Merit said.

"Yep," Max said.

While Max processed the paperwork, Ag showed Merit a row of hearing protection gear displaying everything from a rugged black headset to child-sized pink earmuffs. Merit selected a red folding ear protector set that came in a round zipper case. She also picked out an inconspicuous khaki zipper bag for the gun.

"A lot of people are getting into eye protection. It's up to you," Ag said.

"Do you use it?"

"Not usually," Ag said.

"Then I'll skip it for now," Merit said.

They carried all their loot to the front of the store and joined Max at the checkout area.

"Will that be all?" Max asked.

"Just a minute," Merit said.

She ran to the back of the store and grabbed a book about gun ownership off the shelf.

"When in doubt, read a book about it."

Max added the book to the tally and gave Merit a receipt to sign.

"Thanks for your business," Max said as he handed Merit her ID and card. He gave Ag the heavy shopping bag with handles. It was plain brown paper, no logo or advertisement on the outside.

"Thanks," Merit said.

"Gig 'em," Ag said to Max with his thumb up.

Max returned the salute.

"I should have known," Merit said.

Ag opened the passenger door of his pickup truck for Merit and put the bag on the floorboard of the back seat of the crew cab.

Merit sat lost in thought as Ag started the engine.

"Want some lunch?" Ag asked.

"Sure."

"How about Maria's Taco Xpress? It's on the way."

"Okay." Merit wasn't really hungry.

Ag made his way down South Lamar and parked in front of a building that looked like an architectural quilt. A statue of Maria with raised hands like Evita topped the building. "I'm starving," Ag said.

After they were settled into a booth and had ordered iced teas and enchiladas, Merit lapsed into silence as an Alejandro Escovedo song competed with the noisy conversations around them. Apparently, Alejandro liked it better when she walked away.

"What's up? Did I force you into something you didn't want to do?" Ag asked.

"Of course not. I just have mixed feelings about owning a handgun," Merit said.

"You registered the gun, and you're taking a concealed handgun licensing class, you've followed the law to the letter, and you don't have to shoot anyone if you aren't threatened."

"I know. I just wonder," Merit said.

"Wonder what?" Ag asked.

The food arrived and Merit picked around her plate while Ag forked chunks of hot cheesy tortilla rolls into his mouth.

"Well, are you going to tell me?" Ag asked.

"This salsa has a kick, huh?"

"Don't change the subject."

"I just wonder if my husband would have shot himself if a gun had been harder to obtain?"

Ag put down his fork and looked at her with caring eyes.

"He was so sick and unhappy, he would probably have found another way, but maybe not," she said.

"I'm so sorry."

"We hoped he would get better. The drugs made him depressed."

"Merit, I didn't think. I never met him, so I just didn't think of it. I only want to make you safe. I'm sorry," Ag said.

"It's okay. I just haven't been around a gun since the day I found him in the backyard. I didn't realize it would affect me so strongly. His death was such a shock."

Ag moved around to her side of the booth to sit beside her. He put his arm around her shoulders and they watched the enchiladas grow cold together.

"I had no idea he was thinking of taking his life. He had on such a brave face."

"Is something wrong with the enchiladas?" the waiter asked.

"No. We'll have a couple of Ambhar margaritas, rocks, with salt," Ag said.

Merit arrived home that night after a wasted day at the office. She looked out the French doors at the spot where Tony had shot himself. The grief hung out in her subconscious ready to drift up if given the slightest opportunity.

Betty had been especially gentle to her in the office that afternoon, and had deflected as much client contact as possible. It was partly because of Merit's raw feelings, and partly because of the tequila she had consumed with Ag. Merit assumed Ag had briefed Betty on the gun shopping expedition and lunch conversation. Betty had been her rock after Tony died. Merit didn't know what she would have done without her. Ace, too. Betty stepped in as caring mother and grandmother to both of them, cooking, organizing, keeping them busy and staying involved in Ace's schooling after the initial shock had passed. She was still caring for them, even now, three years later.

Merit looked inside the bag from McBride's sitting on the kitchen table. Pepper jumped up in a chair and poked her nose inside the brown paper.

"Not for you, PepperDog," Merit said.

She took the unpacked bag to the spare bedroom and put it on a high shelf in the closet. She shut the door, then re-opened it and pulled out the book she'd bought. Her hand brushed the gun case.

"Please God, may I never need to use it."

17

Boots, Sonny Nixon, and Rooter sat in Rooter's conference room waiting for Old Man Nixon. Boots, shades on, put his feet up on a chair and crossed them at the ankle.

"We said scare, not harm. What's wrong with you?" Rooter asked.

"Kid was playing with firecrackers. He smoked it. I was just there. I didn't hold him down and make him do it," Boots said.

"Yeah, right," Rooter said.

"Hmm," Sonny said.

"Did anyone see you?" Rooter asked.

"Of course not," Boots said.

Old Man Nixon entered the room like a freight train and sat next to his son. He was the epitome of a Texas fat cat complete with chunky Rolex, monogrammed starched shirt, and a gut that had seen too many T-bone steaks. He put his hand on Sonny's bony shoulder and gave a little squeeze.

"Sonny's been doing a fine job with this so far," Old Man Nixon patronized. "We just need to make sure we're on the same page."

Sonny blew his nose.

"The Estevez brothers cannot win this case. Too much is at stake," said Old Man Nixon.

Rooter nodded.

Sonny wheezed and coughed.

Old Man Nixon cringed at his son and looked down the table at Boots.

Boots pushed his shades up and made eye contact with Old Man Nixon.

Rooter saw it and almost interjected, but a finger from Old Man Nixon held him back.

Boots and Nixon held the gaze for a long time, each measuring the other man. Old Man Nixon gave a slight nod, which Boots acknowledged with his eyes. An agreement was made. No limits.

"Just watch it," said Rooter.

After Boots left, four men in suits entered the room. The two attorneys wore regular ties; their clients wore bolos. Sonny moved to the end of the table. Rooter welcomed the powerhouse men and their high priced lawyers with handshakes all around. They wore the bolos when they were in Texas in order to fit in. They looked like Yankee Doodle Dandies.

"How are y'all," Bolo One mocked a Texas drawl.

"Fine, fine," said Rooter.

All attention was on Old Man Nixon, the kingpin. Sonny was ignored. He sulked at the end of the table.

The bolos were owners of outdoor advertising firms with holdings in the Northwest and on the East Coast. They were out of the jurisdiction of the Texas case, but if Nixon should lose in Texas, the precedent could, and probably would, be applied in other jurisdictions. It was crucial that this challenge to their business model be crushed while it was small and off the radar of the American press and National Congress. The lobbyists they hired in D.C. had donated enough of their money to keep things quiet, so long as a big case didn't cast any aspersions on public voting records.

"Where are we in the lawsuit?" Old Man Nixon asked. "Rooter, bring the group up to speed."

"I've got motions filed that should slow down Merit Bridges for a while. The Estevez brothers rely on her completely. If we can shake her up, they'll fold," Rooter said.

"We're on that," Old Man Nixon said.

"How's that?" Bolo Two asked.

"Just leave it to me for now," Old Man Nixon said.

"We have one large hurdle to overcome," Rooter said.

"What's that?" Bolo One asked.

"There's a case pending before the Texas Supreme Court that's not exactly on point but could be used to sway the judge if we wind up in court," Rooter said.

"What about the mediation?" one of the bolos asked.

"It's coming up fast. We should set the date tomorrow. We've proposed Judge Jones as mediator. We think Merit will accept. Jones has been around a long time and has a reputation for being clean," Rooter said.

"And, is he clean?" Bolo Two asked.

"We're working on it," Old Man Nixon said. "Remember, it's not arbitration, so it's not binding."

"Why not?" Bolo One asked.

"Because we don't want binding arbitration clauses in our leases. It cuts both ways. If the arbitrator finds for the landowner, we all are bound by that decision. Much better to feel them out in mediation and go to court if we have to," Rooter said.

"Good plan," Old Man Nixon said.

"It also gives us another opportunity to run up their legal fees. Choke them in paperwork and billable hours," Rooter said.

"What about this Boots King character? Can he be trusted to hold up under pressure? We don't need a witness," Bolo One said.

"He's got too much to lose to get caught. If anything, we worry about him skipping town if things get too hot," said Rooter.

"Good, then we won't have to pay him," Bolo Two laughed.

"I'll handle him," said Old Man Nixon. "We understand each other."

Sonny shrank further into the seat.

Boots King arrived at Merit's downtown office early one morning while it was dark and before anyone had started the workday. He parked on Lavaca, a few blocks away, to avoid the parking garage cameras. He'd been here before, doing recon, but today had a plan to check her files and maybe get into her safe if she had one. He pulled his Stetson low over his head and, with his back to the side door camera shielding his face, picked the lock to the building. As he entered, he jumped under the camera, back against the wall, and tipped his hat sideways before going down the hall to the stairwell.

He approached Merit's office, peeking out from under his Stetson to scan the floor for cameras and security guards. He didn't see anything, so he went to the double glass doors marked "Law Office of Merit Bridges." He looked inside and ducked just as the security camera swept by the front door in its rotation. He turned his body flat against the wall next to the glass and looked into the office from the side. After the camera had swept the door again, he turned his body against the opposite wall and looked into the office from the other side of the door.

"That camera wasn't here before."

He was sure he hadn't been seen, but he could find no way to enter the office without exposing himself to the camera while picking the lock. He looked down the hall seeking another entrance. There were many doors opening onto the hallway from various offices. He took a guess at a door based on the apparent size of the law office and began to work the lock. It was not yielding. Felt like a dead bolt was holding on the inside. As he tried again, he heard the elevator ding and the rustling of fabric with movement. He froze, and then backed up very slowly into the shadows at the end of the hallway.

Betty walked toward the door humming an old Jerry Jeff Walker standard that Boots recognized, but couldn't name.

Damn, she's an early bird, Boots thought.

If he could catch her before she got to the glass door, and the camera, he could get behind her and force her to unlock the door. The camera could catch his face, unless he placed the hat just so and he couldn't be sure she wouldn't knock it off if she resisted. Maybe he could get the recording once he got into the office and destroy it, but what if the recorder was off site or in the security office downstairs? If he was careful, she couldn't identify him, but then his face might be linked to the break in and mugging.

Betty stopped at the door, keys in hand. She froze for a second. She barely let out her breath, dropped the keys, and reached into her purse, but did not remove anything. Instead, she pointed the end of her handbag at the shadow with her hand inside.

"I know you're down there," she said. "I'm packin', and I'll be glad enough to shoot your ass."

Tough old bird, Boots thought. *She'll probably shoot me right through that purse.*

"Show yourself," Betty said.

She could see the outline of a hat and the pointed toe of a boot at the edge of the light.

Boots stayed in the shadows and assessed his next move. He didn't think she could see him well enough to hit him as long as he stayed in the dark.

Betty backed slowly down the hall with the handbag out before her until she got to the elevator and pushed the button inside.

Still in his hiding place, Boots debated whether to take a quick peek using the keys she'd dropped or take off down the stairs. Flight won out and he left the building the way he'd entered, with his hat pulled low.

"Damn, double damn," Boots said.

18

Merit, Ag, and Val entered the Texas Rose in East Austin at noon. A large yellow blossom was painted over the outline of Texas on the front of the hostess stand. Behind the stand was a bikini clad blonde with a similar yellow rose tattooed on her left breast. The stem and leaves disappeared into the bikini top exciting the imagination of unseen body art. The three looked around for signs of other colorful ladies, but the reception area was closed off from the club proper.

"We're meeting Slag for lunch," Ag said.

Merit handed her business card to the young woman.

"Hi, I'm Rose, Ms. Bridges. I'll let him know you're here." She went up a stairway running to the back of the lobby area toward a door marked "Office".

"I bet all the girls here are named Rose," Ag offered.

"And all have a rose tattoo?" Val wondered.

Merit hummed The Yellow Rose of Texas. All laughed.

Ag watched with appreciation as Rose climbed the stairs in red stilettos. Val stood with his mouth open while Merit admired the fact that Rose could walk upstairs on stilts.

"I love those shoes," Val said.

Merit had never been in a full-blown strip club before, but Slag had pressed her to come down and see his business, and in

Merit's value system, everybody needed a lawyer. She wasn't really offended by the thought of a club of women taking their clothes off if that's what they wanted to do. She didn't like the idea of women being forced into jobs that they didn't care for, however. In all the time she'd known Slag, he'd never shown signs of being that kind of employer. Just the opposite. Regardless, Merit wanted to provide her services.

After a few minutes a man with so many tattoos on his arms it appeared he was wearing a colorful shirt emerged from the office. He came down the stairs twirling the end of a handlebar moustache and smiling at Merit.

"Darlin', good to see you. I've been looking forward to introducing you to the club. We have quite a show today," Slag said as he swept his arm across the room.

Merit and Slag traded air kisses. "You know Ag, and this is Valentine Louis, Val for short. He's my number one paralegal and in law school part time at St. Mary's."

"Good to have you Val, Ag." Slag looked at Val's open mouth and wide eyes. "I take it this is your first time in a strip club."

"Nope," Ag said.

Merit looked surprised.

"I saw a tranny show on video once," said Val.

"Well these are all women, but same concept applies, just a little less burlesque," Slag said as he opened the double doors and waved them in.

The interior of the club was bathed in colorful neon light. Three pool tables lined the rear next to the restrooms. A bar took up over half the opposing wall beside a stepped-up stage area with several floor-to-ceiling metal poles secured to it. Overhead, spotlights highlighted different elements of the bar as ZZ Top sang loudly. A catwalk cut through the center of the club, surrounded by scattered tables. On the runway, lingerie-clad strippers modeled various baby doll pajamas, bustiers with garters and stockings, and long sheer negligees. Some wore pastel and appeared soft; while others sported bold primary colors, leather, and animal prints, making them seem fierce and wild. Something for everyone's fantasy.

Val was able to loosen his jaw another inch or two when he caught site of a pair of crotchless panties with a landing strip shaved into the model's pubic area. Ag seemed detached.

Merit focused on Slag as he pulled out her chair and seated her, and then sat closely on her right so he could speak into her ear. Val waited for someone to pull out his chair, but when no one bothered, he seated himself.

They ordered lunch from a bikini-clad waitress and communicated as best they could over the loud music.

Merit and Slag discussed his new tenant, to be located next door in the adjoining building. Slag owned the entire block on the east side. He had rows of businesses as tenants, making up a strip mall; to go with his strip club, he liked to joke. He handed Merit a large manila envelop with documents. She pulled out the papers, flipped through them quickly, and put the package in her briefcase on the floor.

Val and Ag commented occasionally on the models passing by.

"How long have you been gay?" Ag screamed over the music.

Val recoiled. "Do you realize I could sue you just for asking the question? It's a stupid question anyway, people are born gay, they don't 'get' gay."

Merit heard them, and decided to stay out of it. Slag laughed.

"Well, excuse me for taking an interest," Ag said. "We've never had much of a chance to talk. I was just making conversation."

"Okay, you're forgiven if you're only taking an interest."

"What else would I be doing?"

"Well, it is Texas. You never know if someone is going to hate you or shoot you or try to do you."

"I'm not interested in any of those. Just curious. It's my nature."

The show continued as they ate steaks, baked potatoes, salads, and iced tea. Only Ag had a cold draft with his meal. After a few bites, Merit and Val cut up their food and moved it around on their plates. Ag ate it all, even the potato peel.

As the show concluded, an extremely tall model in a white wedding night negligee was the grand finale. Afterwards, those remaining from the lunch crowd turned their chairs and attention from the runway and toward the stage with poles where the real action started.

Slag leaned toward Merit. "The girl I was telling you about is dancing first. She got a divorce last year, has a kid, and her house is being foreclosed. If you can get the bank off her back, I'll loan her enough so she can get on her feet." He turned toward the stage as Beyonce's "Pretty Hurts" began to play.

Merit had a soft spot for women in difficult situations. Her mother had been behind the curve her whole life. As soon as she got on top of one issue or problem, along came another one. She died never quite understanding how everyone else seemed to manage.

"That's Candy," Slag said.

A short redhead with large breasts began to dance around the first pole. She wore a zebra stripped bra, short plaid schoolgirl skirt, and knee high white socks with black patent leather Mary Jane heels. She began to remove articles of clothing, starting with the top. By the time she was swinging her G-string, Beyonce had solved the problems of all womankind, and the audience applauded loudly.

Slag motioned to Candy, who accepted a tiny robe from one of the two muscled black-clad bouncers. Candy walked over to the table while tying her robe closed.

Slag stood and pulled over a chair from another table. "Candy, this is Merit Bridges and her staff, Ag and Val. She's here to help with the new lease, so I thought she might talk to you about your house, too."

Merit smiled and put out her hand for a shake. "Nice to meet you."

"Likewise, I'm sure." Candy shook hands and popped the chewing gum in her mouth.

"I understand the mortgage company is trying to foreclose on your house?" Merit asked.

"Yes, I got the documents last week. I'm only two months behind on the payments, but I've been one payment behind since my divorce about a year ago."

"I understand you have a child," Merit said.

"Yes, a little boy, Jason. He's in first grade."

Val smiled sadly at Candy and looked down at her shoes.

"Well, I think we can help you. Ag is my investigator. Val does research. Let's make an appointment for you to come to the office and show us the foreclosure docs on your property. We can work with your schedule so you don't miss any work hours."

"Thank you. Thank you," Candy said.

"No guarantees, but we'll do our best," Merit said.

Slag walked Merit and her entourage to the door as Candy returned to the dressing room to prepare for her next act.

"I think she might be turning tricks on the side to make ends meet," said Slag. "We don't allow that through the club, but I hate to fire her. She's hit bottom."

"No family around?" Merit asked.

"Her no good ex-husband moved her and the kid down from Jersey, beat her up on a regular basis, then split," Slag said. "No one to help."

"I understand," said Merit. "We'll do what we can."

Slag nodded his agreement.

"In the meantime, we've run across a shady character named Boots King on another case. Trying to find him. Ever heard of the guy?" Merit asked.

"Name sounds vaguely familiar."

"Any idea where I might look?" Ag asked.

"There's a cockfight once a month in Bastrop County. You might try over there next Saturday night. If he's into drugs, gambling, or vice, he'll probably show up there at some point. I'll email the address when I get back up to the office."

"Thanks Slag. Please keep your ear to the ground," Merit said and looked at Ag.

"I'm on it," Ag said.

"We'll check the credit on your new tenant and see if he looks financially responsible. If he checks out, I'll get a draft of the lease to you by the end of the week," Merit said.

"Good. Thanks."

"Don't forget to have the insurance coverage in place before he moves in," Merit said.

"Right. Thanks, darlin'," Slag said and manifested a second round of air kisses for Merit; tickling her with his moustache. He shook hands with Ag and Val. "Come back any time."

As they walked out, Val said, "I can't wait to tell Betty about this."

All three climbed into Merit's SUV while searching for sunglasses and blinking at the bright light. When exiting, Merit used the backup camera to avoid tapping a large metal sign pole at the end of the parking lot. As they pulled forward, she looked back in the rear view mirror to see "NIXON" in red white and blue lettering on the bottom of the sign.

"I'll be damned, they are everywhere."

19

Merit convened Betty, Val, and Ag in the office conference room surrounded by bookshelves on three walls. Merit had asked Val to pull a few cases from his research. Multicolor flags fluttered at the edges of books stacked at one end of the conference table.

"Okay, everybody. Nixon vs. Estevez. We hope to settle the case in mediation. But there's not enough time between the mediation and the trial date to prep the entire case, so we need to be ready or partially ready just in case mediation doesn't work," Merit said.

All nodded.

"Our main points at trial are, one, the sale was not a true sale because it was between the two brothers; and two, there was fraudulent inducement in the execution of the lease because the option to purchase was hidden in the boilerplate."

"Do you realize what will happen if we win this case?" Ag said.

"Yes, Manny and Tireman keep their property and Nixon hits the road," Val said.

"True, but what happens if you win is that every sign company with billboards around the U.S. comes under scrutiny and their business model falls apart," Ag said.

"Yes, there's much more at stake here than just our case. They will not go down easily," Merit said.

"We should expect more dirty pool," Ag said.

Merit's armpits prickled. She took note and filed it for later brooding.

"Yes, now let's talk about what we do have control over," Merit said.

The group spent an hour going over the legal precedents on point for both issues. They spent another hour going over the cases on point for Nixon's side, which Merit determined to be the four corners doctrine and the binding contract argument.

Merit did a gut check at the end of the meeting and swallowed hard. It seemed about a fifty-fifty chance to win, but she did not offer that comment. Enthusiasm by the team could be the tipping point, and she did not want to dampen that. She smiled and thanked all, then went to her office to mull it over.

Rooter sat mulling at his desk overlooking downtown and the Austin Convention Center. Big business for such a small town just a few years back.

Rooter waited for his assistant to get all three sign majors on a conference call while he pushed the button up and down on the remote for the blinds. Dark, light, dark, light. Rooter popped onto his fantasy football site and checked his stats. He made a player acquisition and placed a bet.

"Take that!"

Rooter checked his win/loss account, smiled and clicked out of the site. He loved to win and money was the scorecard.

"All ready on line two," the receptionist said over the intercom.

Rooter pushed the button, "Good afternoon, gentlemen."

On the intercom, "Nixon Senior here. I've called this pow-wow to let Rooter catch us up on the status of the lawsuit."

Rooter cleared his throat. "We have a strong position right now. I have several attorneys researching case law to reinforce our position in our brief. It will give Merit something to chew on while we continue to get ready for trial. We're letting her believe that the mediation will work so she doesn't fully prepare for court."

One of the voices said, "I thought we had the mediation wired."

"Working on it," said Old Man Nixon.

"We need to be ready regardless," said Rooter. "We can't wait until the last minute for trial prep if something goes wrong with Judge Jones in the mediation. We've never used him before, and there's no guarantee."

One of the other voices said, "Does that mean you'll be running up your fee while we wait?"

Rooter recoiled, "That's up to you gentlemen. If you want me to wait and see I will but we will be unprepared if we go to trial. I'll be in exactly the same position we are orchestrating for Ms. Bridges."

Rooter waited for his hidden threat to seep into the brains of all three power mongers.

Score one for Rooter. These self-proclaimed fat cats have no idea who they're dealing with, he thought.

Old Man Nixon took charge. "Now, gentlemen. This is not the time to trim the budget. We need to pull our war chest together and fund this litigation right now while it's contained in Austin. This is our best shot at testing the option clause, right here in the good old U.S. of Texas. We have a strong Republican as governor, and the mayor is eating out of our hands."

"Big business is on top right now," Rooter said.

"Alright," a deep baritone voice said.

"Alright, I'm in too," another said.

"Good," Old Man Nixon said.

"We'll start making her life hell," Rooter said and made a list of documents he could pile into a box for delivery to Merit.

"Yes, we will," Old Man Nixon said.

20

C andy entered Merit's office wearing a low cut red dress and four-inch platforms. To keep them on, leather straps wrapped all the way up her calf and were tied in a bow just below the knee. Her flaming red hair was pulled into a ponytail that bounced when she walked. Betty heard the doorbell, which was hidden under the carpet in the waiting room, and came out to act as receptionist.

"May I help you?" Betty asked, poofing her helmet hair with her hand at the nape of her neck.

"Yes ma'am. I'm Candy from Texas Rose, here to see Ms. Bridges."

"Well, come on in, honey. I'm Betty. I run this place. The receptionist went to the post office. Don't fall over on those stilts you're wearing. How do you walk in those?"

"It takes practice, but when you get used to it, it's like your legs are extended. I borrowed these from a friend at the club. I can use all the height I can get."

"Well, darlin' you've accomplished that. Let's see if Merit is ready for you."

The women walked down the hall to Merit's office where Betty tapped on the door.

"Merit honey, Candy is here," Betty said.

"Thanks." Merit left her desk chair and shook hands with Candy. "Let's sit over here on the sofa."

"Coffee?" Betty offered.

"I'll have a diet soda if it's free," Candy said.

"Usual for me," Merit said.

Merit settled into a comfy chair by the sofa and balanced a legal pad on her lap.

"Let's see what you've got," Merit said.

Candy handed her a file folder with crumpled papers inside and said, "I've been trying to catch up since the divorce. My son has to have a babysitter after school while I'm working, and it takes most of my tips. I don't see him enough, but I can't leave the Rose."

"Slag tells me you may be breaking some of his rules to make extra money. If you're doing anything illegal, I need to know about it."

"I don't have many skills."

"Maybe you just need some training," Merit said.

"I don't have time or money to go back to school and still pay my bills and raise my son," Candy said.

"I understand. It's hard to get ahead when you're starting over," Merit said.

Betty brought in the diet soda and iced tea with a slice of lime floating on top. "If you need anything else, just buzz me. You're in good hands now, honey." Betty turned to Merit, "Want the door closed?"

"Yes, please."

"I don't know where to start," Candy said.

"Let's talk about the mortgage loan and foreclosure," Merit said.

"Okay. I tried to talk to the bank manager about giving me some extra time, but he said his hands were tied," Candy said.

"I reviewed the promissory note and deed of trust that you signed when you bought the house. That's basically an IOU that you'll repay the loan. The deed of trust is the instrument that allows the bank to step in and foreclose if you don't repay the money."

"Got it," Candy said.

"Reading the correspondence from the lender, it looks like you've missed several payments and caught up on all but one. Your late fee is five percent of the overdue payment of principal and interest, so you're falling further and further behind each month with the penalties. That's all legal, so we can't challenge the late fees."

"Yes, they wrote letters and called. The last time, the loan officer threatened to take my house."

"Well, the harassment we can stop, but our main goal is to get you back on track so you don't lose your house due to the breach."

"So how do I dig myself out of this hole?" Candy asked.

"Good news and bad news. Austin has a strong real estate market so lenders don't mind taking back properties and re-selling them. If we had a lot of junk on the market, they'd be more negotiable so they wouldn't have to deal with undesirable houses."

"I see."

"Under the federal Consumer Financial Protection rules, the mortgage company has to wait until you are more than one hundred and twenty days delinquent on payments before making the first official notice of foreclosure. You're past the end of that period, hence the correspondence and phone calls. Right now, to cure the breach, you need the amount specified in the demand letter."

"I don't have that," Candy said.

"Right, so what I can do is try to negotiate with the lender to get the penalties and late fees dismissed, but I don't know if I can do anything about the mortgage payment itself. That may not be negotiable."

"I don't have that right now, either," Candy said.

"Okay, what do I have to work with?"

"I have a few hundred put back and Slag will loan me a few hundred more. Plus, I have the upcoming payment ready to send."

"That's good. You don't want to miss any more payments while we're trying to work this out. All I can do is talk to them on your behalf and see how far I can get."

"What if they won't deal and I can't get all the money?"

"Most residential mortgage foreclosures in Texas are non-judicial, which means the lender can foreclose without going to court with this type of deed of trust. It has a power of sale clause. See?"

Merit pointed to a section of the document she was holding.

Candy nodded and seemed to follow all the points Merit was making.

"So they can sell it out from under me," Candy said.

"Texas law requires that the lender send you a notice of default and intent to accelerate by certified mail. It gives you at least twenty days to cure the default before the notice of sale can be given. That's the demand letter you got."

"I see."

"Next after that twenty days passes, they have to give you at least twenty-one days before the foreclosure sale. I expect that any day, so we need to get ahead of that notice of sale letter. If you get notice of certified mail in your mailbox, let me know before you go to the post office to pick it up."

"Okay."

"The notice includes the date, time, and location of the sale. We'll check and see if there's anything posted for foreclosure so far. Foreclosure sales are held the first Tuesday of each month between ten and four at the Travis County Courthouse. The property is sold to the highest bidder."

"Who would want to buy my house? It's run down and needs so much work."

"You'd be surprised. There are companies that do nothing but buy foreclosed properties, fix them up and flip them for a tidy profit."

Betty stuck her head in the door after a light tap.

"Your next appointment is waiting," Betty said.

"Okay, we're moving right along here." Merit smiled at Candy.

"I'm so sorry to be a bother," Candy said.

"No way. This is what I do all day long. We're okay on time."

"So the worst that can happen is I lose my house and have to move?"

"Well, there are a few other things that can happen if the fore-closure doesn't bring in at least enough to cover your loan and attorney's fees for the lender. There's a thing called a deficiency judgment following the sale. The mortgage company can go after you for the difference between the sale price and the amount you owe. I wouldn't worry about that right now. Your house is worth more than your mortgage."

"Whew, I don't know if I could ever afford another house if I lose this one," Candy said. "It's the only good thing my ex-husband did for me besides my son."

"Let's don't go that far yet. Let me see what I can do."

"Okay," Candy said.

"About the ex-husband. He's not going to show up and demand half the value of the house is he? I mean, the divorce was finalized and you had a lawyer file everything, right?" Merit asked.

"Oh no, he won't be back. I got the house in the divorce along with all the bills," Candy said.

After Merit and Candy finished their discussion, they walked to the front door. Val was sitting behind the receptionist desk studying *Prosser and Keeton on Torts*.

"Bye-bye, your Honor Candy," said Val.

After Candy parted, Val said, "Nice of you to help her. You know she can't pay you."

"Women do things they don't want to do when they feel trapped," Merit said. "Dancing is okay for some women, but Candy has a child in school now and needs to be home nights. We'll put her on a payment plan."

Betty walked up. "Can you call in some favors?"

"Slag probably wouldn't mind seeing her go to something else. Besides, for her being at the Rose is a temptation. Too easy for her to fall back into hooking," Merit said.

"How so?" Val asked.

"Old regulars probably know where she is. She needs a change of scene to begin again," said Betty.

"For now, let's try to save her house. Val, take a look at the foreclosure notices and see if the house has been posted for Tuesday next. Betty, the paperwork is on my desk. Please open a file and email the particulars to Val," Merit said.

"Will do," both Betty and Val said in unison.

Merit escorted her next client, an elderly widow, to her office. She could hear Val and Betty talking. She paused to eavesdrop.

"Why does she pick up all these stray women? Last month it was that homeless woman over on Pleasant Valley with the dog bite problem," Val said.

"We can't fight every battle, but God does have a way of placing two people together who need each other. Who will help them if we don't?" Betty said.

"I know. I feel for them too, but Merit seems to have an especially soft spot," Val said.

"She does. Her mother was trapped in a bad marriage, and everyone just looked the other way."

"Oh my."

"From that place children either married out or educated themselves out, if they were lucky."

"Hmm."

"I guess Merit wonders how things might have been different if her Mom had a helping hand. I think it might be the main reason she went to law school, a legitimate way to fight battles."

"I never knew," Val said. "I thought I had it rough growing up."

Merit cleared her throat to let Betty know she was listening.

"And, you won't be spreading that around town will you?" Betty said.

"No ma'am," Val said.

Manny was up and out in the crisp air at the shop on South Congress. Every time he looked over at the burnt sign, he could feel his anger at Nixon all over again. He directed a few employees toward repairs on the cars and drove a vintage Volvo into an open bay and onto the car lift. The mechanized elevator was one of the new pieces of equipment they had been able to purchase with the loan money from the refinance. When it arrived and was installed, it was such a happy day. Looking at it now made Manny regret he'd ever bought it.

The day mechanic brought a cardboard box full of parts over to Manny and gestured back toward a homeless looking fellow in dirty clothes.

"This isn't a chop shop, and we don't buy stolen parts. Get that out of here. You want to risk trouble to make fifty bucks?"

"No, not stolen. See," the mechanic said, picking up a carburetor and showing the refurbished sticker on the back of the part.

"You think secondhand parts can't be stolen? Give them back to him and get him out of here. The last thing we need is more trouble."

The mechanic gave the box to the peddler and said, "No thanks."

As the peddler left, Merit and Candy entered Estevez' shop. They could see the charred sign posts still protruding from the ground. Manny came out of his office and shook hands with Merit.

"Manny, this is Candy, the woman I told you about. She needs new tires on her car."

Candy shook hands with Manny and gave him a nervous smile. "I also need an inspection. My sticker shows last month. I don't want to get a ticket."

Manny opened the door and they walked outside to the old Saab. "I think we can fix you up. Can you leave it for a few hours?"

"Sure, but I need my car for work tomorrow," Candy said.

"No problem," Manny said.

"Manny, can you put her on a payment plan? I'll vouch for her. She's going through a rough patch. She has a kid to feed. He's about Emmi's age."

"Is that right?" Manny asked.

"How is Emmi?" Merit asked.

"He's getting better every day. The doctors saved his sight, but he'll have some scarring. He likes being home better than the hospital, and so does his mother."

"Of course. That's great," Merit said.

Manny looked at Candy.

"Sure. We can work something out. You can't drive your kid around on these tires." Manny averted his eyes from her noticeable figure and placed a dime in the non-existent tread of the front left tire.

"Why don't you pull it into the garage and we'll take a look," Manny said.

While Candy pulled the car around to an open bay, Merit turned to Manny. "Don't you need some extra help around here?"

"What do you mean?"

"Well, you were just saying how you needed some help in the office, and she needs a job so she can take care of her son."

"Merit, my wife will kill me if I put a woman like that in here."

"She has regular clothes. I guess. Anyway, she can buy some with the money you'll pay her."

When Candy returned, Manny said, "Candy, I have an opening here at the shop if you can start right away. I need someone to answer the phones, take payments, and open the school one night a week. I also need someone to rotate every other Saturday over at the junkyard on Airport. You can bring your son at night and on weekends, but not here during the day. He and Emmi can do their homework over there."

Manny pointed to the rear of the shop.

"Manny has a school in the house out back where immigrants can learn English as a second language. He's good about giving back that way," Merit said.

"She already has the job."

"That's wonderful," Candy said.

"If you want it. When can you start?" Manny said rolling his eyes at Merit.

21

Merit sat at the defendant's table to the right of the gallery in Courtroom Five. Tireman entered from the holding area and looked around the room. He let out a long deep breath when Merit made eye contact, and allowed the bailiff to walk him over to his chair beside her. The handcuffs remained on his wrists. His knuckles were bruised and scraped red. He had a black eye and a cut on the left side of his chin with a butterfly bandage holding it together.

"What happened to you?" Merit asked.

"I'm holding my own," Tireman said.

"We only have a minute before the judge comes in," she said.

"Okay," he said.

"I spoke with the prosecutor and he acted as if he had no idea about the green card issue. That's a crock because we submitted all that information to his office prior to the first bail hearing."

"Hmm," Tireman said.

"This time, Kim Wan went to the judge in chambers and made him aware of the miscommunication. They're friends from way back."

The judge took the bench and called the room to order.

"The People vs. Tarantella Estevez. Bail hearing," the clerk announced.

Kim Wan entered late and stood in the back of the room. Merit had asked him to be ready to assist if needed. She'd requested his presence to remind the judge that this was the case they'd discussed.

"Ready, your honor," Merit said.

"Proceed."

"We have re-supplied the prosecutor with the defendant's green card plus additional information about his home ownership and business ties to the community."

She handed the clerk a copy of the materials listed.

"Any objection to bail?" the judge asked the assistant prosecution.

"None. We request that his passport be surrendered. We trust your honor to set a reasonable amount," said the assistant prosecutor.

"Bail is set at one-hundred thousand. Cash or bond."

"Thank you Your Honor," Merit said.

Tireman slumped in relief. Merit saw Manny in the gallery make eye contact with his brother. Tireman swiped at his face to hide a tear.

"We'll pick you up when the paperwork is processed," Merit said.

Tireman smiled for the first time in weeks.

After the bail hearing, Merit went outside to use her cell phone while she waited for Tireman to be processed out.

Merit watched her feet as she walked down the courthouse steps to make sure she didn't trip on the worn limestone. When she raised her eyes, a rider came around the corner on a Harley and parked across from the courthouse.

The rider dismounted and crossed the street toward her. He sported dark shades, two silver earrings in each ear, and a metallic belt buckle with an enameled black hog on one side. His t-shirt said "Heel Horses" and his tattoos were a spider on one arm and a skeleton on the other.

She stopped on the sidewalk as he walked straight towards her. He lifted his sunglasses. Chocolate eyes met hers.

In that instant, he knew he could have her, at the first opportunity. She knew he knew. Whether it was physically true or not was irrelevant. She gasped just a little breath.

Did he hear that?

Didn't matter. The deal had already been struck.

"Howdy, ma'am."

"Hi," Merit said. He had very good manners for a bad boy. And, of course, he was about half her age. Hence, the attraction.

"Do you know where courtroom four is?" he asked.

"Yes, take the elevator to the third floor and it will be right in front of you when you get off."

Merit knew that courtroom four was mostly for family violence cases. It made her pause.

He seemed to read her mind.

"Oh, no. I'm just a witness. Subpoenaed to testify for the prosecution," he said and pulled a document out of his back pocket for reference.

"Oh," Merit said.

He extended his hand for a shake.

"Oliver McLaren. Friends call me Tattoo, for obvious reasons."

Merit returned the gesture.

"Merit Bridges."

When he spoke, she noticed that he had a little goatee below his crooked teeth. He'd obviously grown up without braces. He

108

grinned with his eyes as if he knew a secret that she didn't, or they shared one to be made.

Upon close inspection, the spider was spinning a web in the bodywork on Tattoo's right arm. The skeleton tattoo on his left was inscribed U.S.M.C.

Maybe he was a former Marine, Merit thought.

A red buzz-saw blade circled the bones tattoo. *She'd have to inspect that more closely.* He had a shaved head. Probably better for the helmet on the hog.

She handed him her card. "I have to run. Let me know if you ever need a lawyer."

"I will," Tattoo said.

"You will need one, or you will call me?" Merit laughed.

"Both." Tattoo laughed, too.

22

Merit wrapped an email and went into the conference room. Intern Mai, wearing a new shade of orchid lipstick, a Christmas present from Val, showed Mr. and Mrs. Dobie in. She offered them coffee or water and turned to Merit who nodded her dismissal. Merit shook hands and introduced herself to the graying nicely dressed middle-aged couple. They both sported turquoise rings on their fingers, conch belts on their waists, and Mrs. Dobie had turquoise on her tooled leather handbag. They were seated with two large banker boxes before them, a handwritten label on the end of each. "Papa's files" was on one box and "Mama's files" on the other.

"Beautiful ring," Merit said.

"Santa Fe," said Mrs. Dobie.

"How long have you known Kim Wan Thibodeaux?" Merit asked as she seated herself across from them.

"He helped our son with a DUI a few years back. It was good of him to refer us to you," Mr. Dobie said.

"Kids. Yikes. I have one of my own, a son. Teenagers are the worst."

They all laughed.

Merit pointed to a tiny figure in one of her bridge photographs handing on the wall.

"That's him watching the bats fly out from under the Congress Street Bridge."

"Nice photograph," Mr. Dobie said.

"Thank you."

Merit settled into her chair and pulled over a yellow legal pad.

"I understand you have an oil and gas issue. Why don't you start from the beginning and let me take some notes," Merit said.

Mr. Dobie passed Merit a tattered *Last Will and Testament*.

"About six years ago, my mother passed away. My father was already deceased. She left my brothers and me the old family ranch in Live Oak County, just outside of George West, Texas."

"Land and minerals or both?" Merit asked.

"The minerals were still attached to the land since Mama and Papa had owned it so long. We inherited land and oil intact. They had signed an oil and gas lease about twenty years back and renewed it a couple of times with what is now the Line Oil Production Company out of Houston," Mr. Dobie said.

"How much land are we talking about?" Merit asked.

"Six hundred and forty acres exactly," said Mrs. Dobie.

"Were they getting any royalty payments?" Merit asked.

"Yes, they were being paid a twenty-percent royalty interest and got a check every month," Mrs. Dobie said.

"Sounds on the up and up, what's the problem?" Merit asked.

"So far, the land has been included in a Pooling Agreement that my parents ratified. We get paid a percentage of the pool based on the number of acres in the pool relative to other nearby mineral owners. No wells are actually drilled on our land," said Mr. Dobie.

"That sounds standard," said Merit.

"Now, Line has petitioned the Texas Railroad Commission to allow them to increase the density to drill more wells on the same amount of land in the pool," said Mr. Dobie.

"That's pretty standard too," Merit said.

"There was no pooling clause in the original lease. Later, when Mama and Papa signed the pooling ratification agreement, it limited drilling."

"Here it is—it says Line can't drill on the land except in the northwest quarter. There's also an easement in that quarter for trucks to go in and out, and a pipeline goes through there as well." He pulled the document out of the stack and handed it to Merit.

"Now Line is saying that they are seeking the change under forced pooling and want the rules to be different," Mrs. Dobie said.

"I see," Merit said, looking at the document.

"We are in the process of developing part of the land into small home tracts for people to build on, about five acres each. We intend to keep the mineral rights and just sell the land, but if news gets out that the RRC will allow Line to come in and drill these sites, our development will not sell. No one wants to live next to a pump jack," said Mr. Dobie.

"I need to study your documentation. But in Texas, oil is the dominant estate. That means that without further limitation such as in the lease, Line can drill anywhere the Railroad Commission will allow," Merit said.

"We know, but there is no pooling allowed in the lease, and the only allowance is in the ratification, and it does have a limitation," Mr. Dobie said.

"I'm sorry to tell you that just because pooling is not expressly al-lowed, that doesn't mean it's dis-allowed. It just means that the RRC rules apply. That said, you do have a restriction in a document that could be interpreted as an amendment to the lease. It depends on the wording. I'll have to read the documents and do some research."

"Research? Isn't this your area of expertise?" Mr. Dobie asked.

"Yes. My practice includes all things related to land, on or under; real estate, development, buildings, oil and gas, and a little civil litigation where contracts are involved. That's why I use Kim Wan for criminal work, that's his specialty."

"Then why do you need to do research?" Mr. Dobie asked.

"You have an unusual set of circumstances here, which on its face doesn't appear to give you a very good position from which to negotiate," Merit said. "I'm going to need to find a loophole or some case law that gives you an exception to the usual course of dealing. Understand?"

"Yes, I see," Mr. Dobie said.

"If you want me to proceed, I'll need to make copies of your file documents and have you sign my standard contract," Merit said. She pressed the button on the intercom and asked Betty to come in.

"That sounds satisfactory," Mr. Dobie said.

Betty came in with a steno pad and pen in hand.

"Let's draw up the standard representation agreement for the Dobies," Merit said to Betty. Then to the Dobies, "Will you be responsible, or do you need to add your other family members?"

"We are going to be representing all of the family because everyone is scattered across the country. We'll need to have them sign your retainer contract as well, but we can get all that done and back to you," Mr. Dobie said.

"Okay, and Betty, would you please have Mai copy all of these documents and return the originals to the Dobies? I don't want to send them off-site for copying."

"I'll take care of it. Can you pick them up later today or should I have them sent to you?" Betty asked.

Mr. Dobie looked at his wife.

"We can come by around four if that gives you enough time," Mrs. Dobie said.

"Sounds good," Betty said.

Merit turned back to the Dobies. "I'll read through everything and give you a call with an estimate of costs, if that works for you. I bill by the hour, but I think I can give you a good idea of how much time it will take," said Merit.

"That'll work," said Mr. Dobie.

Later that night, after hitting the gym for a much-needed workout, Merit went back to the office and returned her attention to the Dobie files that Mai had copied and Betty left on her desk. Betty had sorted the files into leases and contracts, correspondence with Line, and estate docs, which included the will and letters testamentary of Mama and Papa Dobie. They were in order and the files were labelled and color coded.

Merit began with the contracts and read them from the bottom up, oldest to most current. She found several leases in the stack and several lease amendments changing terms or extending the lease dates. She put sticky notes on the clauses related to pooling, scribbled the date on the yellow post-it for each, and continued on to the correspondence files.

She was hoping to find a way to read the various clauses together to form a logical explanation of the parties' intent to define the location for drilling. So far, she hadn't found the magic string of pearls that tied all the clauses together in her clients' favor.

After going through the correspondence, she noted that her armpits were prickling ever so slightly. She sat for a minute listening for noises in the office, but realized it was not physical danger, but something in the back of her mind that would not stop meddling with her thoughts. She flipped back through the older leases, and there it was, the signature of Meriwether King as witness to a lease dated about eight years back.

"What a sissy name, no wonder he uses 'Boots'. Or was Meriwether an alias to throw people off track? Maybe it wasn't him at all."

Merit went to the copy machine and scanned the document, sending it to her computer. She went back to her desk and composed an email to Ag. She asked him to see what he could do and to get with Chaplain and see if it was the same 'King'. She attached the scanned document, and hit "SEND".

"Finally. Maybe we have a lead on this guy."

23

Betty went onto the Travis County website to search for Candy's foreclosure. Merit had asked her to make sure it wasn't posted for the next sale on the Courthouse steps. Betty had only attended one foreclosure ceremony with Merit. It seemed archaic to her to have a batch of people gather on the steps of the courthouse in the morning and have attorneys tantamount to auctioneers read the deed of trust documents and ask for bids. *Like a herd of kid goats trying to get to the tits first*, she thought.

When Betty and Merit had attended, the bank's attorney was selling a property owned by one of Merit's clients and she wanted to make sure there was no collusion in the sales price or with the buyer. The bank's attorney read the foreclosure documents and then asked for bids. Several people bid the price up to what Merit thought was fair market value, so the property was sold and the buyers had to prove that they could have the money to the bank that afternoon. It was all such a dramatic scenario, Betty had been excited by the whole process. Now she could see how a foreclosure practice could get very old, very fast.

She completed her tasks online and sent an email to Merit that Candy's house had not yet been posted for foreclosure. Betty was certain Merit would be happy that she had time to try to work with the bank. Now she just had to do her magic.

Merit and Ag parked in the office garage at about the same time. Ag called out to her.

"Hello, Counselor. Didn't want to come up too fast without giving you notice."

"Hello, Ag. Thanks, my startle response has been working overtime lately."

Everyone had been on high alert since Betty's encounter with the man in the cowboy hat who they guessed was Boots King.

Ag took Merit's briefcase and walked her to the glass door. He fumbled around, pulling instead of pushing, finally got the door open, and held it for her to pass.

How many times have I opened this door? Ag asked himself. *What a klutz I am today.*

He pushed the button for their floor and she brushed her shoulder against him as she entered the elevator. He could smell her perfume and thought it smelled 'blonde'. Ag breathed in the aroma of sweet fragrance notes until they arrived at the appointed floor.

"Thank you," she said and walked down the long hall toward the office.

Ag stayed by her side. The piped in music played the instrumental version of 'To All the Girls I've Loved Before'. The two hummed the melody in harmony, Merit not seeming to notice the accompaniment.

As they continued down the hall, oncoming office personnel caused Ag to drop behind Merit to allow single file passage. He looked at her hair, back, waist, bum, and legs. He felt himself grow warm and swallowed. After the others passed, he reluctantly returned to promenade and opened the office door for her. This time, he focused so he could get it on the first try. She smiled at him, took her briefcase and went down the hall to her office.

For such a smart gal, she sure is blind to me. I'm going to have to make a move, Ag thought. He snagged a cup of coffee from the break room, composed himself, and joined Merit in her office. He was so nervous around her these days. He wished he could just go back to the way it used to be.

The heart wants what the heart wants, he thought.

Merit wrapped a phone call and called Betty in to take notes.

"Okay, go," Merit said.

Ag flipped open a pocket note pad like police detectives carried.

"What is the latest on Tireman's case?" Merit asked. "Has APD found any physical evidence to tie him to the arson or involuntary manslaughter?"

"No, they are sure he committed the crimes, but as far as I know, they don't have a witness or anything like DNA. It all burned up in the fire," Ag said.

"That may will help with a plea. I'll tell Kim Wan," Merit said.

"That's it for now on that," Ag said.

The discovery of the moniker, Meriwether King, had given Ag a new avenue to search for Boots. It was time to report.

"What about the Dobies?" Merit asked. "Did they come up with anything?"

"I interviewed Mr. and Mrs. Dobie at their home. They remembered little about him, but they recalled enough to lead me to believe that Meriwether and Boots are most likely the same King. Their description of him was similar to the other leads we've had," Ag said.

"Good news," Betty said.

"The company that he worked for had no forwarding address, but I did get his prior address to Chaplain. He's going to see where it leads and get back with me," Ag said.

"Great. At least something," Merit said. "Could you two coordinate the follow-up?"

"Can do. Hope you find him," Betty said to Ag. "This Boots character is as slippery as snail snot."

24

Merit left her home in a rush toward the office. She'd over-slept after drinking too much wine the night before while sitting in the backyard. She usually resisted looking over the spot where Tony had sat, but now and again she'd sink into a terrible loneliness. On those days, she'd go outside to feel sorry for herself. This usually happened when she drank by herself. She hated that, drinking alone and feeling sorry for herself.

At the end of the block, she noticed a black 4x4 with a naked woman chrome emblem on the front grill. She had seen that on eighteen-wheelers on the highway, but never on a pickup. It looked like a Playboy bunny silhouette. Something made her armpits prickle and she stopped for a moment and looked around. No one seemed to belong to the truck, and it was parked near a neighbor's home that she didn't know very well. She decided to shoot a pic of the license plate, which read KNG69. She had the odd feeling she'd seen the truck before, but Texas has lots of trucks. She also took a picture of the dual wheels in back. Not all Texas trucks had that.

Boots watched Merit back her SUV out of her driveway then he ducked behind a neighbor's fence. Since he couldn't get into her office right now, maybe he'd find something at her house that would help

Nixon. Mostly, he just wanted to go where he didn't belong, violate the privacy of his target, and show that there were no barriers to keep him out if he wanted in. He planned to leave a few telltale signs to make her worry. He felt pleasure at the thought of her fear.

He waited a moment to make sure she didn't return for some forgotten item and entered the side gate into the backyard. No cameras here.

He looked into the glass along the back of the house. He could see a small dog asleep on a rug in the sun that was shining through the panes. He tried a few windows, but all were locked. There was no doggie door that he could see. He stepped up on a deck with French doors leading into the dining room. He used his knife to shave away a bit of the wood, popped the lock and went in.

A brindled small breed terrier began to bark and jump on Boots' leg. She rolled over on her back exposing her tummy for rubbing.

"A real guard dog," Boots said.

He pushed the dog aside and looked around. He thought he heard something. He stopped, listened for a moment, and then systematically checked each room. Must have been outside. When he reached the home office, guest room combo, he rifled a small desk in the corner, but was disappointed when he found nothing on the Nixon case. He looked through a desk drawer and found a few files, one on a property in Port Aransas, Texas, and one on a private school in Houston, Texas. Boots snapped a pic with his phone of the address in each file.

"Must be where her son goes to school. Might come in handy later." He carefully restored the files to the drawer.

Along the wall were shelves filled with cameras, lenses, tripods, cleaning equipment, and other photography equipment. He'd seen

Sonny Nixon with a similar Nikon camera as the one on the shelf. *What a waste of time taking pictures of things*, he thought. There was a funny looking file cabinet with thin horizontal drawers. He pulled them open and found stacks of photographs, black and white in the top drawer, color in the second. In the third, there were stacks of eight by tens of a male child with blonde hair and hazel eyes. *Must be her son*, Boots thought. Some were in the toddler years, and others had the pre-teen look.

In the second from the bottom drawer were hundreds of pictures of bridges. Some were the same print, but most were different bridges around the Texas Hill Country and over Lady Bird Lake in Austin. Boots had no idea if the photographs were any good, but he flipped through a few and recognized some of the bridges.

Lastly, he pulled the bottom drawer, but it was locked.

"Hmm."

He pulled out a slender blade on his knife and popped the lock in seconds. When he pulled open the drawer, he saw dozens of pictures of young men aged twenty to thirty-something. Most were naked or in provocative boxers and tighty whities. He flipped through the photos and admired some of the abs and pecks. Not his taste, but nice specimens of male anatomy. He wondered if she knew these men or just used them as models for photography. He recognized a totally nude man in one of the shots.

"Where do I know him from?"

He took a few souvenirs and restored the file drawers to their original status, but left the bottom one unlocked.

Boots moved onto the master bedroom, looked in the closet at all her fancy clothes and estimated over one hundred pairs of shoes. A real clotheshorse.

Next, he checked the kid's room. There was a picture on the nightstand of a man and a boy standing by a kite flying contest sign at Zilker Park. Must be the kid's dad. The bed was made, and nothing was out of place. Looked like he hadn't been there in a while, too neat.

He looked into the living room and the dining room and passed into the kitchen. The usual, fridge, dishwasher, stove, nice big breakfast table in a window nook, apple wallpaper. Cheerful. He lit a cigarette from the gas stove and contemplated what to do next. He opened the refrigerator door and stood there staring at the food deciding if he wanted a snack. He smoked his cigarette as he foraged, snacked on some dry cereal that smelled like wet rope, then drank from the milk carton and put it back in the fridge.

Satisfied for now, he crept from the house the same way he'd come in. He made his way to his truck and out of the neighborhood.

Betty took the call from the Tarrytown Pet Clinic. She jotted some notes and went into Merit's office.

"Seems that Pepper has gone strolling around the neighborhood and wound up in the Tarrytown Post Office," Betty said.

"What?" Merit asked.

"Your vet called. Someone brought Pepper to the clinic based on her vet tag and they are holding her there. Said they'll keep her for an hour before taking her to the shelter. Cost is fifty dollars," Betty read from the notes.

"Damn. Well, it's better than the shelter. She'd be covered with fleas," Merit said.

"Want me to send Val over to get her? You've got a meeting in ten minutes."

"Please. If they know who brought her in, please get the name. I'd like to thank them."

"Oh, yeah."

"Loan him your key. Please tell Val to make sure and lock her in the house. When I get home, I'll make sure she hasn't dug a hole in the yard."

"Will do."

"Thanks."

"I wonder how she got out," Betty said.

"She hasn't done that before. The gas man may have left the gate unlatched."

"Was she in the yard?"

"I didn't think so. Weird."

Betty joined Merit in her office at the end of the day's work.

"What's on your dance card for tonight?" Betty asked.

"I was thinking about going out later. Hayes Carll and Buddy Guy are playing at the Saxon Pub. I might hit Stubbs. I think Robert Earl Keen is playing at The Continental Club."

"Hot date?"

"No, just meeting some friends."

She intentionally didn't invite anyone from the office. Merit had not mentioned Tattoo. She knew Betty would not approve, especially after the recent fiasco with John, and she wasn't comfortable sharing her sex life with her staff.

She liked Tattoo, but had no intentions of getting involved, and he was only playing around. That's what it was really, sex and a good time. That's the plan, only a little fun. No more husbands for her and the disappointment that comes with that. She needed fun in her life. That's all. If she and Tattoo showed up at The Broken Spoke or anywhere else at the same time, no one would be the wiser.

Whom she danced with was private.

Merit arrived home late from the night out with Tattoo. She had decided to go to his place so she could leave when she wanted. She let Pepper into the yard and watched her relieve herself so she wouldn't make a run for the hole she'd probably gotten out of earlier. She made a mental note to walk the fence the next morning and plug Pepper's escape route.

She was exhausted, and hungry. She fed Pepper and then went to the fridge to forage for a snack.

Something was off. She smelled tobacco smoke coming from the refrigerator. She sniffed around to see if something had caught fire, but the smell was only in the fridge. There was a small pile of ash or dog dirt or something on the floor right at the door.

She felt prickles in her armpits and jerked around, but no one was there. She thought of the gun in the drawer in the bedroom, but grabbed a cast iron skillet off the stove instead. She went through the house turning on lights and looking behind doors, then laughed at herself and went back to the kitchen.

It must have been the leftover chile rellenos, she thought.

She stood in the kitchen and changed her mind. She'd promised herself never to ignore the danger sign of the armpits. She went back through the house one more time. In her office things were out of place. Everything was present, but it was just a bit askew. Nothing she could put her finger on.

She thought about calling Tattoo or Ag, but she didn't want the complications of either of them in her home at two a.m.

She re-checked the locks on the doors and took Pepper with her to the bedroom. She closed her bedroom door, which usually stayed open, and went to bed for a restless night's sleep.

Merit tackled a large stack of files that Betty had left the night before. Ag dropped by the office to give Merit an update on his latest conversation with Chaplain.

Betty showed him into Merit's office. "I'm stayin," she said.

Ag and Betty sat in the guest chairs across from Merit's desk.

"Tell him," Betty said.

"What's up?" Ag asked.

"I think someone was in my house yesterday," Merit said.

"Was anything missing?" Ag asked.

"No, but I'm sure I left Pepper inside. I always do. And, when I opened the fridge, I could swear I smelled cigarette smoke. A file cabinet that I always lock was unlocked."

"Maybe it was Val when he took Pepper home from the vet," Ag said.

"I asked him. He said he didn't open the fridge or go past the back door. Just let the dog in and re-locked," Betty said.

"If you'll loan me a key, I'll run by and check it out," Ag said.

"Good idea. If her office was catty-wompus, someone was in there," Betty said.

"I'm on it," Ag said.

"Where are we on locating our star witness?" Merit asked.

"Chaplain can't find this Boots King character," Ag said. "His name isn't on any apartment lease or house deed in Travis County, and he doesn't have a car registered in his name. APD found the same info we did from the landman's association, but they hit a dead end there too."

"That dog don't hunt. He isn't a ghost," Betty said.

"No, but he knows how to hide, apparently in plain sight. Chaplain's a good man and APD is good, but they do have limited resources."

"I've spot checked Nixon's offices, but not seen anyone matching his description go in or out. I can't sit on it all day," Ag said.

"I have a subpoena drafted for him to testify."

"The witness subpoena is worthless if we can't find him to serve it. If someone doesn't want to be found, it's pretty easy to hide in Texas," Ag said.

"I know that. What about Emmi? Who else could it have been with the same description he gave Manny?" Merit asked.

"It's Boots King all right. Probably behind all this with Nixon's blessing. There's just no proof he committed any crimes," Ag said.

"What does he have to do? Kill somebody?" Betty asked.

"I could hire someone to watch the office all the time, but I think it would be a waste of money. He and Nixon have to know that APD is looking for him with regard to Emmi's injuries and all the rest," Ag said.

"Told you. Snail snot," Betty said.

"What about the old address for Meriwether King and the license plate from the truck outside my house?" Merit asked.

"Dead end so far. Chaplain is doing everything he can. The guy is just nowhere," Ag said.

"What about the cockfights Slag told you about?" Merit asked.

"King's been there, but he's not come back lately. I've got a few guys looking out for him, and I'm going myself on Saturday," Ag said.

"Well that does it. I'm packin' and both of you better too," Betty said.

25

Merit and Ag entered Bull's Eye Firing Range in Oak Hill. Ag shook hands with the owner who was behind the counter.

"Bull, this is Merit. Merit, Bull."

They nodded a greeting. She noted Bull's thick neck and hairless cue ball with thick floppy earlobes and tiny little lips under a black moustache. He looked like a bald Mr. Potato Head.

"Could we get a couple of B27 targets and an extra box of .380 practice rounds?" Ag asked.

"Coming up," Bull said.

Bull pulled three large sheets of paper from below the counter sporting the silhouette of a man with a black multi ring target on his chest. There was an X in the center and rings out to the number seven on the outside.

"I'll bring the targets. Take lanes three and four," Bull said.

"This is the standard target required for the CHL shoot in. Bull still does the long version of the CHL class for people who are serious about learning," Ag said.

"What's the short version?" Merit asked.

"It's streamlined now, but I want you to go the full monty since you've not been around guns much."

Merit and Ag entered the indoor shooting range on the side of the warehouse building and put their cases down on the counter at the head of lane three. Ag unzipped Merit's khaki case and put her Ruger on the counter with the barrel facing forward toward the target area. Bull joined them, handed Ag the ammo and pushed the IN button to bring the target caddies forward for Merit's lane. He clipped the B27 on the caddy and pushed the button to send it back down to three yards.

"You load it like this," Ag said.

Ag handed Merit one of her clips and he took the other. He started pushing bullets from the box into the clip. Merit copied his actions until they both had the clips fully loaded.

"Now, you slide it in here and the clip locks into place. Always have the safety on while you're loading the pistol and while you're at the range. Take it off just before you're ready to shoot," Ag said.

"Got it."

"Try it first without shooting. You can see if you like one hand or two hands. If you want to, hold it with your right hand, since you're right dominant, and cup your left hand under your right."

"Like this?" Merit asked.

"Looks great. Now, pull the slide back and release it to put a round in the chamber."

Merit and Ag both popped their ear protectors on their heads. Merit picked up her gun, clicked off the safety and pulled back the slide as Ag had shown her.

Ag stepped behind Merit and she aimed through the sight and shot five rounds. She set the gun down on the counter and Ag pushed the button to bring in the target. All five were in the circles, but none in the center.

"Good. Now try to squeeze the trigger a little slower and get control of your aim. Line up the notch in the sight, and then gently pull the trigger. Keep your eyes open when you shoot, and open your stance a little."

"Got it."

"Send the target down to seven yards, the CHL class teacher will have you shoot in at three, seven, and fifteen yards."

"Okay. Let me try again." She sent the target back down the lane, situated herself with her legs apart, and squeezed. She felt more in control and shot off two more rounds.

Ag brought the target back toward them. "Nice."

Ag moved over to lane four and started his practice, letting Merit build a relationship with the gun on her own. After they had both shot up a box of ammo, and Merit was feeling properly introduced to the pistol, Ag packed up his equipment to go.

"Your class starts in fifteen minutes. I'll leave you to it," Ag said.

"Okay. You're not staying?" Merit asked.

"You can handle this. I've already taken the class remember? And I know the instructor, so hands off."

"You spoil all my fun," Merit said.

Merit signed into the class, filled out the appropriate forms, had her picture taken for her concealed handgun license, and took a seat in the back of the room. The class reminded her of a defensive driving course she'd completed once to get out of a speeding ticket. There were twenty-one participants, eight women and thirteen men.

The instructor entered wearing camouflage military style pants, black combat boots, and a 9MM Glock in a holster strapped to his thigh. His t-shirt was so tight over his muscled thirty-something-year-old physique that the words "Bull's Eye Firing Range" stretched to look like graffiti on a wall.

"Today and tomorrow, you will learn the rules for carrying a concealed handgun in the state of Texas. You will learn when it is appropriate and inappropriate to do so. You will also learn when it is legal and illegal to do so," Muscles said.

"Isn't that the same thing?" a class member chimed in.

"Pretty much. Texas law requires this four- to six-hour course, or something similar, to obtain a permit. Our course covers the use of force, gun safety and storage, dispute resolution, and Texas laws."

"Sounds like high school," the heckler said.

"No high school ever issued a handgun license," Muscles said.

"Are you the gun police?" the heckler asked.

"Technically, it's not gun, it's pistol. Gun is used for shotgun or bigger equipment," Muscles said.

"Excuse me, pistol police," the heckler said.

Several class members, including Merit, glared at the heckler. He shut up.

"After the instruction, you must pass a fifty question test, and shoot on the firing range. Assuming you pass, you must then apply and pay a fee to the state, which issues the license. We'll do all the paper work here and check it for you before you send it in with your money. Any questions?"

The class members turned to the heckler again, ready to pounce if he opened his mouth.

A class member, wearing a UT t-shirt, raised his hand.

"Yes?" Muscles said.

"What was the paperwork we did before taking the class?"

"That was to make sure you were approved to obtain a license if you followed the regulations to do so. No need to take the class if the state won't give you a license anyway," Muscles said.

Intramural raised his hand.

"What is the law about openly carrying a handgun on campus?"

"The law evolves around open carry during every legislative session," Muscles said.

Merit couldn't envision herself with a six-gun on her hip.

"Let's hold the rest of the questions until we finish tonight. Most of them will be answered during the course of the class," Muscles said.

Muscles demonstrated gun safety with his Glock and rifled through the class sign in sheets for the pistol type each classmate was going to use.

"Those of you planning to use less than a 9MM may want to rethink your choice of pistol," Muscles said.

Merit raised her hand. "Why's that?"

"If you are forced to defend yourself, you will want the highest level of protection available."

"I was told by the salesman who sold it to me that it was perfectly sufficient for self-protection, especially since I can easily conceal it in my purse," said Merit.

"Well, I disagree. I'd hate for you to find yourself in a position of weakness," Muscles said.

"Weakness?" Merit said.

The next day after work, Merit drove herself back to Bull's Eye to finish the class. It was a very comfortable setting for her. She had received her law license many years ago, but had continued to study every year to maintain her credentials. This was just one more area of the law to learn. What she was nervous about was the shooting part at the end of class.

Muscles took his Glock out of the holster with is right hand, released the clip into his left hand, and held up the pistol for the class to see. He demonstrated gun safety and explained as Ag had about keeping the safety on when not firing the weapon. He re-emphasized the need for the 9MM as the smallest gun he would recommend for self-protection and pointed at Merit and her .380 for emphasis.

Merit's face flushed pink and she pressed her lips together.

"Why don't you let her shoot you and see if it works?" the heckler said.

Maybe I like this guy after all, she thought.

"Well, there's no requirement that you take the class with the gun you intend to carry," Muscles said.

He didn't mention the .380 again.

Muscles went over all the rest of the Texas laws that he hadn't finished the day before, and explained the 51% notice signs in restaurants and bars. Merit had seen the signs and always wondered what it meant. She learned that all alcoholic beverage retailers must post one of two firearms signs. One sign is for stores selling alcohol to go, or establishments where alcohol sales are less than 50% of gross receipts. It warns that possessing a concealed handgun without a license is a felony.

The sign Merit had seen round Austin bars was the second sign that had a big 51% stenciled in red over the words. This sign had to be posted in establishments where on-premises consumption of alcohol constitutes more than half of the gross receipts of the restaurant or bar.

The warning on this sign is that possession of a concealed weapon on the premises is a felony. In other words, if it was primarily a restaurant, the gun was allowed, but if it was primarily a bar, nix the gun. Merit guessed the law originated from a time when cowboys got liquored up and shot up the town. No real reason to believe that was true.

It was interesting to learn new law about a different subject than she usually engaged, and the class went by quickly. The written test was easy. All the questions were directly out of the class curriculum and mostly in the handouts. The rest were in the booklet from the Texas Department of Public Safety, which she had studied earlier that day.

After a short break, and while another instructor and Bull graded the written tests, Muscles took the class into the firing range and watched to make sure no one shot another classmate as guns were pointed in the wrong direction or mishandled. More than once, he pushed a classmate's hand down onto the counter with the gun flat to prevent a mistake. He walked around, lectured, and gave pointers. It appeared that all classmates had learned how to safely handle their weapons. Next, he instructed the class to load the guns and attach the targets to the caddies for the shoot in.

"This CHL class requires you to shoot a course of fire in three strings, twenty rounds at three yards, twenty rounds at seven yards, and ten rounds at fifteen yards. So let's start with the targets at three and see how you do," Muscles said.

Merit attached her target to the caddie and sent it down the lane with the OUT button as Bull had shown her.

"The first string will be one shot in two seconds, five times; two shots in three seconds five times; and five shots in ten seconds one time," Muscles said.

Merit loaded the Ruger, put on her red ear protectors, and released the safety. She held the pistol in her right hand, cradled the gun and right hand with the left, separated her high-heeled feet, and put the gun down in low ready position.

"Raise your weapon. Fire," Muscles said.

She raised the gun into eyesight, gently squeezed the trigger five times per instructions, and then lowered the gun to the counter. Muscles walked down the backs of the shooters and looked at each pistol, making sure the barrel was pointed down the lane and not at nearby classmates.

"Move your target out to seven yards, pick up your pistol, and fire on my command twenty more rounds. Five shots, ten seconds, one time; two shots four seconds, one time; three shots, six seconds, one time; and five shots fifteen seconds, one time. I'll call off each interval," Muscles said.

The class followed his instructions, and shot on his command then checked the targets to see how they did. They put on the last clean target and sent it down the lane to fifteen yards per Muscles instructions.

"Lastly, fifteen yards in ten rounds. Two shots in six seconds one time; three shots in nine seconds, one time, and five shots in fifteen seconds, one time."

The class did as they were told until an entire box of ammo had been loaded and dispensed while following the gun safety rules established by Muscles, Bull's Eye Firing Range, and the State of Texas.

"If you didn't do so well this time, don't worry," Muscles said. "You get three attempts to pass with a 70% score out of 175 points. The inner rings, eight, nine and ten are five points a shot; the seven ring is four points a shot, and anything else on the target is three points a shot."

Merit did some mental math.

"Take your targets out to Bull and he'll grade them for you," Muscles said.

The class began to assemble their targets, pistols and empty ammo boxes to leave.

"If you didn't get at least a 90% score, you should seriously consider additional training to improve shooting ability. Bull will set that up for you if you need it. Thank you," Muscles said.

The class members mumbled "Thank you," and filed out the door into the store toward Bull.

Merit wrapped up her paperwork, shook hands with Bull, and walked outside.

Ag was sitting in his truck waiting for her by her Beemer.

"How did it go?"

"I shot a ninety-eight percent in a short skirt and high heels! What did you expect?"

Ag laughed. "Nothing less. Hop in, we'll celebrate."

Merit arrived home from her celebration with Ag and her CHL class feeling strangely de-stressed. There was something about shooting that discharged a lot of pent up energy. Maybe it was the hyper focused state she entered to remember all the rules, follow all the instructions with the sighting and squeezing of the trigger. It was a lot like meditation, being totally present to one thing to the exclusion of all the clutter in life. She got a sense of how shooting could be a sport and a hobby apart from self-protection and violence.

She took the clip out of the gun and put it in the nightstand along with the Ruger. She still wasn't ready to keep a loaded pistol in the house, and she certainly wasn't going to carry it around every day, but she was legal now; Betty and Ag were happy. She now had the option if she needed it.

She looked out the window at the spot where she'd found her husband, dead, blood all over the ground, gone from her for good. She closed the drawer to the nightstand and got into her empty bed.

26

Merit arrived early at her office to prep for the mediation. Manny Estevez would be joining her in about an hour and she wanted to go over her strategy one last time before they went to the mediator's office. Merit could hear music through the overhead speakers and smell coffee brewing when she opened the door.

"Morning, Betty," she yelled into the void that would soon bustle with activity.

Betty joined her and walked her to her desk.

"Mornin' darlin'. You're early today," Betty said.

"Big day today. You're early too."

"Got a problem."

"Uh oh. What now?"

Betty peeled back the end of a manila envelope and slid the contents onto Merit's desk. John Brewing wearing nothing but his weatherman smile in eight by ten glossies splayed out.

"Came in the mail," Betty said.

"How?" Merit said.

"Did you check your photos when the smoke smell was in your refrigerator?"

"Oh no."

"There's no return address. It was postmarked Austin. Nice package." Betty turned one of the pictures sideways to get another view.

"No note?"

"Nope."

"It's some coincidence that this arrived right before the mediation," Merit said.

"I'm sure," Betty said.

The office phone rang and they both ignored it. It rang again and then Merit's iPhone played John Brewing's quacking duck ringtone. Merit picked it up.

"Hello," Merit said. "I just got them."

She listened.

"I don't know who sent them," Merit said.

She listened again as her face turned pink.

"An apology?" Merit said. "I don't owe you a thing. If anything, we're even."

Betty looked flabbergasted. "The nerve."

Merit and Manny sat at a long conference table in the law firm of Jones and Tawny. Jones Senior, father of the named partner, was a retired judge and now of counsel to the firm. He led the firm's mediation and arbitration division and worked part time when someone needed a powerful hand to help settle a dispute out of court. Under the clauses of the sign lease that Manny had executed, good faith mediation was required prior to any trial to resolve conflicts. Since this mediation was voluntary, Merit envisioned a mutually agreeable resolution. She had hopes that it would end the fighting and allow Manny and his family to return to some semblance of a normal life. She had agreed to use Judge Jones, although Rooter had suggested him. Jones had a good reputation on the bench, and he was seasoned in this type of dispute. This would be an evaluative mediation, meaning the judge would counsel both parties on the strengths and weaknesses of their cases. He would also gauge each party's likelihood of success if the dispute proceeded to litigation, and try to use that information to leverage a settlement.

Rooter and Nixon had been set up in a different room so that Judge Jones could go between the two parties. That way he could focus on each side's arguments and points of law without the other hearing the opposition's case strategy.

Judge Jones, graying and distinguished, entered the conference room and addressed Merit and Manny. "As you know, this is a mediation, which is voluntary. It is not an arbitration, which may be binding in court. Your actions here today will not affect the outcome of the trial that is pending before Judge Hightower. Our goal today is to see if we can work out a compromise that both parties can live with, and to see if we can end this conflict and dismiss the lawsuit."

Merit nodded. She was well aware of how mediation worked. She had explained it to Manny in her office earlier, but it was good for him to hear it again from Judge Jones.

"I've already spoken with Rooter and Sonny Nixon. They are willing to drop the lawsuit and relinquish any claims on the land for an extension of the lease to fifty years for one dollar a year rental," Judge Jones said.

"Fifty years!" Manny said.

"That's absurd," Merit said, "Fifty years for fifty dollars."

"It's an opening offer to get things rolling," Judge Jones said.

"It's insulting. That is an encumbrance on the title of the land that will cause many problems if the Estevez family wants to sell it.

The area is going from warehouse and workshops to mainstream business. No bank or grocery store is going to buy the property with a forty foot sign at the door," Merit said.

"No, I won't take that," Manny said, "They're trying to steal from me again."

"Give us a minute to discuss a counter offer," Merit said.

Judge Jones left the room and Merit turned to Manny.

"What about a five-year lease for free just to get them off your back, then you can take the damn thing down and they'll be out of your life," Merit said.

"Do you think they'll take that?"

"No, but we have to start far enough away to give us some room to move. I'm sure that's what they did with the fifty-year offer."

"Okay."

Merit knocked on the door and Judge Jones came back in. She presented the counter-offer and they waited for Judge Jones to go work on the other side. It was his job to try to grind each party down over the course of the four hours they had set for this encounter. The hope was that the judge could get them closer and closer together until, like magnets, they set on a certain point and snapped into a final deal.

Merit and Manny waited, and waited.

Finally, Judge Jones returned. "I've really worked them over, and the best they'll do is a twenty-five year lease for one thousand dollars a year, with an option to renew for ten additional years at five thousand a year."

"That gives them thirty-five more years at well below-market rent. That's not much better than fifty years. Don't they realize that if they lose, the sign comes down next month?" Merit said.

"That's the offer," Judge Jones said. "They think they have a good case, and don't think they'll lose, so they're basically offering you this deal to save attorney's fees."

"What do you think?" Merit said, wondering where his experience told him the case would end.

"I think they have a good case. They have a contract, in writing, with the option to buy at the price Mr. Estevez sold to his brother. It's pretty clear under the four corners doctrine that the deal was made."

"What about the fraud in the inducement? That would allow the court to go beyond the four corners of the document and consider the intent of the parties. Using this Boots King character to trick my client should create an exception to the four corners doctrine."

"Maybe," Judge Jones said. "But it's a risk, and they appear to have deep pockets. They may be able to outspend you at trial."

"I don't doubt that," Manny said.

"What about the spirit of the law?" Merit said.

"It's hard to capture a spirit."

"The contract was clearly meant to apply to third party purchasers. Manny and his brother didn't sell, they just re-arranged their assets," Merit said.

"Young lady, you know a corporation is a separate entity under the law. It's just like selling to another person," Judge Jones said.

"Yes, but it is an extenuating circumstance that the trial judge must consider. Have you told Nixon and Rooter that?"

"Oh yes, they're aware," said Judge Jones.

"Let's go to ten years for one thousand dollars a year and a five year option to renew at fair market rate to be established at the time of the renewal," Manny said.

"Are you sure?" Merit asked. "We've come a long way from getting the sign off your land to giving them fifteen years."

"Yes," Manny said, his shoulders slumping.

Merit nodded. Judge Jones left the room to make the counter offer and Manny fumed. He paced in a three-step pattern in the corner of the room.

They waited and waited again. Finally, Manny excused himself. "I'll be right back."

Manny went to the men's room to cool off. He splashed water on his face and wrists. He looked at himself in the mirror. Could his family tolerate any more of this? Between the con man, the lawsuit and the hospital bills, he was feeling the strain. He might have to sell something to pay Merit if the case went to trial. He needed to settle. Maybe he could work out something on the attorney's fees. How much more could he take? He went into a stall and sat on the toilet with his clothes on. He pulled some tissue from the roll and wiped his forehead with it.

Rooter burst through the door laughing with Sonny and Judge Jones behind him.

"They'll fold any time now," Judge Jones said.

"How can you tell?" Sonny asked.

"I've stressed the risk at trial and the high attorney's fees. It scared them," said Judge Jones.

"Good work," Rooter said.

Manny saw red. He kicked open the stall door and burst into the room.

Judge Jones recoiled and Sonny stepped behind Rooter. Manny balled up his fists, then an extreme calm rolled over him. He walked out of the men's room leaving the three in silence.

By the time Judge Jones and Rooter returned to the conference room, with Sonny obviously absent, Merit and Manny were packing their files.

"We have a counter-offer," Rooter said.

"How much of your retirement is Nixon paying for Judge Jones?" Merit asked.

"You're obligated to see this through mediation, Merit," Rooter said.

"Good faith is a requirement. We mediated. It's over," Merit said, scowling at Judge Jones, who ducked his eyes.

"Taken any good photos lately?" Rooter asked. "Maybe a little beef cake? Some soft porn?"

Merit threw the files into her briefcase and snapped the latch.

27

M erit waited in line to valet park her Bimmer at the W Hotel on Lavaca Street. Valet parking and fancy hotels were all part of the new Austin. The W was next door to the Austin City Limits music venue. She had fond memories of great entertainment at ACL: Asleep at the Wheel, Emmylou Harris, Ruthie Foster. Last time she'd been, she'd seen a taping of Bob Schneider. That was back in the Sandra Bullock days. The W wasn't even in existence when Bob and Sandy were dating.

How had Austin gotten to be such a big city? Almost overnight. Merit hated the traffic, but she didn't mind the great food. Barley Swine, Uchi, Franklin BBQ, they all rivaled any good restaurant in the country. Even Sandra Bullock had a restaurant in town, Bess Bistro. Foodies loved it. Merit had been meaning to try a new place, called Jezebel, where the waiter took down the diner's preferences through a questionnaire then the chef cooked a meal to suit the customer's tastes. What would they think of next?

She left her key in the cup holder and arranged the slit in her gown so she could get out of the car gracefully without flashing her panties at anyone. Photographers snapped her photo.

Merit took the ticket from the valet.

"Keys in it. There's no place to put it in the ignition," Merit said.

"I've driven these before," the valet said.

"Thanks."

Touchy. Merit walked down the sidewalk. She missed the ten-foot tall Gibson guitar that once was standing on this corner. She wished Gibson and the city would organize another installation around town.

Merit arrived at the door, showed her invitation, and merged into the crowd. She spotted a bar in the corner and made her way over. She passed a waiter holding a tray of beautiful tidbits that smelled like fennel and garlic. She snagged one little pastry puff and popped it in her mouth.

"Coolio!" she said.

"We're pouring Texas wines tonight," the bartender said. "All donated by Bending Branch, Duchman, Texas Legato, and Llano Estacado. I recommend the Bending Branch Cab."

Merit noticed his fabulous thirty-year-old build under his tuxedo uniform.

Double coolio, she thought, reading the label on a colorful bottle.

"What's The Turk?" Merit asked.

"A Cab Syrah blend out of Paso Robles California. Proceeds go to Nobelity Project. Local writer named Pipkin developed it, I think," the bartender said.

"I'll try it," Merit smiled her best smile.

He poured the wine through a bubbler to accelerate the breathing process and handed it to Merit. That's when she saw the wedding ring on his left hand.

"Thanks," she said.

Merit moved on. No home-wrecking for her. Even cougars had their standards.

Merit navigated to the huge framed photographs on the far wall to locate her donation. She'd been supporting Women's Safe

Place since it had been in existence. This year, the fundraiser was a silent auction of photography of vintage Austin. The theme was retro and Merit had photographed the sign at Sandy's Hamburgers on Barton Springs Road. She had taken a black and white shot of the tall frozen custard on a cone that comprised their sign in neon and superimposed it over a pic of the Barton Springs Railroad Bridge. Her signature was scrawled across the bottom. So far, the photo had gotten four bids, starting at three fifty increasing twenty-five dollars per bid. At this point, Women's Safe Place would make four hundred twenty-five on her pic.

"Not bad."

"Nice shot."

Merit looked up from the bidding sheet to see Sonny Nixon looking almost handsome in his tuxedo and bow tie. For once, his nose was not running.

Must have taken Zyrtec, Merit thought. *Couldn't I have one night away from these goons?*

She smiled politely.

"Hello. Sonny, how are you?"

"Fine, thanks. Didn't know you were a photographer," Sonny said.

"I try," Merit said.

"Rooter's over there, if you want to say hello," Sonny said.

Merit looked at him to see if he was kidding, but he had a straight face.

What an idiot, she thought. Men could always play the game and go have a beer. Women were different. If you were their adversary, you usually stayed that way.

"I'll catch up with him later," Merit said.

"What did you use for the photo?" Sonny asked.

"I have a Nikon D4S."

"Nice," he said.

Sonny fumbled awkwardly avoiding eye contact and pulling at his cummerbund.

"You shoot?" Merit asked.

"Used to. I was a photographer in college," Sonny said.

"Not anymore?" Merit asked.

"Gave it up, you know. It was the love of my life. Still have some of my original equipment," Sonny said.

He looked directly at her for the first time. He seemed so sad she almost felt sorry for him.

"It's never too late to start it up again," Merit said. "Sometimes I don't shoot for months, but it all comes back next time I pick up a camera."

"Nah, I've got to be at the office most of the time now. I have a responsibility. My mother's money started the company before she died. She wouldn't like what's been done with it," Sonny said.

"I didn't know," Merit said.

"I've said too much. Enjoy your evening," Sonny said.

He began his fidgeting again and disappeared into the crowd.

Boots drove his pickup to Donn's Depot on West Fifth and parked in front of a railroad crossing sign. He spotted both Nixons inside. After Boots ordered beer for all at the bar, Old Man Nixon, Sonny, and Boots settled into a booth in the back. Sonny was squashed between his father and a wall of colorful advertisements. Boots hoped the Depot was not about to become a casualty of the growing economy along with so many other great joints around town.

"You picked a nice spot," Old Man Nixon said.

"I don't move in your circles," Boots said.

"I understand. Just kidding," Old Man Nixon said.

The bartender brought over the longnecks, no glasses.

"You called me," Boots said.

"Since the mediation fell through, I want you to up the ante on that Texas Lady Lawyer," Old Man Nixon said.

"How high?" Boots asked.

"Throw her completely off balance without taking her out. We don't want them to hire another attorney. Just make it so she can't think straight," Old Man Nixon said.

"Take her out?" Sonny said.

"I said without taking her out," Old Man Nixon said.

"Physical harm cannot be on the table now or later," Sonny said.

"Your call," Boots said to Old Man Nixon.

"We'll take it one step at a time. Give her something to worry about and let's see how the case goes," Old Man Nixon said.

Sonny looked at his father.

"What would Mom think of all this?" Sonny asked.

"Mom's not here," Old Man Nixon said.

"I miss her every day," Sonny said.

"You're just like her. She made you weak," Old Man Nixon said.

"I didn't come here for a trip down memory lane," Boots said.

"Right. Let's get this lawyer lined out and we'll figure out the rest later," Old Man Nixon said.

"How much money do you need?" Sonny asked.

Boots enjoyed every minute of it.

28

The next day after work, Merit parked in her garage at home. The motion of the car activated the outdoor lighting. She looked around, checked her armpits to see if she had any little prickly inklings of danger, felt none, and went into the house. She dropped her briefcase on the kitchen table and held the door open for the dog to go out.

"I'm sorry you had to wait so long, PepperDog."

She filled one bowl with kibble and rinsed out the other, adding fresh water. She nibbled on her pink polished fingernail. She selected a nice Malbec from the wine cooler and popped the cork out with the screw.

The wine was sweet and fruity, full bodied just the way she liked it. She let Pepper back in, locked the door, and began to undress as she walked toward the bedroom.

The house felt empty with Ace away at school and John no longer expected for a late night romp. Tattoo had not yet received an invitation to come over.

She flipped on CNN in her bedroom, and then turned it off immediately, when her armpits prickled just a little.

A noise outside? Was it the TV? Was she hearing things? She walked on eggshells these days.

She peeked out the blinds. Saw nothing. The lack of motion detection had shut out the lights and there appeared to be no movement to re-activate them. Still, something felt off. She looked toward the neighbor's fence but couldn't see anything out of the ordinary.

She went back to the kitchen, grabbed her purse where she had left it on the counter, and brought it to the bedroom. She took out the Ruger, released the safety, re-set it, and put the pistol on the nightstand. She undressed, put on a robe, went into the bathroom, and filled the tub.

As Merit soaked in the water, she melted into the wine buzz, the bubbles, and the feeling she had protection if someone came through the door. The combination gave her peace. She took a huge breath, and finally relaxed even though she was in the tub and the gun was in the bedroom.

Boots circled the neighbor's yard and watched Merit's shadow move behind the shades in her house. He could see her holding something as she sat on the bed, but couldn't see what it was. He crept around the edge of the yard, avoiding the motion sensors for her outdoor lights.

What a joke. A false sense of security at best, useless if someone really wanted in, he thought.

Boots could see Merit fiddle with something then put it on the bedside table. He watched her shadow undress, put on a robe, and leave the bedroom.

Boots saw the bathroom light go on and her shadow move around the window. It looked like she was running a bath.

"Your time is coming. I can have you anytime I want you," Boots said.

He was happy, excited actually, just to watch and know what he could do if he chose. He wanted to make it last.

"Foreplay," Boots said.

Merit and Ag took Red River on the east side of downtown, past Darrell K Royal-Texas Memorial Stadium, and toward Bastrop County. It was late, but they'd heard from Slag that cockfights were a thing of the night and if they wanted a chance to catch Boots King, they needed to become night owls, too.

Ag had the picture from Chaplain that was grainy, but hopefully good enough for an ID. They also had the descriptions from Emmi and Betty. Since the mediation hadn't worked, it was more important than ever that they serve Boots and have him testify in court.

When they started seeing piney woods, Ag took a left and drove several miles down a caliche road hitting potholes and limestone protruding through the hardpan. He pulled his truck into a row of pickups and SUV's along a cedar break and killed the engine. They sat for a while looking around and breathing heavily in the dark. To the left at the end of the drive was a metal building that looked like a workshop. Behind it was an old wooden barn that had been propped up with odds and ends of wood and scrap. Half the roof appeared missing and a faint light glowed through several large cracks in the board walls.

Three burly men entered the workshop throwing light across the ground until the door closed behind them.

"Looks like the front building is the clearing house for the barn. We can either go in as paying customers or climb around this cedar in the dark and try to get a look," Ag said.

Merit fidgeted with the window button, which didn't move the glass because the engine was turned off.

"Let's wait a minute and see if any women go in," Merit said.

Up, down, up, down on the window button.

"What is that smell?" Merit asked.

"Pigs. Over there is a pigpen. See the hogs moving in the dark behind the fence."

"Yuck! Makes me reconsider bacon."

"Stop stalling. What's it going to be?"

"I'm deciding. Did you know cockfighting is legal in Texas under Section 42 of the Penal Code?"

"You're kidding."

"No. It has to be for medical experimentation. I looked it up."

"And when does the medical part come into play?"

"I guess when someone gets arrested and needs an excuse for cockfighting, which is otherwise illegal."

"I bet that works," Ag said.

"No. But neither does anything else. Stronger legislation was passed in 2011, but as you can see, it's still going on."

"You're stalling," Ag said.

"Okay, let's try around the side of the barn, if we can get there without breaking our necks," Merit said.

"Good call. You have too many teeth in that beautiful smile to pass for trailer trash," Ag said.

"Thanks, I think," Merit said.

Ag pushed the button on the overhead light so it would not come on when they opened the doors. They both slid out. Merit rested her door gently against the car then quietly pushed it closed. She pulled her ball cap snug on her head and touched the

Longhorn logo for luck. Ag joined her and they picked their way through the cedar along a limestone ledge to the side of the barn. When they were about halfway there, they could hear the voices inside cheering and swearing.

Merit and Ag found cracks in the wood at comfortable heights for each of them and stared at the mayhem inside the barn and the world's oldest spectator sport. In the corner the three burly men they'd seen enter the outer building were taking cash from a frenzied crowd of about fifty men. The three yelled out bets like a trader on the stock market floor and moved money from one hand to the other depending on which bird was being blessed with the will to win. Merit expected a bunch of rednecks, which they were, but she didn't expect to see so many men wearing expensive boots, monogrammed shirts, and Rolex watches. Apparently, cockfighting drew spectators from all economic strata.

The two gamecocks, one mostly black and the other mostly red, were in cages in a wooden cockpit made from boards like the barn. Behind each cage was a handler poking the birds with some sort of stick, which inspired them to move about.

In the center of the ring, there appeared to be blood on the floor with feathers stuck to it.

After the bets were made, the spectators moved into the bleachers and an announcer called for the fight to commence.

"Starting round two. This will be a gaff fight."

He rang a bell and the two managers opened the cages and pulled them off the stage as the gamecocks jumped out. The birds began to strut around the ring facing each other and bristling their feathers. On the spurs of the cocks were long, sharp, dagger-like attachments transforming their spurs into knives for maximum injury. The steel blades were sharp, causing the announcer, who was also the referee, to steer clear of the weapons.

"Is this a fight to the death?" Merit whispered.

"It can be. The first bird to go down and stop fighting loses."

"Do you see Boots King?"

"I don't think so," Ag said.

"Me either."

The birds reared up on their feet and puffed their breasts at each other. It happened so fast. With neck feathers fanned and wings whirring, the birds jumped up and parried at each other. They strutted the pit and calmed some. The handlers picked up the birds, blew on their backs, and yanked at their beaks. Next, they held the two birds beak-to-beak reigniting the frenzy, then dropped them on the stage.

The roosters rose up, then kicked and dueled in mid-air, striking each other when an opening occurred.

The red cock flew at the black bird spurring him in the side with his gaff-enhanced spur, causing blood to splash across the floor. The black cock regained his balance and went after the red cock again with his beak and feet, slashing his abdomen with the gaff.

The red cock was stunned and shifted his weight from one foot to the other.

The black cock went in for another slice, taking the red cock down for a quick finish.

Merit looked away as the barely breathing red cock was discarded in a barrel near the game pit.

Boots King pulled into the end of the line of parked cars at the cockfight arena and sat in his truck finishing a beer and a joint, followed by a cigarette. He saw movement between the parking area and the pigpen and watched to see what it might be. At first he thought it was the cops finally raiding the place after years without detection or caring or both, but one of the figures was small and wearing a ball cap. Maybe it was kids trying to sneak in without paying or someone taking a leak out back. He watched a while longer as the two figures moved to the side of the barn and appeared to look inside. He exited the truck and began to move toward the two silhouettes.

Boots watched Ag turn his head from the game to the parking lot and back again. As Boots made his way around the edge of the cedar break, he saw Merit's ponytail swinging from beneath the cap and knew it was her. Boots identified Ag as well, but didn't think they had recognized him. Boots halted when Ag and Merit turned and stood up straight.

After a moment, Boots advanced further into the cedar break and saw Ag take a step toward him. The front door of the venue opened and light shone around the parking lot as a couple of rowdies left the warehouse counting their winnings. The stream cast enough light for Boots to see the Glock in Ag's hand.

Boots knew if he could see the gun, Merit and Ag could probably see his face. The rowdies started toward their vehicles near the cedar break. Losing his anonymous advantage, Boots lowered his gun out of sight, backed slowly down the row of trees, and returned to his truck.

Boots left the parking lot as Merit and Ag hastily made their way to a pickup at the end of the row. As Boots drove away, he vowed to fight another day. He was serious about hurting them. He was not just up to mischief any more, he was as single-minded as the black gamecock.

29

The day after the cockfight, Boots King arrived at Merit's house in Tarrytown and entered through the same dining room door he'd entered before. He'd waited for her to leave for work, and waited as usual to make sure she didn't return.

It's time to teach the bitch a lesson, he thought.

He would have to avoid the cockfights now. One of his favorite forms of entertainment.

Nixon had briefed Boots on the mediation. The signage corporations had hoped the mediation would settle the whole matter and end this mess once and for all but Judge Jones had opened his big mouth and Merit had learned that he was in Nixon's pocket. They were going to trial, and Boots had to make sure that Nixon won. If he took Merit out of the picture, Manny would just hire another attorney. He had to make sure she was rattled enough to lose the case. A little distraction was in order, and maybe some fun too.

He went into the same office he'd viewed before and looked through the desk. Still nothing on the Nixon case.

"Too bad."

Boots turned off the heat and checked to make sure all the windows were closed.

He looked in the cabinet under the bathroom sink and found a generic brand of Drano and several cleaning products. He dumped some of the liquid in the bathtub and around the kitchen sink with the stoppers plugged in. He poured the remaining products into a wine bottle, out of the recycling bin, and stuffed a wad of paper towels into the neck of the bottle.

He raised the top on the stove and blew out the pilot light, then turned on all five burners and let the gas enter the room.

He went into the hall closet to blow out the pilot light on the hot water heater but found a box on the wall that said "Tankless" on the sticker. He couldn't see how it worked, so he closed the door and continued through the rest of the house.

Satisfied, he went outside through the French doors in the dining room and looked into the house through the glass from the backyard. He looked at his watch and timed the minutes to let the gas fill up the house.

When Boots was certain that he had waited long enough, he pulled out his lighter and lit the wad in the wine bottle. He took aim at the kitchen window and threw the bottle through it. The kitchen exploded. He could see the dog run down the hallway through the French doors. The fire progressed quickly through the rest of the old house catching and expanding as it went.

Hearing the explosion, several neighbors ran out of their houses and toward Merit's front yard. Several had cell phones out dialing 911 as they ran.

Boots cut through the back of one neighbor's house, and made his way unseen to the street in front of Merit's home. He hung back for a while, and when the crowd swelled, he joined the neighbors to enjoy the fire. Boots stood mesmerized. Trance-like while feeling the heat of the bonfire of wood, furniture, glass and fallen brick.

When Boots heard the fire engines coming, he was shocked to see where he was. He had stayed too long. He made his way down the side street to his truck, reluctant to leave his favorite motion picture.

"Showed her."

Merit pulled up to the smoldering remains of the house too late to make any difference. She stood at the curb crying and watching the steam rise off the embers still smoking on the ground. She looked over the mess into the backyard, but Pepper was not there. She feared the worst.

Betty and Val pulled up and ran to Merit. They held onto her arms on each side and Betty cooed in her ear.

"It's going to be all right baby. Hang on. Hang on," Betty said.

Val was fighting back tears. Betty did the talking.

"That bastard. It's going to be okay," Betty said.

"I left Pepper inside. Ace will be crushed," Merit cried.

Betty and Val went mute.

"All Ace's baby pictures, all my photography, my grandmother's hutch, all gone," Merit cried harder.

"Oh darlin'," Betty lost the battle with her tears.

A few remaining neighbors were talking to the firefighters. Merit saw Ag pull up in his truck. She made eye contact and saw him go over to question the fire chief.

"Any idea if it was an accident?" Ag asked.

"Doesn't look like it. We'll know more in a day or two. Ms. Bridges have any enemies?"

Ag looked over at Merit as if asking permission to share. Merit nodded.

"She's working on a couple of tough cases. There've been threats. You should coordinate with Chaplain at APD."

"Will do," the fire chief said and turned to Merit. "In the meantime, get some protection. Whoever did this is evil and serious. Looks like he wanted to put on a show."

Ag moved over to Merit and hugged her. Betty hugged them both and all three were silent as Merit cried into Ag's shoulder. Val cried too, and put a hand on Merit's back.

"How do I tell Ace? How can I possibly tell him? His father, now Pepper," Merit said.

"It will be okay," Betty cooed.

Merit felt Ag let her go. She saw him scanning the scene.

"Like a man to look for something to fix," Merit said. "This can't be fixed. It will never be okay."

A neighbor from down the street came toward the crowd with a squirming wet Pepper in his arms. "I don't know how she got out, but here she is. All in one piece," he said to Merit.

Merit grabbed Pepper from his arms and squeezed her so tight the wet fur ball yelped and dripped. She cried harder, so hard she couldn't find her voice.

Betty spoke for her. "Thank you. It means so much to her."

Merit nodded at him and finally said "Thank you. Thank you so much," to the neighbor and the heavens above.

30

Merit went to Betty's and began to work the phones while Betty sent Val to Nordstrom at Barton Creek Mall to pick up a few pairs of jeans and shirts for Merit. First call Merit made was to her best friend from her undergraduate days at Rice University in Houston. Joy was Ace's godmother and her closest confidant. It gave Merit a great deal of comfort knowing that Joy was nearby if she or Ace needed her, like they did now.

"Joy, this is Merit. Something terrible has happened," Merit said.

"Are you alright? What's the matter?" Joy asked.

"My house was burned down. I'm involved in a really intense case against a bunch of shady characters, and it's gotten dangerous. I need you to get Ace from school and hang onto him until I can get there to pick him up."

"Of course. Of course. Be careful. I'll do it right now. Do you need a place to stay? You're welcome here," Joy said.

"I'm going to take him to the beach house in Port Aransas until Ag can get things sorted out with the APD," Merit said.

"Okay, I'll have Ace here when you arrive. I'm so sorry," Joy said.

"Don't take your eyes off of him until I see you. Is Tucker around? Can he help?"

"He's at the office, but I'll have him meet me at the school. I'm on my way."

"Thank you so much. I'll see you in a couple of hours," Merit said.

Merit took Pepper into the shower and scrubbed the soot and muck off both of them. She was blow-drying Pepper's fur when Betty came in with the clothing.

"Here, darlin', this is the best we could do, but I think they'll fit," Betty said.

She handed Merit the shopping bag and took over drying Pepper.

"I'll have your suit cleaned while you're gone," Betty said.

"Don't take any chances going out alone. Ag is going to Chaplain at APD to see about having some additional security for you and Val. If they can't cover it, he'll hire private. I don't want anything to happen to you," Merit said.

"Don't worry darlin'. You know me. I'm a survivor. But I'll be careful, and you too. Call me when you get to Houston," Betty said.

"I will," Merit said.

"Do you have everything you need?" Betty asked.

"This should get me by for a few days. Thanks. I've also got clothes at the beach house."

"Do you have your pistola?" Betty asked.

"It's in the car," Merit said.

Merit worked the phones on her way south to Houston. She had Betty release intern Mai to study until further notice, with a guarantee that her paycheck would be mailed to her in the interim. Merit also had Betty advise the building's cleaning superintendent to beware of going into her office alone late at night. She made sure Ag had sufficient security for the remaining office staff, which she'd pared down to Betty and Val. She didn't think the intruder would be foolish enough to return, but better to be safe.

Next, she called her old mentor in Houston from her former firm. Woodard "Woody" Preston had been an attorney at her first firm out of law school in Houston, before she moved to Austin to open her own shop. He was an old time lawyer, traditional and extremely ethical. He loved the law and made it his personal life's work to preserve the Constitution. He had sworn her in when she'd passed the bar. His favorite saying was "the law is a seamless web". That had stayed with her since the first time he'd said it, when she was a baby lawyer and anxious to learn.

She called and worked her way through the maze of receptionists and assistants at Bell and Bright, one of the largest firms in Houston, and finally got Woody on the phone.

"Woody, I'm in trouble. I need to see you. I'm on my way to Houston now," Merit said.

"I'll be at the office all afternoon, or I can meet you after. Are you in danger?"

"Yes, and I need to get Ace to make sure nothing happens to him. Can you meet me after work at Joy's?"

"Of course, what do you need?"

"This case. It's gotten out of hand. I don't know which way to go next to protect my client and my family. I need to talk to you."

"I'll be there."

Merit woke up the next morning in her house at the beach "in the dark night of the soul". She replayed her conversation, from the night before with Woody, over and over in her mind. His warnings echoed in her brain. He'd seen disgruntled clients and the opposition in a case go off the deep end before. He'd reminded her that sometimes the need to win trumped all logic and fair play. She would recover, he'd promised. It did not make sense to her that someone would destroy her home for money or meanness. Nothing made sense to her at all.

Her dreams had been worrisome. Images of fire and the smell of smoke stayed with her. She loved her house in Port Aransas, and was chagrined to find that the dark cloud she was attempting to escape had followed her down to the Gulf Coast. She meditated and wrote in her journal, but it didn't help to lift the gloom.

She finally got out of bed and made a pot of her favorite tea. Neither Ace nor Pepper stirred in the bunkroom. She let them sleep. She took a cup out onto the deck and watched the waves roll in and out, willing herself to take deep breaths. Her Austin home was gone. A monster had come into her life and no matter how much she struggled, she could not release herself from his grip. Her beautiful antique furniture, her carefully selected wardrobe, Ace's baby pictures, her photographs and cameras, all gone. All taken from her by a viper who'd been thrown into her life and turned it into a snake pit.

She tried to figure it out. She tried to see her way forward. She tried to remember Woody's advice. She tried to cry. She tried to scream. She tried and tried until she tired of trying and just watched the water. In and out, swoosh and splash, roll and recede. The rhythm began to sooth her and the tea warmed her hands. The creamy milk calmed her tummy. She settled, breathed, settled further.

Ace opened the patio door holding Pepper's leash. The dog nuzzled Merit's leg with its cold nose and Merit gave her a long stroke down her back.

"Morning, Mom. I'm going to take her out. I'll be right back," Ace said.

"Okay, Peaches. Do me a favor? Take her to the dunes so I can see you. I don't really want you out by the driveway until we get a few things sorted out." She didn't want to scare him any further. He had taken the news about the house better than she had thought he would. Being away at school had given him a break from his old room and young child toys.

She thought they were safe, as few knew they had left town, but he needed to be on alert to any possible danger. Better to scare him a little than remain silent and have him caught unaware.

He stood before her clearly not comprehending the level of danger. He hadn't seen the house burn, she had. He hadn't thought that Pepper was dead, she had. The love in her heart when she looked at his messy bedhead blonde hair and crooked smile was overwhelming. She could not bear it if anything happened to him. He was her heart. She choked back emotion.

Ace pecked her on the cheek. "Sure, Mom. Don't worry."

"I'll get some breakfast started in a minute," she said.

Merit settled herself and returned to her process. She was safe. Ace was safe. Her staff was safe. Pepper was safe. That's what was important.

She had not remodeled her Austin home since her husband had died. She had never given herself a fresh start because she wanted Ace to feel as if he had a familiar place to return to from school. She wanted him to remember his growing up years and the happy memories he'd had with his father. As for her, she had never been in love with the place since she'd found Tony that day. Thankfully, he had gone out to the backyard and was sitting in a lawn chair when it happened.

But, it didn't just happen, did it? He chose. He chose to leave her, and Ace, and life and love. He had taken a hateful gun and pulled the trigger and made a statement that could never be unmade.

"I don't want to live with you anymore," he had said with his final act.

He had bought the gun as part of his plan. Had he deliberately gone in advance, bought the method of his final breath, hidden it from her and waited? What was he thinking while he waited? Did he hate their life together so much that he could not bear it any longer? The therapist had said that suicides didn't have much to do with who was left behind. It was only about the person leaving. That didn't feel true. He had left her, and she had failed him. She had failed Ace by not saving his father. She would never let anyone hurt her or Ace like that again.

She broke into sobs and turned her head so that Ace could not see. She cried until she could not cry another tear, and then she became angry. How dare this Boots King try to take what was hers? How dare Nixon use her misery to fatten his bank accounts?

She would go back to Austin and find some way to fight, to reclaim what was hers, to protect her son and restore peace. She would begin again. She would not let anyone steal away her life.

Merit took a long walk on the beach after breakfast. She'd always loved the bird life along Mustang Island. The waves were full of diving gulls munching on lunch. Cranes and heron walked their long legs along the surf hoping a fisherman would cast off a leftover carcass.

Betty called to discuss living options in Austin.

"How is it down there?" Betty asked.

Merit held the phone up above her head.

"Hear the gulls?"

"Yes. I can almost taste the sea salt," Betty said.

"Find a place for me to live?" Merit asked.

"There's not a lot to choose from. Most of these realtors are like tits on a bull, totally useless," Betty said.

The boom had caused a shortage of housing in Austin, and finding a long-term lease was not going to happen quickly. Merit would need time to settle with the insurance company and decide whether to re-build or buy new. Lots of decisions to be made and she was not in a place to make them.

"Some realtors are spoiled with the healthy market. No need to hustle these days. The ones that do work hard don't have much inventory," Merit said.

"I found a rental near your old place in Tarrytown on Bridle Path, but it won't be vacant for a few weeks."

"I want something different. Maybe downsize to a condo close to the office," Merit said.

"How about a high-rise? I called Bob Strickland at Loft Space. He has a two bedroom two bath unit with an office in the Warehouse District. He can lease it to you for a year until you decide what you want to do. If you don't like it, you can move anytime," Betty said.

"I've never thought of myself as a loft person," Merit said.

"Austin has changed. You live alone. There's a doorman and lots of security. They accept small dogs. Before you know it, you'll be as happy as a dead pig lying in sunshine," Betty said.

"I don't know," Merit said.

"There's a waiting list all over town. We were lucky he had not committed the unit yet. The best alternative is an executive suite hotel. You'll love that," Betty said.

"Yeah, right. It's just the thought of moving and starting over. I just can't face it."

"There's nothing to move. You can try high-rise living for a few months and see how you like it. I'll get you set up while you're gone with a bed, dishes and TV. You can decorate when you get back. Rest. Take a vacay with Ace and enjoy your time off. The nest will be empty soon and you won't need a yard or a big space anymore."

"Okay."

"Good."

Betty always won, Merit thought, *but she always knew what was best, so she should win.*

31

B oots entered the junkyard on Airport Boulevard through the back fence. He worked his way slowly in and out of the maze of cars taking care not to be seen by any of the shoppers. It was near closing time, and only a few stragglers were left circling the car carcasses and scavenging for parts. Boots didn't see the little bastard that had smoked the firecracker. Good. He didn't need anyone sounding the alarm today. He needed to find Tireman. Make a point. Send a message. It was irrelevant whether Nixon would support his decision to go beyond their directives. They'd have to go along, or he'd just remind them of what he knew, where he'd been, and what he'd done all on their behalf. He didn't need their permission.

He regretted he couldn't use his weapon of choice, fire. Wouldn't this place make a beautiful bonfire? Too bad there was no gas left in all these old wrecks. Nothing left here to burn except maybe the office. That might get too much attention, but was tempting.

Tireman rounded the corner and started taking a carburetor off of a wrecked Honda Civic. The customer stood beside him pointing and giving instructions as if he knew more about engines than Tireman. Tireman patiently listened and nodded and put the carburetor in a cardboard box. He handed it to the customer and sent him to the office for payment. The last customer of the day.

Tireman started shutting down the lot and signaled to a sexy looking woman working in the office to chain up the gate.

When Boots and Tireman were alone, Boots stepped out of hiding and called out, "Hey Tireman, how's that nephew of yours?"

"He's getting better. Do I know you?" Tireman asked.

"Too bad, I thought I'd gotten one more wetback out of Texas."

"Qué?"

Tireman's eyes sparked recognition. Boots moved toward him.

Tireman opened up the trunk of an old Honda and tossed the spare tire and jack on the ground. He moved towards Boots slapping the tire iron against his thigh.

"It was you who hurt my Emmi," Tireman said.

"That's right. What are you going to do about it?" Boots said.

Boots stepped sideways as Tireman charged him with the makeshift weapon. Boots pulled his 9MM from the waistband of his jeans and fired. Just as he pulled the trigger, Tireman hit Boots' arm with the tire iron sending the gun spiraling under a stripped down Volvo. Boots had underestimated him.

Tireman swung the tire iron at Boots head and Boots grabbed the curved end and twisted. The tire iron somersaulted over and over and landed in a pile of black truck tires. Boots recovered quickly and hit Tireman with his right fist, then kicked at him with his pointy boot. Tireman dodged both blows and punched Boots in the gut. Boots doubled over and Tireman kicked toward Boots' cojones. Boots deflected Tireman's foot, grabbed and twisted it. Tireman landed on the gravel and Boots kicked him with the point of his boot, making contact.

"Uh!" Tireman grunted, then punched Boots in the knee with his fist.

172

"You bastard!" said Boots, backing up.

"I know who my mother was. Do you?" Tireman recovered and ran like a billy goat, butting his head into Boots' chest. Boots struggled to regain his balance.

It enraged Boots further that Tireman had perchance hit on his biggest shame. Boots pulled a metal scrap off the nearest wreck and as he spun around, Tireman ran right into it. Tireman fell to the ground, hit his back on the jack he'd tossed, and didn't get up. He lay there groaning as Boots retrieved his gun from under the Volvo and tucked it in his waistband at the small of his back.

Boots grabbed Tireman by both feet and dragged him toward the office. He opened the door and shot at the redheaded woman as she scrambled under the desk. Taco ran away from the sound, toppling a stack of hubcaps. They clattered across the floor like Frisbees, and sounded like thunder.

"I'll take care of you in a minute," Boots said to the sexy redhead.

Boots grabbed a bungee cord off a hook on the wall and bound Tireman's feet to the old bench car seat.

Boots saw the redhead run for the window, breaking the screen and spraying gravel as she landed outside. She scooted out of site behind the nearest car as Boots aimed the gun and fired. The shot missed her and took out the window of her embrasure, sending glass flying.

"Damn," Boots said. He rarely left a witness.

Boots picked up a can of gasoline and poured it over the car seat, desk, and floor of the office. He twisted a piece of newspaper into a torch, flamed it with his zippo, and lit the gas as he backed out the door.

Boots saw a car pull up to the gate as the redhead ran toward it waving and shouting. He recognized Tireman's brother, Manny, who floored the car and sped up the driveway toward the office. Boots tucked the gun in his waistband and took off toward the back lot through the cars as the flames began to leap around the office. He found a hiding place to watch the mayhem. He could not let his artwork go without audience.

Manny grabbed the fire extinguisher from his vehicle and began to spray the flames. Boots saw Manny hand the extinguisher to the redhead and run through the flames and into the office. He watched Manny pulled Tireman free of the building as it exploded into full flames and sprayed debris across the gravel yard.

Boots was thrilled. He could not have orchestrated a better show. He became dizzy with the spectacle of it and rubbed the gun tucked in his pants.

"Tarantella! Candy! Llame una ambulancia! Call an ambulance!" Manny said.

The redhead ran to Manny's car, pulled out a cell phone and dialed 9-1-1.

Boots saw Manny lean over Tireman.

"Hold on, Hermano," Manny said.

"He hurt Emmi. It was him," Tireman gasped.

Manny bent over Tireman and rocked back and forth.

Boots knew Tireman was gone, the office was gone, and the fire department, sirens blaring, were too late.

"I win," Boots said.

Manny left the hospital and his brother forever. He drove the Austin streets for a while and eventually parked at the Highway 360 overlook. He could see downtown and the hospital where his brother's beaten body lay lifeless. He finally broke down in the privacy of his car. He cried the first tears he'd shed since Emmi was born. He thought about how hard Tarantella had worked his entire life. He thought of Emmi and the scars that would never leave his youthful face.

He remembered his promise, upon leaving Mexico, that his Mexican Mafia connections would be left behind and that his new life in America would be the end of those ties. He knew that asking a favor of his old friends would put him, his business, and his citizenship in jeopardy. He knew he would be obligated to them forever if he made that one phone call. If he were ever publicly connected to his old life with Banda de Mexicanos, his business would be forever suspect. The reputation and credibility he had fought so hard for would not survive.

He looked at the downtown skyline and let his eye follow Congress from the Capitol south through SOCO to his small part of the world. He couldn't see the auto shop, but he knew it was there. His anchor to Austin and Texas and America, his sangre, sudor y lágrimas—his blood, sweat, and tears.

Manny grew quiet, and then he grew angry. One should never make a decision while angry, his mother had often said. What would his mother think now if she were alive? What would she think of the thug who had killed Tarantella and was evading the law and justice? What would she say now? He knew. There was a point that one's enemies should not cross over. There was a point where even his docile sweet madre would no longer turn the other cheek.

"Madre de Jesús, forgive me." He crossed himself, picked up his smartphone, and dialed the country code for Mexico.

Rooter and Sonny met with Old Man Nixon at Rooter & Brown.

"What's up?" Old Man Nixon asked.

"Sonny asked me to set this meeting so he could talk to you about a few business things. I don't necessarily agree with what he wants to do, but I do work for Nixon Outdoor Advertising, and it's owned by both of you," Rooter said.

"You have the floor, Sonny," Rooter said.

"I know you told Boots King to burn down Merit's house and to kill Tireman. I want no part of this business anymore," Sonny said.

"Whoa. I don't need to hear any of this," Rooter said.

"First of all, King is acting on his own. I didn't tell him to go that far," Old Man Nixon said.

"I was there. The message was clear," Sonny said.

"Well, if that were the case, which it's not, you'd be an accomplice as well," Old Man Nixon said. "Remember that your signature is on record on the affidavits."

"I've admired you most of my life, Dad. Actually worshipped you as a child, but I've had enough," Sonny said.

"You've never stood up for anything in your life," Old Man Nixon said.

"Well, I'm standing up now. As soon as the trial is over, I want my half of Mom's money out of Nixon Outdoor Advertising. I've tried to love you in spite of everything, but all you do is insult me." He turned to Rooter. "I have to get out while I can. Rooter, do what you have to do to make it fair and legal," Sonny said.

Old Man Nixon's face reddened. He stood, towering over Sonny.

"You ungrateful bastard. You're out when and if I say you're out."

Merit, her staff, and a substantial part of the south Austin blue collar community joined Manny Estevez and his family at the graveside of Tarantella. The day was gray and drizzly and the crowd arranged umbrellas overhead, side by side, in a black makeshift tent. The dirt, mounded next to the grave, melted and slid down the hillside.

Manny and his wife held little Emmi between them. The little boy's right eye was bandaged, and his left eye was crying. The priest spoke of Tarantella's honesty, devotion to family, and work ethic. He recognized the grieving family left behind. He prayed and made the sign of the cross over Tireman's casket.

"In the name of the Father, the Son, and the Holy Spirit. Amen."

"Amen," echoed the grief-stricken.

After the service, Merit saw Manny join a group of about eight or nine men who stood apart from the rest of the congregation. Merit assumed they were Tireman's family from Mexico, but something was strange about them. They moved in like a web around Manny and his family. Manny was speaking to them in rapid Spanish. He pointed to Merit and Candy, and the leader of the group nodded as if he understood Manny's instructions.

Ag situated Merit, Betty, and Val in his truck and filed into the line of cars exiting the cemetery.

"Who were those men that Manny was talking to?" Merit asked.

"I think that was the Mexican Mafia," Ag said.

"No. How could you tell? Are you making that up?" Val asked.

"Been around," Ag said.

"The one in the front was so ugly he could scare a buzzard off a gut pile," Betty said.

"They were all carrying guns," Ag said.

"Should we be worried?" Merit asked.

"For Manny maybe. Looks like he might be taking matters into his own hands," Ag said.

"For our safety?" Val asked.

"If anything, you should feel safer," Ag said.

"Well, bless their hearts," Betty said.

32

Merit packed up to leave her office.

"I'm going to the firing range with Ag. He wants me to keep practicing," Merit said.

"Good. After Tireman we all need to double up on our security," Betty said.

"I'm trying," Merit said.

"How did you do at your last shoot?" Betty asked.

"Hit the bullseye inner ring three times."

"Go girl. Regular Annie Oakley."

"Wasn't she from Oklahoma?

"Ohio, I think."

"Hmm."

"I think Ag is starting to get sweet on you."

"Nah. We're just friends."

"That moon dog look he gives you."

"No way."

"Yes, way."

"You've got that one wrong."

"Well, just don't accidentally shoot him."

"Yeah, that's what I'm afraid of. Now what do I do with this gun?'"

"Just keep practicing. Hopefully, you'll never need it," Betty said.

Merit met Ag at the Hill Country Outdoor Firing Range in Oak Hill. They planned to run out to Nutty Brown Cafe for a beer and a burger after practice, and this range was on the way. Besides, Ag had said he knew the owner.

"Hopefully, this one's a Longhorn," Merit mused as she parked her BMW and unloaded her gear. Ag was waiting for her by the office.

"Hello, beautiful. I've already paid and had them put up targets," Ag said.

"Howdy, gunslinger. Ready to shoot?" Merit asked.

The range was a narrow stretch of land with a huge mound of dirt at the end. Bullseye targets were nailed to upright pieces of plywood in front of the dirt barrier. At the other end of the range, Merit and Ag placed their guns, ear protection, and extra ammo on a wooden table that was about waist high. To the right of them there were low boxes where other shooters laid on their bellies and fired rifles like snipers.

"Don't think I'll be doing that," Merit said as she pulled her scarf around her neck against the chill. The sun was about to go down. Even though it was still daylight, she could see the moon and the sun out at the same time.

She and Ag hustled into their ear protectors to block out all the noise around them and loaded their clips in silence. After they were set, Ag pointed at one of the targets and held up three fingers. Merit lined up on target three and Ag started firing at target two.

After they'd exhausted their clips, they looked at the targets through binoculars. Merit was inconsistent in her accuracy. Ag hit the bullseye almost every time. When the snipers left, Ag lifted his ear protectors and gestured for her to do the same. He stepped up next to her and the length of his body came in contact with hers. She took an unconscious half step back to allow space between them. Ag pointed to her Ruger.

"Look Merit. Don't put your finger all the way through the trigger guard. Just push it through enough for it to comfortably fit on the trigger and pull it back. That creates a space between the remainder of the finger that is along the frame so it does not touch the pistol and press it off line. The less movement and contact the better for consistency."

"Like this?"

"Right. Now press the trigger straight back so there is no sideways movement."

"I get it."

"Now, hold the gun up like you're going to shoot."

Merit raised the gun toward the target.

"Your eye has three focal points when you aim the pistol, the front sight, the rear site and the target. The rear site will be a bit blurry and the target the most blurry," Ag said.

"Yeah, it is a little fuzzy."

"Target shooters usually use what they call the six o'clock hold. You sort of let the inner black part of the target sit on the front site like a clock face at six o'clock. That way you have the pistol aimed correctly."

"That seems a bit awkward."

"There is another method of shooting for action or combat that involves no sighting. It's totally instinctive, which is probably more your style. A Fort Worth police instructor taught it to me. You look at nothing but the target. You instinctively point the pistol at the target stretching your arms out all the way like pointing a finger at an object."

Merit pointed and looked at the target.

"You might see your pistol or finger a tad bit in the periphery but that is not a big deal," Ag said.

"I see," Merit said.

"The instructor told me stories of abused women who had never held a firearm before. They desperately picked up a pistol and just pointed it at the bad guy and popped him good. No training or learning to interfere with instinct."

Merit practiced pointing and shooting and didn't let herself think about popping anyone or anything but paper.

Merit felt gravity release like the drop of an elevator. She pulled the trigger over and over without thought or design. She awoke to the realization that the gun was not an animate object destroying and killing from its tiny bullet mind. It was an extension of her—her arm, her hand, her finger on the trigger.

Merit's face was warm. It was a choice whether the gun would be shot. Her choice whether harm would come from the weapon she had feared for so long. She was a thinking, trained, choice-making human who would use the gun as a threat, as a security blanket, or as a weapon of protection. She had decided long ago that killing for killing's sake was not her sport. What she had finally come to grips with was whether she could safely own a gun, maintain it, and secure it from those who would cause harm if they were to obtain control over it. She would use the gun as she'd been taught in alignment with her principles and values. She was free from the fear of it. Free from the worry of what others thought about her having it. Free from the fear that she might cause harm to herself or others with it. It was exhilarating to release a fear she had held so long. A fear she had concretized at Tony's death.

Merit's breathing relaxed and confidence increased. She removed her protective ear-wear and checked her accuracy with the binoculars.

"Not bad, all shots on the target, and most of them in the inner three rings. Nice work," Ag said.

Merit smiled. "Thank you. Thank you for this. Thank you for helping me feel safe."

Ag swallowed, his Adams apple bobbing, as he diverted his eyes from hers.

Merit picked up her box of ammo and began to reload the clip. She kept the safety on while, at Ag's request, a young man ran down the range to staple on new targets. When it was all clear, she replaced her ear protectors on her head and began to fire again. Her breathing was even and her focus was intent on fine-tuning her aim. It felt more like a sport now, like golf or swimming, something she could improve on. It felt like what it actually was in the real world, not what she worried it might become in her fearful mind.

After practice, Merit and Ag continued on Highway 290 through Oak Hill and into Dripping Springs. They pulled into the Nutty Brown Cafe and found a table outside among the oak trees with a toasty heater nearby. A guitar player covered an old Bob Wills' standard. They ordered beer and burgers.

"Has Chaplain seen anything of our friend Boots?" Merit asked twisting the edge of the menu.

"Not a peep," Ag said.

The beers arrived and they contemplated Boots and the case while sipping suds made in the 512 area code.

"You'd shoot him if he threatened you, wouldn't you?" Merit asked.

"What if Tireman had had a gun instead of a tire iron?" Ag asked.

"He might be alive, maybe not," Merit said.

"King better not come after me. I'll shoot him in a heartbeat," Ag said.

"How can you say that as if it's nothing?" Merit asked.

"It's not nothing, it's something, a big something. And, we need to find him before he hurts someone else," Ag said.

"How do you look for someone and stay away from them at the same time?" Merit said.

They focused on the beer.

"I know what will cheer you up," Ag said.

"Oh yeah?"

"How about a little wager on the game at Jerry's World in Arlington next week," Ag said.

"Longhorns vs. The Fighting Irish at Cowboy Stadium? What do you have in mind?" Merit asked.

"Well, it is the College Football Playoff National Championship, so I think it deserves at least a few bucks," Ag said.

"I'm taking Texas, so I guess that leaves you with Notre Dame," Merit said.

"I'd take whoever was playing the Longhorns. How much?" Ag said.

"Trying to win my money with little Indiana Leprechauns?" Merit asked.

"Those Irish are a tough bunch. I'll even give you points. You'll need 'em," Ag said.

"Smack talk. No way. Even bet," Merit said.

"How about a home cooked meal by the loser. I hear you can crank out some nice pasta," Ag said.

"I know you can't cook," Merit said.

"I can grill."

"In the winter?"

"In Texas there's always a warm day or two for grillin."

"True. You're on," Merit said.

"I've already won," Ag said. He smiled.

"In your dreams," Merit said.

33

Trial preparation was tedious and demanding. Merit invested the time to drive to Houston to see her mentor face to face. It also gave her a chance to visit Ace and make sure the security Ag had arranged for her son was being carried out.

Maybe she and Ace could have some dinner at one of her old favorite restaurants from college days, or at least a beer and root beer at Kay's by the Rice campus. She couldn't focus when she felt her son was out of her protective reach. She'd been texting him so much he finally emailed her a YouTube video of the harm caused to children by overprotective parents. After that, she started texting the security guard instead.

If she made good time to Houston, she planned to replace two of the suits she'd lost in the fire. The trial was going to require that she wear something besides blue jeans, the one suit Betty had cleaned, and the suit she'd brought back from Port Aransas.

She left Austin on south Ben White Boulevard, drove by the new airport, and took Highway 71 toward LaGrange. The three-hour drive gave her time to work the phones, set up dinner, and think through her strategy. She set the cruise control at seventy-five miles per hour and the BMW floated down the road, almost driving itself.

Boots King pulled in behind her when she left her house and followed her across town. "Where is she going?"

When Merit stretched out on open highway, Boots realized she was leaving town and he'd not packed a bag.

"Road trip."

Boots called Old Man Nixon from the car.

"She's up to something, but I don't know what. Yet," Boots said.

"Well, keep tabs on her just to be on the safe side. Manny Estevez seems to be staying close to the shops and home. I'll have someone drive by and check on them while you're gone," Old Man Nixon said.

"Roger that. I'll report back when I know something," Boots said.

Boots pulled in behind her when Merit stopped for gas and a bathroom break in Sealy. Boots thought she'd spotted him sneaking around the corner of the building out of the men's room. When she didn't react, he let out a breath.

Why am I so worried? It's not like we've been introduced. She did see me at the cockfight, but it was dark.

He heard her radio station advertising Houston KILT and dialed it in so he could listen to the same songs she was playing as he drove along some distance behind her.

On the way into Houston, they passed a string of horses with riders, and horses pulling covered wagons, on the side of the highway. Boots had forgotten that it was time for the Houston Livestock Show and Rodeo. A banner on the back of one of the wagons read, "Los Vaqueros Rio Grande Trail Ride". She wondered if Ace's class was going to the rodeo again this year.

On their way around Loop 610, Boots watched Merit pull off, park, and run into Neiman Marcus in the Galleria.

Boots stayed with her car in the parking lot, taking the chance that she was only shopping and not having some clandestine meeting in Houston's most popular shopping mall.

Boots was beginning to wonder if he'd followed her for nothing but a shopping spree when she finally arrived downtown and entered a skyscraper with a sculpture out front that looked like a huge tinker toy. He followed her into the parking garage and took the stairs into the lobby of the building. He exited in the corner and watched her sign in at the security desk and board the elevator. He approached the security desk and clandestinely checked her destination on the clipboard, Woodward Preston. Penthouse. Boots looked up at the building directory. The penthouse housed a law firm.

"Is there a men's room on this floor?" Boots asked.

"Round the corner on the left."

Boots entered the men's room and called Nixon. "She's visiting a lawyer named Woodward Preston."

"I'll get Rooter on it. Get back here. I need you."

Merit met with Woody in his wood paneled office in downtown Houston. The firm had every indication of success, but was inviting as well. Woody welcomed her with a warm smile and a hug. She loved the feel of his tweedy jacket and the smell of pipe tobacco in his gray hair.

"Woody, I am straining the resources of my firm with this case. Every time I ask for discovery, Rooter covers me with paper that takes all my staff extra hours to sort out. I've hired temps, but that only gets me so far, and it's expensive. I'm exhausted. Even Betty is complaining," Merit said.

"Can your client pay you?" Woody asked.

"Eventually, but it may take longer than I want to collect," Merit said.

"You can always come back to work with me," Woody said.

"You can't afford me anymore," Merit laughed.

"How about the insurance on the house," Woody said.

"I should receive that after the investigation of the fire, but I don't want to finance my client's cases with my personal assets," Merit said.

"And you shouldn't," Woody said.

"And worse, I don't know my next step with the case," Merit said.

"There's merit on both sides," Woody said.

"I think my biggest weakness is that the document clearly says that there is an option to buy, but the admonition to have an attorney read it is buried in the fine print."

"You're right. It is in a really small font, and the new statute requires that it not be hidden in the boilerplate. Check the statute on the warning requirements," Woody said.

"I did, but the lease was signed before that was passed. The analogy helps me with the fraud angle, but it doesn't completely win the case," Merit said.

"Yes, a deal is a deal in Texas. Don't go crying to your mama after you sign on," Woody said. "So what's your argument?"

"That the lease was void on its face because it was designed to fraudulently obtain the execution of Manuel Estevez," Merit said.

"That's a start. So it never took effect as opposed to voidable, which would mean that it took effect and then was cancelled," Woody said.

"Right, and if it never took effect, it didn't exist and therefore, Manuel is not bound by the contract," Merit said.

"There's the problem with his actions. He allowed the sign to be placed on his land. So he acted as though he were bound."

"That circles back to the fraud. If he was tricked, he may have acted in good faith when Nixon did not," Merit said.

They caught up on personal things, Woody's oldest in law school, Ace's first semester away from home, and the Longhorn's new coach.

Merit felt fortified and ready for the fight.

"I think you're in good shape. Go to it, my dear. I'll walk you out."

Boots went to his truck and waited while he watched Merit's SUV. He wasn't about to drive back to Austin without some sort of payoff. He didn't care what Old Man Nixon said. Maybe he would visit her kid. He had the address from the files in Merit's home office. Or, maybe he'd follow her a bit longer. Scare her a little.

She finally came down the elevator arm in arm with an elderly gentleman in a beige trench coat and plaid hat. He opened Merit's car door, gave her an affectionate peck on the cheek and went back in the elevator. Boots saw the elevator numbers stop three floors up and as Merit circled the drive down, Boots circled up. He saw the gentleman leaving a parking space in a vintage Cadillac and pulled in behind him. The elderly man left downtown Houston and travelled through Montrose and into River Oaks. When the Caddy pulled onto Kirby Lane, Boots shot up behind and gave it a rub on the bumper.

"This is fun, and she'll be even more off her game with her old sweet sugar daddy in the hospital or dead."

The Caddy swerved and swiped the side of a parked car. The driver regained control and turned onto a side street to escape. Boots followed and bumped him again. The Caddy slowed down, but Boots used his powerful truck to push him along. The gentleman seemed to barely hold the car in the street and avoid oncoming traffic. He began to honk his horn over and over, then held the blast while he drove.

Boots rubbed the Caddy again and watched for a good catch spot.

The Caddy sped up and pulled away from Boots.

Boots saw his chance as the road took a sharp turn to the left. A house with large statuary was dead ahead. He picked up speed, rubbed the Caddy again, and then pushed faster.

At the corner, a River Oaks Security vehicle started its lights and siren and pulled in behind Boots as he passed. Boots gave one final shove on the Caddy and took the sharp left turn on three tires. The Caddy careened into the sculpture and stopped with a jolt. Boots went to the next block, made a U-turn into oncoming traffic, and drove back past the wreck.

Boots saw a shaky Woody being assisted by a couple of good Samaritans. Woody slid down the side of the car and sat on the asphalt gasping for breath.

Boots chuckled.

The River Oaks security vehicle passed him in the other direction. When he saw the rent-a-cop make a U turn and head back, Boots took off. He saw the security car in his rear view mirror for a time until he lost it on Shepherd in the traffic. Boots hoped the driver wasn't close enough to get his license plate.

Ag met with Chaplain regarding the subpoena on Boots King.

"This guy isn't a ghost," Ag said, "and thanks to Merit and the River Oaks security guard getting the license plate, we should be able to locate him. We know he drives a truck that's bigger than Dallas with dual rear wheels. Why can't you find him?"

"We have an APB out on his truck description in case he's changed the license plate, but no luck. Do you know how many 4x4s there are in Texas?"

"I know. It's just that Merit is beside herself with worry. He's following her and has attacked her mentor. He's like a father to her. I don't think she could live with herself if something happened to him or anyone on her staff."

"I understand. The bastard's not staying in Austin as far as we can tell, and there are no family members in the area."

"What about family outside Austin?" Ag asked.

"He has a sister in Tyler, but she says she hasn't seen him years," Chaplain said.

Chaplain creaked back in his desk chair and rubbed his hand across a full head of hair.

"Are you still staking out Nixon's offices?" Ag asked.

"Of course. The bastard hasn't been seen around there, and Nixon says he no longer works for them. Rooter has asserted attorney client privilege. He says if he knew, he wouldn't be able to tell us anything, but insists he doesn't."

"It's not only about service of process anymore. He's hurting people, Chaplain. We need to find this guy."

34

Merit and Val sat in the library at her office with dozens of law books stacked next to the client files.

"I've got a conference call with the Dobies on their oil and gas lease problem. Can you handle this until I get back?" Merit asked.

"Sure, I'll try to have a memo for you on your final questions by the end of the day," Val said.

Merit closed the door and settled into her office just in time for Betty to announce the conference call from the Dobies.

"Hello."

"Hello, Ms. Bridges, we are hoping you have some good news for us," said Mr. Dobie.

"Are you all there?" Merit asked.

"We're here," said Mrs. Dobie and several other voices.

"Okay. I've carefully read the oil and gas lease, and I have done some research on your facts," Merit said.

She flipped through a yellow legal pad to the notes she wanted.

"I think you have a fifty-fifty shot at keeping the drilling in one quadrant of your land if you sue. That's not very good odds with an oil company in Texas."

"That's not good news," Mr. Dobie said.

"What I think would work better is to try to negotiate with them. Talk amongst the family, see what's the least intrusive solution that you can live with, and then give me some parameters for talking with Line Oil. I suggest you use the seismic reports in your file to guess where Line Oil would most likely want to develop. See if you can arrange your subdivision layout around that area. After you define the parameters, I can see if they will take a sure thing in the area they are probably going to want to drill," Merit said.

"So dangle a carrot and see if they bite?" Mr. Dobie said.

"Right, and part two is to get something for yourself that you need," Merit said.

"Such as?" Mrs. Dobie asked.

"For example. It appears that the best site for drilling is in the middle of the back of the six hundred and forty acres. If you can give Line Oil the corner they already have plus the middle of the back, which they don't have, you may be able to negotiate the building of a road through the acreage to the back of the section. That way, they can get in and out to the drill site and once they are finished, you have a nice road to structure your subdivision around."

"We'd have to do a cost analysis. It might work," Mr. Dobie said.

"Yes, that would be a good step. See how much the road costs and offset it by the amount lost with the inability to sell the extra land. If they are close to the same, you can call it a wash and save attorney's fees and headaches," Merit said.

"That's a good idea," Mrs. Dobie said.

"I have some contacts at Line Oil. When you get your ducks in a row, give me the plan and I'll float it by them. If they like it, we'll do a full proposal to their development department."

"Ten-four," Mr. Dobie said.

"It's always better to avoid a lawsuit if you can," Merit said.

35

The trial started the next day. After the preliminaries, Old Man Nixon took the stand. He wore a black suit with an open collared white shirt that stretched tight over his gut. Cowboy boots, no tie. Rooter questioned him first, laying the usual groundwork about the agents used by Nixon Outdoor Advertising, the lease, and basic business matters.

Merit had prepared all night for this moment and was ready with her questions when Judge Davis gave her the cue to begin.

"Mr. Nixon, do you expect this court to believe you knew nothing about Boots King's tactics in defrauding my client?" Merit asked.

"Yes. I do. I was not there when Mr. King spoke with Mr. Estevez, and neither were you or anyone else for that matter. I educate all my contract workers to be forthcoming and fair in their dealings on my behalf."

Merit looked at the judge. "Approach?"

Judge Davis was a quiet man, large in his black robe, but serene, like he knew the secret of inner peace.

Judge Davis looked at the document Merit handed to him and nodded. Merit, in turn, handed the document to Old Man Nixon.

"Mr. Nixon. Please look at the lease before you and read the clause marked 'Option to Purchase,'" Merit said.

"In the event of an offer to purchase said property, Nixon Outdoor Advertising shall be notified, in writing, and given thirty days to match such offer or pass. In no event shall the transfer of the land void, cancel, or affect the lease in any way and the lease shall attach to the land and not the parties to the lease."

"And, is that clause in the small print on the back of the lease called the boilerplate?" Merit asked.

"Yes, but so is half the lease. The front is only to set up the parties, the land description, and so forth. The meat of the agreement is on the back, along with this clause."

"I see. And, since it is a lease, why would you, or anyone approached by you, expect to find this clause in the lease?"

"We assume they can read, and the document clearly admonishes them to hire an attorney if in doubt about their rights under the agreement," Old Man Nixon said.

"Mr. Nixon—" Merit began.

"Besides," Nixon said. "We don't take anything more than they would get anyway. We match the price they are offered. We don't discount it a dime."

"Except in the case of my client, who did not sell to a third party at fair market value," Merit said.

"We can't know that," Old Man Nixon said.

"Since the option attaches to the land, you get to ride this gravy train through subsequent purchasers. Doesn't that diminish the value of the land by limiting its use?"

"That's balanced out by the rents we pay and the advantages of income for future owners."

"Do you really believe the small rents you pay cover the value?"

"Yes," Old Man Nixon said. "We pay the national average."

"How do you know what the national average is? Have you been price-fixing with other sign companies?" Merit asked.

"Objection," Rooter said.

"Sustained," Judge Davis said. "Stay on point, Ms. Bridges."

"Yes sir."

"Isn't it true that your agent, Boots King, pushed my client to execute the lease while hiding the option clause, and goading him into foregoing an attorney's advice before signing?"

"No, my contractors would never do that," Old Man Nixon said.

"As you said, you weren't there, so you wouldn't know what was said to my client. That's all," Merit said.

Rooter was on his feet.

"Re-direct, Your Honor," Rooter said.

Judge Davis looked at his watch.

"Be brief," Judge Davis said.

"Mr. Nixon, how do you know that your agents, including Boots King, did not lie to Mr. Estevez or any of the other landowners where your signs are located?" Rooter asked.

"Objection," Merit said.

"Exception, Your Honor. Course of dealing," Rooter said.

"Go ahead," Judge Davis said.

"Continue, Mr. Nixon," Rooter said.

"I know because we always do it the same way every time. Each contractor is instructed to act in exactly the same way using the same script with each landowner. They are to point out the option clause and allow the landowner time to meet with an attorney if they so wish."

"Every time," Rooter said.

"Yes, every time. In all our years in business, we make sure there is never an exception," Nixon said.

"How do you make sure?" Rooter asked.

"We shop our sales people and independent contractors," Nixon said.

"What do you mean shop them?"

"We set up quality control through helpful businesses who act out a situation with our team members. We send out a new agent and record his actions through hidden camera. That way, we can be sure they understand the importance of their interaction with our new business associates," Nixon said.

Merit stood.

"Your Honor, during discovery we requested all information regarding Boots King and this transaction and were not presented with any such video or documentation," Merit said.

"Mr. Rooter?"

"The videos and records are used to monitor the agents and then destroyed. If it got out that Nixon was shopping the agents, their actions might be contrived. These records are gone, so there was nothing to present," Rooter said.

"We'll reconvene after lunch," Judge Davis said.

Rooter turned to Merit with a smug smile.

Sleaze bag, she thought.

Sonny Nixon saw the exchange and watched his father swagger down the aisle of the courtroom. *All power, no substance.* He thought of his mother and her generosity to people her whole life. He remembered stories of when his maternal grandfather started the sign company and ran sequential Burma-Shave signs along countryside fences. His favorite was: Every Shaver . . . Now Can

Snore . . . Six More Minutes . . . Than Before . . . By Using . . . Burma-Shave. His mother and her father met with the farmers and ranchers, had coffee around their kitchen tables, and treated them fairly and honestly. If a rancher didn't want signs anymore, they simply took them down. The company was not the megacorp that it is now, but with the small business back then, his mother always seemed to feel good about her work, her charities, and her friends. Sonny hadn't felt good in so long, he'd forgotten what the sensation was like.

Manny supervised as Banda de Mexicanos set up their headquarters in the Heart of Texas Motel on Highway 290 East. He had reserved four rooms, two men per room, plus an extra room for overflow, equipment, and visitors. Manny pulled the crew together in the extra room and filled them in. He advised that Boots King had been sighted near the cockfights in Bastrop County and in several bars around Travis County outside of Elgin. The motel's location allowed Banda to monitor both cities and all the outer counties. Manny had no idea he was driving back and forth to San Antonio. Neither Manny nor Banda considered alerting their Hispanic brothers there, as no connection to San Antonio had ever been made. All indications were east of Austin, so they put their brothers on notice in LaGrange, Columbus, and Houston.

Manny had told them that finding Boots King to testify was crucial to winning his case, but more importantly, vital to keeping everyone safe until the trial was over. Banda had years of experience in the same shadows where Boots lived, and if anyone could find him, it would be them. Banda spread out to all known locations each day and prowled the haunts at night. Manny had requested daily reports. Thus far, no Boots.

Banda had been less than an hour behind him at the cockfight in Bastrop County two days ago, going on a tip from Manny. Since then, no sightings. That same night, they reported that they had seen his black 4x4 with the emblem of a naked model on the grill, but had lost it on I-35 in five o'clock traffic, and had been unable to pick it up again. Banda was good, but Austin was an unfamiliar city, and Texas was a big state. There was a learning curve. Boots was always one step ahead of them.

Thanks to Candy, the APD had a composite of Boots' face. Manny provided Banda a copy of the drawing along with all the information he had gleaned from Merit and Ag on Boots' whereabouts.

Manny made sure neither Candy nor Merit knew that Banda was in Austin. Banda's plan was to show the composite around the bars and hangouts where Boots might go and see if they could get a lead on him. They were aware that APD was doing the same, but there were places that Banda could go that APD would not know about.

Neither Manny nor Banda knew that Old Man Nixon had limited Boots' activity after he had killed Tireman. If Old Man Nixon had known what Banda intended to do to Boots, he might have left him active. It would solve several problems for Nixon and the Bolos. They couldn't take that chance, however, as Chaplain might arrest him and Merit might force him to testify before Banda could take him out. It was all supposition anyway, as Old Man Nixon had no idea Banda was in town. Maybe the old guy should fear for his own life. So far, Manny had not given the word, but if he did, there would be vengeance for Tireman and little Emmi, and there'd be nothing Old Man Nixon could do to stop them.

How would Old Man Nixon and Boots feel if the tables were turned and they felt the fear in the pit of their stomachs for a while? Manny thought.

Banda had been of little help so far except to protect the Estevez families and secretly watch over Merit and Candy. Manny knew he was going into trial the next day with his co-jones blowing in the wind, but at least he knew he could focus on the suit without worrying that some monster would hurt another member of his family.

Merit and Kim Wan left the courtroom through the swinging gates with Rooter right behind. She felt eyes on the back of her head, turned around abruptly, and saw Rooter staring and smirking.

"Why are you looking at me that way?" Merit asked.

"I can't believe you made that argument in open court," Rooter said.

"As opposed to your argument that was so truthful and convincing?"

"This is a trial, what does truth have to do with anything? Don't tell me you still buy into that officer of the court routine."

"Right, it's all about the win for you, Scooter, no matter who it hurts; and for the record, you took the same oath I did as an officer of the court."

"Don't call me Scooter."

"How does it feel to be disrespected? Now you know how my client felt when you drilled him."

"It's not the same thing. Yours is a personal attack. I went after him for business reasons."

"It was personal to him. What do you call family, his livelihood, his dream of making it in this country?"

"I call it a pipe dream. The American Dream is long dead. Big business rules now, and you know it," Rooter said.

"I know no such thing. My dreams are still intact and so are my client's. It's a shame you lost yours, but we are not giving in to your beliefs. We are protecting our beliefs, and when you are alone in your office working late at night, you can remember that."

"I'll be out celebrating with the hottest chick in Austin, and you'll be getting ready to lose this case tomorrow."

"Those jurors are not like you. They won't vote with you. The jurors know the struggles of my client and they will vote with him."

"You'll never get to a jury vote. Here's my motion for Judge Davis. I'm presenting it first thing tomorrow. It's a matter of law. There's nothing to decide. I'll give you tonight to work on your reply, just to be fair," Rooter said.

"Thanks a lot. You mean so you can gloat. I didn't know you had the word fair in your vocabulary. Do you have this rigged too?"

"No need. Four corners doctrine. Legally, your client signed the contract, was paid good money by my client, and he has to live with the deal he made. He wears big boy pants," Rooter said.

He handed her a document.

"You can't prove fraud because it's my client's word against yours. The judge will take it from the jury in the morning. Just wait and see," Rooter said.

"And this Boots King character who executed the lease. He just happens to be out of your reach?" Merit asked.

"Exactly. Long gone."

"You can smile all you want, but don't think for a minute I've forgotten what a lying, cheating prick you are."

"Oh, I remember. Seen Woody lately?" Rooter said.

Merit ignored the elevator and went for the stairs. She was furious that he knew about Woody and relished in the threat to his life. Every step she took down to the first floor filled her with more dread.

She knew Rooter had a legal point that the judge would have to consider. If she could only find someone to corroborate Manny's testimony that Boots King lied to him. If she and Ag had only been a little faster at the cockfight. Maybe they could have followed him and at least told Chaplain where he lived. Ag was still trying. Merit had asked him to look for one more night.

As promised, the next morning in court, Rooter moved for Judge Davis to take the case from the jury and rule from the bench on the point of law. The judge had the jury temporarily removed. After the room settled, with a nod he cued Merit to begin.

"Your honor, we have my client's word against Mr. Nixon's as to whether there was fraud in the inducement of the contract. That is a question of fact, and a matter for the jury. They must decide whom they believe," said Merit.

"Your Honor, I move that there is no one to corroborate Mr. Estevez's testimony regarding the fraud by an agent of Nixon. There's been no proof that my client knew of the fraud, and it cannot be proved from the testimony we have. Therefore, the fraud is unprovable on the facts and the court must rule as a matter of law that the four corners doctrine applies to the lease," said Rooter.

"The jury can decide if the fraud has been proved through Mr. Estevez' statements." Merit pointed to Manny sitting at the plaintiff's table. "The four corner's doctrine is modified by the statements of Boots King, Nixon's agent."

Judge Davis took a deep breath. "Though it pains me to do so I cannot see a question for the jury. In Texas, contracts are sacrosanct. We do not re-write agreements in court. Your client is not a child. He knew or should have known the ramifications of executing the lease."

"But, Your Honor . . ." Merit said.

Rooter kept a straight face, but Merit saw his foot tapped the side of the defendant's table.

The judge brought the jury back into the courtroom and dismissed them with thanks.

While the jury filed out the side door, Merit took their measure. Each one looked at Manny with sympathy. Merit knew she had them. So close and yet so far.

There was mumbling in the gallery. The press scribbled on note pads. John Brewing had apparently gotten off the weather desk because he was there with a camera crew. Merit could still feel the cleat marks up her back.

"Order," the judge said. "I'm ready to rule. The four corners doctrine states that the entire agreement of the parties must be in writing, and the merger clause in the lease assures that the entirety is in the document. Mr. Estevez executed the document and was paid a consideration for his agreement. The lease term was for a time certain and during that time, the option clause was activated by the sale. I find for the defendant. The lease stands."

Merit looked at Judge Davis as if he'd shot her. She knew there was risk in her argument, but she genuinely thought she'd met the burden of proof without the agent, Boots King, being present to testify.

Merit's heart broke when she looked at Manny. He appeared confused, then angry. He looked at his wife and they shared a glace. Merit knew they felt shame for their inability to protect themselves against the complications of another country, another language, and a set of rules that were both foreign and seemingly unfair. She felt guilty that she had let them down.

Merit returned to her office to find the entire staff waiting for her, except for Mai who had a test the next morning, and was still on study leave. Betty met Merit at the door with a glass of Malbec and a hug and they joined the others in the conference room.

Kim Wan had decided not to join them, as he had not seen his wife or children in days. His fees would have to be considered and discussed later.

"What a mess," Merit said.

All the books around the walls seemed to mock her with their details and rules and loopholes.

"We lost. I guess it was fair and square, I trust Judge Davis, but it doesn't seem right," Merit said.

"I looked for Boots King right up to the last minute. He's nowhere to be found," Ag said.

"I know. It's not your fault. No one else has been able to find him either," Merit said.

"It's not your fault," Val echoed.

"Sun don't shine on the same dog's tail all the time," Betty said.

Ag looked around as if their assurances were fruitless. He seemed to be exhausted like everyone else.

Each took a drink and sank into their individual thoughts with glazed expressions.

Merit remembered the look in Manny's eyes when the judge announced the verdict. She thought of the firm and how much it had invested in this case.

"The law isn't everything I thought it was," Val said.

Merit waited for Betty to weigh in. It seemed she had nothing else to say.

36

Merit took a much-needed break and scheduled a trip to Port Aransas. She drove through Houston, picked up Ace from school, and took him south for a quick trip to the beach. She needed a weekend with some family time and wanted a quiet place to lick her wounds and consider her next move. Ace napped in the car for a while with Pepper in his lap until they reached Victoria and stopped for Texas junk food and a bathroom break. Ace poured a couple of Dr Peppers from the fountain and Merit selected a big bag of Fritos. Leaving Victoria, they dropped down and drove along the Texas Gulf Coast munching and putting their troubles behind them while admiring the wildlife and blue waters. They noted the birding trails and tried to name, in alphabetical order, all the birds they'd seen on their many trips to Port Aransas. Merit had been using games like this since the day she'd learned that Ace was dyslexic. When he was small, his favorite was monkey in the tree.

"There were three monkeys in a tree, two more climbed up the tree. How many total monkeys were now in the tree?"

"Five," Ace would squeal with delight at knowing the answer.

Merit became very creative over the years at inventing teaching games.

Although they could have crossed over to Corpus Christi and taken South Padre Island Drive across the JFK Causeway Bridge, they always took the TxDOT ferry. It was part of the experience to realize that on one side may be trouble, but on the other was freedom, escape, paradise.

They reached the ferry in Aransas Pass around sunset to cross over the Corpus Christi Ship Channel. Ace pointed out his favorite sights—sailboats, pelicans, gulls and palm trees. Merit saw him let out a deep sigh. Things apparently had been stressful for him lately as well.

"I love it here," Ace said.

"Me too." Merit took her own deep breath.

Merit drove the BMW, following the flagger's gestures, onto the Michael W. Behrens, one of the older ferries with the wheelhouse in the middle. As soon as the parking brake was set and the ferry departed the dock, Merit and Ace jumped out of the car and ran to the front of the boat. Pepper watched with her wet nose on the windshield.

They only had about fifteen minutes during the crossing to spot their little friends before the ferry docked on the other side in Port Aransas. They actively scanned the water on both sides. To the left over by the fishing pier, there they were, a pod of about ten dolphin jumping and swirling in the water. No matter how many times she saw them, Merit never took for granted the miracle and wonder of the beautiful creatures. She felt that she could commune with them in her mind. She could see that Ace felt the same way and hugged him close.

They rejoined Pepper in the car and watched the ferries on both sides docking and undocking, moving across the water in a dance with no apparent rhythm, but never colliding or interfering with another boat in the channel lane. Merit drove the SUV off the ferry on the Port Aransas side, down Cotter to the beach, and along the waves to their home away from home. They went to bed with the moon reflecting in the surf.

The next afternoon, Merit sat on the deck of her Port Aransas house drinking wine from a plastic cup and watching Ace and Pepper play on the beach. She could have gotten a wine glass, but the occasion didn't seem to warrant it.

Merit watched for signs of anyone who might approach Ace. She had been looking over her shoulder so long it had become a habit. Fear had become second nature, and she hated that constant reminder of danger. She took a breath and tried to relax. Hopefully, Boots King was far, far away now that she had lost and she had nothing he wanted.

Merit had spent months on the lawsuit, endangered her office staff, lost her home, and put her son and Woody in the path of a maniac; and still she had not won. She had exhausted the financial resources of her client, and even if she agreed to cut the bill, which she probably would, the impact on both Manny Estevez and her office would be devastating. Rooter's team had managed to take the day either by skill or on a technicality; either way it stung.

She guessed the whole gang was at the Petroleum Club right now, celebrating and gloating, showing all of Austin big business how the firm of Rooter & Brown had taken down the Law Office of Merit Bridges. Nixon, Sonny, and the boys were probably counting their money and making plans for the rape and plunder of the next small businessman.

Merit thought back over the past months. She thought of Tireman and how he had burned the sign and started the first domino falling. That domino crashed into the mediation with Judge Jones in the back pocket of Nixon. The next domino was poor Emmi attacked with the smoking firecracker. After that, her home was destroyed. Poor Woody was almost killed. The harshest blow was the loss of Tireman. Merit knew Boots King had killed him. Everyone knew, but he could not be found and APD seemed to be at a loss for what to do next. Of course, they would keep looking, but would he ever surface? Maybe it was best if he didn't. Every time he came within a mile of her or her loved ones, something bad happened.

One domino falling after another until the last had fallen when she lost the case and she was out of options. There was nothing left to do. She had no more tiles to play.

At least she hoped that Boots King was out of their lives forever. What purpose would it serve for him to continue to terrorize them? The case was over. Nixon Outdoor Advertising, there's a company to remember. How in the world did they get away with it year after year, hurting one business owner after another? How did they always come out on top with the little guy always wondering what hit him?

Merit went inside and re-filled her cup. She looked at the photographs on the wall that had always brought her peace; rolling waves, sandy dunes, pelicans flying. She looked out the window at the blue sky. Nothing brought her comfort. Nothing felt familiar. She could not stay in hiding forever, even if it was a paradise. She would have to go home to a glass box in a tall building that had only a bed and a flat screen. She could spend time with Tattoo, but that didn't appeal to her either. He was fun, but fun wasn't what she was after. She wanted another shot. She wanted to take back a little bit of what Nixon, Rooter, and King had stolen from her, her staff, and her clients. She wanted justice. How could she get it? What could she do?

She poured the last of the wine into the cup and listened to the waves.

Ace waded into the surf and waved up at her. She ignored the wine, grabbed her hat and walked down to the beach. She smelled the sweet brine and let the sound of the ocean wash away her fears. She gave thanks for the sun and springtime. She was grateful for this place. She was grateful that her son was safe and that Pepper was alive. She was grateful for her life.

After the trial and a brief meeting with Nixon, Boots King left Austin in the dark of night and drove along I-35 to San Antonio. He had won. Nixon and Rooter had taken the trial lawyer down, but he, Boots King was the big winner. His bonus was in his pocket, courtesy of Old Man Nixon, and he was dreaming of far away places where he could spend it.

He preened in the rear view mirror and sang along with George Strait.

He looked up at the signs along the way from Austin to San Antonio with the red, white, and blue Nixon logo along the bottom. He had leased over eighty percent of them and he was proud to see his handiwork dotting the highway along the Texas Hill Country. Forget the view, forget the driving distractions, capitalism wins again.

"Take that, Dad! What con did you ever pull that was this good?" Not to mention Tireman and that snotty-nosed kid, Emmi. He'd taken them all down along with Merit's house. This was a good gig, and he deserved his nice fat bonus.

Maybe he would move to Tennessee, or Virginia, or out West. He liked California. It was going to be too hot around here for a while. He had eluded the APD so far, but they were eventually going to catch onto him. Maybe he'd start thinking of a new name; Boots King was getting a little too well-known.

He needed to lay low. Maybe New Mexico for some fun in the sun. Cancún would be nice, but with the changes requiring passports at the border, he was out of luck unless he got a fake. That seemed too risky right now. He'd heard that APD had a warrant out for his arrest for murder. He'd really lost it that day at the junkyard. Probably a little overboard, but he just couldn't stop once he'd gotten started. Oh well, one less Mexican in the world was no big deal.

He reminded himself to change license plates again. He may have to pop the Playboy bunny off the grill too. Too bad, he really liked that decal. Maybe he should have the truck re-painted.

Could he actually take a vacation? He'd become so accustomed to the thrill. Boredom didn't suit him.

Nixon had some connections with the Bolos out west. After a nice vacation on his bonus, Old Man Nixon would hook him up. There was always a need for someone who'd do what he was willing to do.

He had created a nice niche business. Wasn't that the buzzword these days? Niche? He laughed to himself.

37

Merit popped her head into the break room at the office to find Val grabbing a yogurt from the fridge.

"How's it going, Val? Keeping up with school?" Merit asked.

"Great. How was the beach?"

"Wonderful," Merit said.

"I've been listening to the class recordings on the way to San Antonio and back. It's really paying off," Val said. "Today I covered the elements of negligence: duty, breach of that duty, and proximate cause of injuries."

"Good work," Merit said.

Merit thought St. Mary's Law School was a good fit for Val. The University of Texas did not have a night school or part-time program, and Val didn't want to move to Houston to take advantage of South Texas' great set up for working students. St. Mary's didn't have the prestige of the other Texas law schools, but Merit didn't think Val intended to go into big law anyway. What was the old joke? The A students became judges, the C students became millionaires, and the B students worked for the C students.

"I emailed some new assignments. No rush," Merit said.

"Okay. I'll take a look. Today I counted the Nixon signs between San Antonio, Schertz, Kyle and Austin. There are fifty or more of Nixon's and a bunch more with competitors' logos dotted along the highway and blocking the view of the Hill Country."

"Yeah. Last time I drove to Port Aransas I counted as many along that way too. It's gotten completely out of hand."

"Really ugly. The highway's not too bad, but along the small towns you can't even see the scenery anymore."

"I know," Merit said. "Crazy. How many burgers can one eat? How many television shows can one watch?"

"Well, I wouldn't go that far," Val laughed.

"Yeah. Well, the Estevez case is over, but we still have other clients. Please check the new assignments, but they're not urgent. By next week is fine."

"Before you go, could you answer a couple of questions for my torts class?" Val asked.

"Sure, shoot."

"Well, I understand intentional torts, but what about negligence. What if a person didn't know if they were negligent when they did something? And, what about the class action suits? Does a company have to know they did something wrong, or can they just make a mistake?"

"Sometimes it involves intent, and sometimes it's what they should have known," Merit said.

"How about . . ." Val said.

"What? Wait."

A light bulb went off over Merit's head.

"Fraud, class action. All the signs along I-35. Signs on the Gulf Coast drive. It could be a class."

"I'm taking the class. What class?" Val asked.

"No, not that type of class. Take some notes. I need you to check this out in the library right away. Why didn't I think of that before? It may not work. But, it might," Merit said.

Merit felt the room was spinning. She bumped the heel of her hand on her forehead like the V-8 commercial.

"What? What might work?" Val asked.

Merit sauntered into the Texas Rose to the beat of a Lyle Lovett tune about ladies and wives.

Rose, the latest tattooed hostess, dialed the phone for Slag before Merit could ask.

"Ms. Bridges is here."

Slag bounded down the stairs with arms open and started air kisses before he reached Merit's cheek. "Darlin', so good to have you."

"Thanks for seeing me on short notice. Is there a quiet place we can chat?"

"Let's go to the bar, it's early for the heavy drinkers, so it should be quiet enough."

After they sat, Slag said, "What would you like?"

"Do you have Dublin Dr Pepper?" Merit asked.

"Sure, and I'll have a Coke," Slag told the bartender.

"I wanted to talk to you about the Nixon sign out front. Do you have a copy of your lease?" Merit asked.

"Yes, I do. I haven't had it for long, about three years. Brings in a nice little income every year. There's usually a liquor ad on it, which isn't bad for the club. Is there a problem?"

"Maybe, maybe not. If I could take a look at your lease and

maybe ask you a few questions, it might help another client of mine," Merit said.

"Absolutely, fire away." Slag motioned toward a tall brunette in a purple thong and red tassels. "Brandy, would you bring the 'Nixon Sign' file from the office upstairs. It's in the back cabinet."

"Right away.

Merit sipped her icy drink. "Mmm."

Slag smiled. "We aim to please."

Merit turned to Slag. "Not that it was necessary, but is there a reason you didn't have me check the lease for you? I've read all your other contracts and leases."

"Not really. It was just so short. More like a receipt book than a legal document. I read it myself, and since I could cancel it after the third year with a month's notice, I just signed it."

"Did you notice anything about selling your property?"

"No, it doesn't say anything about that. It's just a lease. The guy who walked me through it said it was just a lease."

Brandy returned with the file and handed it to Slag with a smile and a slight curtsey that made her breasts bounce.

"Let's see," he said and handed the lease copy to Merit.

"Hmm," she said, reading from the light of the flashlight app on her iPhone.

"Find it?"

"Not yet. Maybe nothing." Merit pulled a small magnifying glass with a light out of her briefcase and began to scrutinize the fine print.

"You're making me nervous."

"Here it is," Merit said, pointing to the middle of a paragraph.

"Here what is?"

"It's an option clause. If you ever sell your property, either now, or anytime after the sign is removed from the site, you must offer Nixon a right of first refusal at the price you've been offered. It's in the boilerplate."

"What? Let me see that. I didn't agree to that."

"I'm sorry, but you did. My other client did too."

"No," Slag said.

"It also applies to anyone who buys your property, even if you cancel the lease. It's called a covenant that runs with the land, not with the owner of the land."

"He lied to me. I'll kill that son-of-a-bitch!"

"Who?" Merit asked.

"Some guy in cowboy boots and sunglasses. I don't remember his name."

"He didn't witness your signature. Looks like Brandy did. What did he look like?"

"Tall, thin, he might have broken broncos in a past life, rugged."

"Sounds like Boots King, the guy I asked you about when we met with Candy."

"Oh shit! I didn't remember him at the time. What can I do about this?"

Back at the office, Merit found some quiet time to read the research memo Val had prepared on class actions.

She had a grasp of the basics, but she'd asked him to summarize the background so she could get it all clear in her mind before she went into the advanced cases. His memo went back over the common areas where class actions suits were filed. The more famous ones fell into about three categories. First were energy-related and included the lawsuits involving the Exxon Valdez oil spill in Alaska, the BP Gulf oil spill, and the collapse of Enron. Second were the drug company suits, including the diet drug Fen-Phen, Vioxx, and leaky breast implants. Third, there were the environmental-related suits, Pacific Gas & Electric in Hinkley, California, made famous by the movie *Erin Brockovich*, and the suits after Hurricane Katrina. Lastly, there were a couple of stand-alones, tobacco companies for concealing smoking dangers, and securities fraud perpetrated by Tyco, MCI, and AOL-Time Warner.

What was required by the court to certify a class was easy to enumerate. Merit had already surmised that Rooter would probably evaluate each of these requirements to see if he could attack their case on the failure of any or all of them.

Merit skimmed over the rest of the introduction to the requirements. First, he listed numerosity: the class had to be so numerous that a joinder of all members is impracticable. Ag had found over one hundred, and they were still signing up landowners, so that was covered.

Secondly, commonality: there must be a common claim to each class member giving rise to the cause of action. They had fraud in the inducement of one type of lease, so Merit thought that would do it, maybe.

Third was typicality: the class representative had to have a claim arising from the same course of conduct as the rest of the class. Merit had Ag working on that one.

Lastly, adequacy. The plaintiffs must show that they would fairly and properly protect the interest of the class. Merit's reputation was spotless. Kim Wan Thibodeaux had a good record as well.

"Bingo," Merit said.

Ag stood at Merit's office door and looked at the back of her head and blonde ponytail. He memorized the slope of her neck and the way a few hairs found their way out of the hair band and fell around her collar. He could smell her perfume drifting over like the curl of a finger beckoning him toward her and under her spell. What would it be like to kiss that spot? What would she think of his kisses and caresses? Would she like him as much as her boy toys? Could he make her understand how he felt about her?

He imagined entering the room and locking the door behind him. He took off her jacket from behind as he kissed the nape of her neck. He slid his arms around her shoulders and unbuttoned her blouse. One button, then another, then another as he nibbled her ear and breathed warm air into it. He cupped her full breasts feeling the lace of her bra in his hands. She leaned her head back against him and he nuzzled her hair while he pushed his hands into the band of her skirt.

"Hrrmph." Betty cleared her throat behind him in the hallway.

"Oh." Ag jumped and blushed. He composed himself and knocked on the door frame.

"If wishes were horses, then beggars would ride," Betty said as she moved on to her desk.

Merit raised her head from the memo she was reading and smiled at Ag.

"You rang?" Ag said.

"Hey Ag. Come in. Have a seat. Want coffee?" Merit asked looking back at the page.

"No, thanks. Just had a cup with Chaplain. But, I'll take you to the Broken Spoke tonight for a beer and a dance."

Merit held up a finger to let her finish a sentence.

"Okay, ready. What were you saying?" she said.

Ag froze then fumbled with his notebook.

"Uh, nothing," Ag said.

He flipped further then found the right page.

"Chaplain has all but closed the case on Tireman and Emmi. He said if we get anything to let him know, but they assume, since the case is over, that Boots King has fled the jurisdiction," Ag said.

"The case may not be over. That's what I called you about."

"But, I thought we'd lost."

"We did lose the Estevez case, but I'm trying to get another bite at the apple. Val made me think of it."

"Val? Little law student Val?"

"Right. I want you to make a list of all of the Nixon signs between here and San Antonio, and then I want you to see if you can match them to a landowner. If there's no building or address on the site, see if you can locate the owners through the tax records."

"Okay. What's the plan?"

"I'm going to try to certify a class for a class action suit."

"All the sign owners together?"

"Yes, but it's a long shot. And, we need to find a representative of the class. Not Manny, he's already had his day in court, and not Slag, he's too controversial. We need a good class representative since this will be a test case."

"Who?" Ag asked.

"I don't know yet, but I need a plain vanilla white good old boy, married, with kids, who goes to church every Sunday and votes Republican."

"Are you kidding? That should be a piece of cake in Bexar and Hays counties. If it were Austin, we might be in trouble."

Austin had long been identified as a blue city in the midst of a red state. Any time there was a national election and the news networks color-coded the votes, Austin stuck out like a bluebonnet in a poppy field.

"Let's start putting together a list of those with signs and interview them to see if they have the option clause. While we do that, someone will hopefully surface with the proper pedigree to be our class representative," Merit said.

"What if we can't talk anyone into it? Republicans don't like suing big business," Ag said.

"They don't like being swindled either. If someone was tricked into signing the option clause in the lease, he may be mad enough to help us out. If we can get a big enough group together, maybe we can get the media involved and put some pressure on the court to certify the class."

"You think it will work?" Ag said.

"Even if we can't certify, Nixon won't like being outed."

38

Ag drove south on the I-35 feeder road and spoke into a recorder, noting the approximate location of each Nixon sign as he passed. He also snapped a pic of the advertisement on the sign and estimated how far it was from the highway and adjoining tract, if he could tell. This would aide him later in locating the land on a tract map for the signs sitting on vacant land. The ones with businesses were easy; he just jotted down the address, or the name of the company on the building. If there were a lot of information, he'd stop and take a photo. The signs on vacant land would be more difficult, but he had some great landmen in his address book, and he'd be calling them for help. He noticed a new sign in front of a Stripes service station in Buda, and another in front of I-35 Self Storage in Schertz. Both had Nixon logos at the bottom of the advertisements.

Ag's neck hurt from looking up for so many miles. He took a break in San Antonio and lunched on cheesy enchiladas, refried beans, and rice at Mi Tierra. The freshly-made tortillas were so hot he had to toss them from hand to hand to cool them a bit before rolling. He had no idea that Boots King had been rolling tortillas there just days before, and was less than three miles away packing for his departure to higher ground.

Ag turned back toward Austin and repeated his research while driving along the feeder on the other side of I-35. There were more signs on the east side going toward Austin, so it took him even longer to complete the task.

The next part of the plan was for Ag to spend an entire day circling Austin streets, and maybe another day looking for Nixon signs in greater Travis County. He might also take a drive down to Port Aransas, per Merit's request, if they didn't have enough plaintiffs from the I-35 and Travis County signs. She had indicated that at least one hundred landowners would be necessary to try for the class certification. It wasn't a rule, but it seemed the minimum to get the court's attention. From the looks of his list and numerous micro cassette tapes, there would be no problem finding one hundred.

The next step would be to figure out if they had the option clause in their leases. To do that, each landowner had to be contacted and vetted. If the clause were in the lease, they would need to be signed as a client. If no clause, or if they knew about the clause before signing, they could not become a member of the class. If the contracts were just leases without the option, there would be no fraud and therefore, no class. Merit had assured Ag that Nixon was using the same lease. Hopefully, a leopard didn't change its spots.

Merit sat in the conference room that Betty had turned into a war room for the lawsuit. Betty had organized the file boxes and paperwork into logical sections. There was a box for each geographical area containing a file for each landowner along I-35, in Austin, and in Travis County, that Ag had located. Merit sipped hot tea with milk to warm up. Fortunately, winter only lasted a few weeks in Texas. That morning, she had seen a few signs that spring might be right around the corner. The fallen leaves had turned to compost and there were a few irises and Easter lilies starting to send up green shoots in the flower boxes around town. She still found it strange to take an elevator to the ground level from her condo and walk to work. It did not feel like a normal Texas event, but it was becoming one.

Betty came in with a stack of newly created files and Merit watched her organize them in their proper places in the boxes on the conference table, and the folding tables along the wall. There was a computer printout posted by the door that cross-referenced the land tracts to the owners' names alphabetically. The filing system might change later, but right now, it was more important to Merit to see where the signs were in relation to each other than who owned them.

Ag had done an excellent job finding the signs, he and Val had researched the landowners with the help of a few contract landmen, and Betty had organized the "whole damn mess" as she'd called it. Most of the files contained copies of the Nixon leases, and most of them had highlighted sections in the boilerplate showing the option clause in yellow.

If Merit were able to establish the class, all members of the class would be notified of the proposed settlement and its terms. Class members could either accept their portion of the settlement or "opt out" of the settlement, declining to accept the settlement funds and instead pursuing their individual claims in a separate lawsuit. It was win-win because they could decide later.

This was a big day. Ag was bringing in two plain vanilla white-bread male plaintiffs who owned properties with signs containing the Nixon option clause in their leases. Merit was hopeful that one of the two could be the class representative. Ag had warned that both were committed to the lawsuit, but neither was on board as point man. She needed to get started with the lawsuit, and needed a lead plaintiff to do so.

She didn't want Rooter getting wind of the research she was doing, and the landowners had been warned of the need for secrecy. The contract landmen had signed confidentiality agreements, and her staff was on alert regarding shredding and locking down of documents at the end of the day. With all the precautions, it still was a lot to expect over one hundred landowners with spouses, employees, and friends not to let slip to the wrong ears about the plan to file the class action suit. She desperately needed to find the class representative and get Nixon served.

Betty whispered at the door, "The first one is here, Odell Packing. Now, don't piss him off."

"I won't. I won't. Show him into the conference room and bribe him with a cup of your fantastic coffee. He'll be begging to work with us," Merit said.

Betty laughed and went to the reception area where she escorted Mr. Packing and Ag to the conference room. Merit had taken the single file on Mr. Packing from the war room and waited for them to settle in.

"Thank you for coming Mr. Packing. I know Ag has told you very little about what we're doing here, and I appreciate your giving us your time without a full explanation," Merit said.

Mr. Packing looked like ex-military gone a little pudgy. He probably had insurance with USAA. He had a buzz cut, was clean-shaven, and wore a suit that required dozens of polyesters to be harvested for the honor of its creation. He shook hands with Merit and sat between her and Ag at the conference table.

"I know there are questions in the Nixon lease, and Ag has explained the trick with the option clause. I'm willing to be part of the lawsuit, but I'm not sure what else you need from me," Mr. Packing said.

"First, let me explain that although we have an interest in your individual case, we have a much larger interest in bringing a class action by combining your case with that of all the other folks in a similar position. Let me explain how a class action suit works."

"Okay, but keep it simple. I know very little about the law, much less lawsuits," Packing said.

"Gotcha. There are other landowners who executed the Nixon leases and allowed them to place signs on their property. Most had similar terms to your lease, three years, then renewable each year thereafter unless notice was given before the end of the year. Not all, but most had the hidden boilerplate clause that gave Nixon an option to purchase if the land was sold, even if the lease had been terminated."

"How did some of them have different leases?" Mr. Packing asked.

"They struck out the option clause and initialed it," Merit said.

Mr. Packing looked sheepish. Merit noted his discomfort.

"Ninety percent of the landowners missed it," Merit said.

"Okay, that much is clear. What's the hard part?"

"There are a couple of hard parts. First, the landowner has to sign an affidavit that he was lied to in order to entice him to sign the lease. It's called fraud in the inducement."

"Well, that Boots King fellow did lie to me. He told me that it was a simple lease and that there was nothing in there except to give notice when I wanted the sign gone," said Packing.

"Yes, and you can sign an affidavit to that effect as did the other landowners."

"We're still meeting with others to get those signed and notarized," Ag said.

"Yes. You're right on time for that," Merit said. "Did anyone else witness the conversation between you and Boots?"

"No, we were alone in my office," Mr. Packing said.

"We are trying to locate Boots King," Merit said, "but frankly, don't have much hope of finding him. In his absence, we are hoping that the number of affidavits, all stating that his tactic was to lie and advise against legal counsel, will carry the day and overcome the need for his presence."

"No problem. I can swear to what he said," Mr. Packing said.

"Great. The second hard part is that we need a class representative who can be the lead plaintiff. All the other plaintiffs would be part of the class, but they don't all show up in court. We need a face to put on the group, one that is upstanding and respectable, one that frankly looks like yours," Merit said.

All three sat quietly while the news sunk into Mr. Packing's Caucasian respectable brain.

"I've looked at the profile you filled out with Ag." Merit pulled it out of the file and flipped to page two. "We know you are well regarded in the Schertz business community, you belong to the Lion's Club, the Rotary Club, attend the First Methodist Church of Schertz, and coach little league for your son's team. You are the picture of respectability."

"Well, thank you," Mr. Packing said. He pulled on his right ear lobe and contemplated the situation.

"There's not a whole lot extra for you to do," Merit said. "Mostly, you'd need to be present at the hearings and any negotiations that may arise. You'd also have to appear in court during the trial. If you are not the representative, but just part of the class, you don't have to attend those meetings or go to court."

"That doesn't seem too hard, what's the catch? What are you not sayin'?"

"No catch, but you do need to know there have been threats against those who've opposed Nixon."

"I have a gun," Mr. Packing said.

"Of course you do," Merit said. "Permitted?"

"Yes," Mr. Packing said.

"Okay. Then we just need to ask you a big personal question," Merit said to Mr. Packing, then exchanged a look with Ag. "Is there anything in your background that could be attacked in terms of your character?" Merit asked.

Packing stalled.

"I know we all have secrets, and we're not here to judge," Ag said.

"It's just that, if you are called to testify, you need to be beyond reproach, no character flaws that can be used to make you look like a habitual liar, someone who would deceive for profit or gain," Merit said.

"Anything you tell us is covered by attorney client privilege. It will never leave this room," Ag said.

"This is a really personal question to ask, based on how little we know each other," Merit said, "but we have to know before we go any further. Have you had an affair? Cheated on a business partner? Broken the law? Done something that you're not proud of?"

"Well, I have not lied, cheated, or stolen in my life. I do, however have some memories of, let's say, leave time when I was in the U.S. Navy. This was before I was married, mind you. It might be frowned upon by my church. I wouldn't want that to come out."

Merit stifled a laugh and turned it into a smile.

"That's not an issue. Nixon would not be able to pry into anything that old or irrelevant," said Merit.

"That's great," said Ag.

"If you agree, I think you are our class representative," Merit said.

"Let's get those cheatin' skunks!" Mr. Packing said.

Merit finished drafting the lawsuit and prepared it for filing the next day in the Texas State Court of Travis County. She'd had Val research CPRC 15.002(a)(3), which allowed for the filing where the defendant company has a principal office. Nixon had its primary corporate office in Dallas, so she could have filed there. They also had a large division office in north Austin, and it was a no-brainer to file locally in lieu of taking long road trips.

Alternatively, according to the statute, she could file in a county where the substantial part of the cause of action arose. Since the fraud was also committed in Hays and Bexar counties, those might have been a suitable venue in addition to Travis County. That was risky because Rooter might challenge and win on a venue change to Dallas. She didn't want him to get any early momentum. If this was going to work, she needed to score first, and keep driving the ball and intimidating him until she reached the goal line. After weighing all the options, she decided to keep it close to the office and have the opportunity to serve Nixon immediately.

"Travis County it is," Merit said out loud.

She left the office late, picked up a roasted chicken and veggies at Whole Foods, and went home to her condo that still felt like a hotel. She looked out over downtown and put a checkmark on the positive side of high-rise living for the view. Music too. No matter how much Austin changed, or where she lived, Austin still had the music as its heart and soul. She hoped it would always be "The Live Music Capitol of the World".

She slept fitfully while contemplating the work she'd completed thus far. She got up and went to the office early the next morning to polish the petition and add some bells and whistles.

The cause of action complained that Nixon Outdoor Advertising, Inc. had fraudulently induced each member of the class into executing a document by materially misrepresenting what was in the contract, that the representation was false, and that the speaker knew it was false and made the representation with the intention that it be acted upon. The complaint further stated that indeed the claimant did act upon the misrepresentation, causing him to suffer injury.

Val had thoroughly researched Johnson & Higgins vs. Kenneco Energy, and Merit relied heavily upon the case in drafting the lawsuit. She had hit all the marks required in the Johnson case, and hoped the judge agreed.

The complaint prayed for relief in two ways. First was the request of extinguishment of the entire lease. If the court refused to void the entire document, she pled in the alternative for the removal of the offending clause from the lease. That gave her one drastic remedy, knocking Nixon completely out of the lives of her clients. It also gave the court a second way to play Solomon. They could allow Nixon to have the leases as agreed, but take out the clause that was not agreed on. It was risky, and she was in a way giving the court an easy out when she'd preferred the initial outcome. However, she could not in good conscience argue that her clients had not agreed to at least some form of lease and signage on their property.

Next, she asked for one dollar in compensatory damages and ten million dollars in punitive damages. Actual damages would be hard to prove because each case was different depending on the value of the land involved. Merit knew this was her weak link and decided to play the damages in a range that didn't make the plaintiffs look greedy, but still high enough to be a threat to Nixon.

All this, of course, was done in the name of Odell Packing and the class of over one hundred and twenty-five members, plus additional members to be added to the class. Leaving it open-ended would allow Ag and Val to continue to locate landowners, obtain affidavits, and name additional plaintiffs, if newly discovered. Over one hundred participants would allow the court to see that the mass action consolidating the plaintiffs into one group would be more efficient for the court system than each filing individually.

It would also let Rooter know that Nixon was exposed and that Merit's little band of merry men were digging up all of Nixon's nasty garbage. She hoped to threaten him not only with the Texas class, but also with a possible national class. That would draw attention to the billion dollar outdoor advertising industry across the entire United States. Merit guessed that was the last thing Nixon wanted.

Merit was going to have Val file the lawsuit early in the morning to give Ag time to locate and serve Old Man Nixon. Merit planned to be with Ag when he handed Nixon the papers. She would not miss the look on his face for her entire legal fee. She only wished Manny could see it too. Maybe Old Man Nixon would be willing to take a selfie with her to commemorate the occasion.

"Nah, probably not."

Merit was already at her desk when Val arrived early in his best vintage Hugo Boss suit and Kenneth Cole loafers. He had on a rather long western duster overcoat that made him look like a cowboy out of *Young Guns*. No hat, of course, that would have been too much, even for Val. Merit thought it was too warm for the coat, of course, but drama was required for such an auspicious day. She expected no less from him.

Merit knew he didn't even have to go outside, as e-filing had been mandatory in Travis County since January 1, 2014.

Betty joined the party with a stack of printed pages, which she handed to Merit. She looked Val up and down.

"Isn't it a tad warm for that getup? In case you didn't notice, spring has sprung," Betty said.

"I want to be in my power suit when I press the key," Val said.

Merit schooled him with every detail of the filing plan. She wanted no mistakes. Val was to file with the Travis County District Court at 8:00 a.m. when it opened. As soon as he received a file-stamp number registering the suit, he was to text it to Ag who would add it into the service of process documents.

Merit then gave Betty her instructions. If the press called, Betty was to avoid them, giving Merit and Ag a clean shot at serving Nixon unaware.

On the street at exactly 7:45, Merit and Ag travelled out of the parking garage toward east Austin and Cisco's Bakery. Cisco's had long been the gathering spot for various public officials, including congressmen and lobbyists. Businessmen also filled the tables between politicians in hopes of garnering favor and being in the know before all of Austin heard what was up next. Paramount were the huevos rancheros, migas, and hot biscuits served to those willing to wait in line for the privilege of dining. Old Man Nixon and Sonny had breakfast there regularly, without having to wait of course. Ag's recognizance indicated that they would be there today, Monday, the way they always started the business week.

Merit and Ag stood near Ag's truck, which was parked around the corner from Cisco's. Merit looked at the time on her watch, and then at Ag.

"Are they inside?" Merit asked.

"Old Man Nixon is in there with a bunch of his cronies. Sonny's not here today," Ag said.

"We only have to serve one of them as an officer of the company," Merit said.

"What's keeping Val? Check your phone," Merit said.

"I just checked. It will buzz when he texts," Ag said.

"I know. I know. I just want to get this done," Merit said.

"We will. Hang on," Ag said.

They paced the sidewalk, periodically checking the phone.

BZZZT.

"Finally!" both said at once. Ag looked at the screen.

"We're on," he said.

Ag turned around so Merit could use his back as a desk. She scribbled the filing number into the pleading at the top of the first page.

Merit and Ag went around the corner, entered Cisco's, and bypassed the line. They waved to the hostess as if they were regulars. Their mouths began to water at the smell of the cooking food, but they had no time for breakfast today. They went into the back dining room, which had large glass windows looking out on East 6th Street and a row of budding crepe myrtle trees. They located Old Man Nixon and his fat cat buddies having their buttery biscuits and coffee.

"Hello Mr. Nixon. We have a delivery for you," Merit said.

Old Man Nixon wiped his hands on paper napkins. He and his buddies did the half stand bump and re-seat before a lady. It was habit.

Ag took the blue-backed complaint from the inside pocket of his maroon jacket and served Old Man Nixon in front of over fifty hungry politicos, locals, and Longhorn fans.

"You've been served," Merit said.

Merit watched Old Man Nixon drop his napkin and stare after them with his mouth open showing a half eaten biscuit. He opened the blue cover, and began to scan the pleading. His face turned as red as the checkered table cloths.

Ag smiled and recorded the time and date in his notebook. Merit took his arm and he escorted her from the cafe.

"Coolio," Merit said.

39

B anda de Mexicanos reconnoitered at the Heart of Texas Motel
to strategize their next move. They had been given Boots
King's address in San Antonio just moments before from their
insider at the APD. Apparently, Chaplain had traced Meriwether
King through several address changes and had located a rental off
Loop 410. They were told that Chaplain and his detectives were
going over to see if they could take Boots into custody. Ag Malone
was invited by Chaplain as a courtesy because of all the work he
had put into the case to facilitate Boots' location.

Banda de Mexicanos was planning to arrive first, and if Boots
King was there, eliminate any further action by APD or anyone
else, for good. Banda was more like a singular unit than individuals.
They moved together like birds in flight turning in unison with
little conversation or instruction.

They loaded their SUV and two trucks with firepower and
caravanned down I-35 as fast as they could go without attracting
attention. They slowed down to under sixty-five miles per hour
around the Buda speed trap, and then picked up the pace again
near Schertz.

When Banda left Loop 410 and entered Sierra Springs, a west
side neighborhood near Sea World, the lead SUV took over and
the two trucks dropped back. The stragglers hid in the area, and

waited for instructions. The SUV parked one block from the house number they'd been given and watched the target house for a few moments. They didn't see any lights or activity, but couldn't be sure there wasn't a truck in the garage.

Knocking on the door seemed too risky, as alerting him to their presence might cause him to go for a weapon. A ploy to get in was considered and discarded.

Worried that APD might show up any moment, the SUV called the trucks into action and the gang entered the yard through a gate in the back fence. The shades were pulled on all the windows, so all they could do was burst through the door, hope the element of surprise would catch Boots King off guard, and take him out before he got one of them.

Crash!

Down went the back door and the men rushed the house, checked each room sequentially and found nothing but smelly trash, empty boxes, and a sink full of dishes.

Too late.

The crew swiftly exited the house the way they came in, and left the neighborhood the way they'd entered.

Commonality of cause of action was the primary issue of concern to Merit. She had Val spend some extra time researching this element of the certification requirements. The question was whether the class had enough common elements to be considered a class by the courts. Merit had requested a full memo and copies of all the cases. She would do her own research later to expand her understanding and plug any holes.

Merit sipped her tea and organized the folders with the cases in them that Val had copied. She started with the file labeled Wal-Mart Stores vs. Dukes. This was a Supreme Court case, which narrowed the circumstances appropriate for class action suits. In Wal-Mart, the class asserted that managers in more than two thousand local stores had used discriminatory tactics. The Supremes noted that each store was managed independently and therefore the conditions at different stores did not present a common question. The court decertified the class.

To get around Wal-Mart, Merit needed to prove that Nixon used fraud to induce the landowners to execute the lease. Establishing that fact would resolve the claim central to the validity of each one of the claims. It would take it out in one stroke.

Merit next turned to a file with an antitrust suit, Comcast Corp. vs. Behrend. In Comcast, the Supreme Court in 2013 held that there was no evidence the plaintiffs had suffered a loss under the single theory that matched the liability. The Supremes, on appeal, decertified the class in Comcast.

"Not good news."

Betty popped her head in the door.

"How's it going?"

"Not sure. So far, Val's briefed a lot of cases that aren't on our side," Merit said.

"One thing I've learned about the law is that it always swings back and forth until it settles in the middle. Usually, it's just about being in the right spot by the time the case is decided," Betty said. "The scales of justice."

"Right, more like a pendulum. Who taught you that?" Merit asked.

"You did," Betty laughed.

"Thanks, I needed that," Merit said.

Merit returned to the memo and files. Val had included an insurance policy case, Life Partners, Inc. The insured asserted claims for breach of contract, breach of fiduciary duty, and unjust enrichment. The trial judge ordered the certification of the class. The appellate court confirmed, but the case was still ongoing.

"One for our side," Val said.

She read several more cases that were helpful to certification in the Nixon case and started wrapping it up. She placed the information back in an oversized file bucket and locked it in her credenza.

Betty popped in again. "I'm going to call the escort to walk me to my car if you're not ready to go," Betty said. Merit had a new rule that everyone who left the office after dark have a security guard see them out.

"I'm ready," Merit said.

40

"Ag is waiting for you," Betty said from the office door. Merit went down the hall to her office passing dozens of photographs of bridges and remembering where she took every shot. She would plan a big day for photography when all this was over. Maybe even a day at the beach with Ace, if the lawsuit were ever finished. She knew class action suits could go on for years, and she was going to run out of money before Rooter was through with her. She had some contacts with a few big tort firms and would have to bring them in eventually. For now, it was her baby.

Merit and Ag did a strategy recap in her office. Both were weary, but still committed to the plan for the class action.

"Chaplain and I missed King in San Antonio. Looks like he'd been gone a few days, but we found a broken back door and fresh tracks all through the dusty floor," Ag said.

"Why would someone break down the door?" Merit said.

"Maybe someone else is looking for him too," Ag said.

"You mean someone like Manny and his buddies?" Merit asked.

"Don't know. Just sayin'," Ag said.

"Okay. Let's not go there. What about the class action suit?" Merit asked.

"Still tracking down the last of the landowners," Ag said, "I'll keep you posted on our progress."

"Sounds good. Other news, we also have an agreement with Line Oil." Merit read a document in the file before her.

"Great. So they went for building the road and drilling in back," Ag said.

"Yep. Win-win," Merit said.

"If that's all on that, I have something else I'd like to talk to you about," Ag said.

Merit looked up at the tone of his voice. "Okay, that sounds ominous," Merit said.

"Remember the day we bought your gun and you told me about your husband's suicide?"

"Yes," Merit said, holding her breath.

"Well, I did some checking," Ag said.

Merit stood up angrily.

"Hear me out, Merit. Please," Ag said.

"How dare you meddle in my personal affairs? I thought you could be trusted. I am not one of your research projects, and neither is Tony."

"Hold on. I have something to tell you that I think you'll want to know," Ag said.

Merit sat back down and pouted, but did not speak.

"I chatted with Chaplain at APD on our drive to San Antonio to apprehend Boots King. Chaplain told me that when they investigated the suicide, they were told that Tony had gotten word that afternoon that his cancer was not curable. He was told there was no hope left. There was nothing further they could do."

"What do you mean? No one told me this," Merit said, choking back tears.

"They assumed you knew. It was in his medical records from the Cancer Institute. They probably played it down for fear of a lawsuit."

"What? They told him that day? I never opened the records. I couldn't bear to read them."

"Yes, that day. There's something else," Ag said.

"Do I want to hear this?"

"I would, if I were in your shoes," Ag said.

Merit didn't respond.

"Tony spoke to his doctor about physician-assisted suicide. He said he was afraid of being kept alive by machines in the hospital. He didn't want to suffer and he didn't want you and Ace to suffer or pay for large hospital bills. He thought preserving his life without regard for the quality of his life was inhumane."

"Oh God. What if I had been there, maybe I could have stopped it. What if he hadn't had the gun? If things had been different."

Merit knew in her mind that the suicide was not her fault, but she could not get past the guilt in her heart. Was she at fault? Did she not try hard enough? Was there any stone she'd left unturned?

"Tony was not making the decision because of depression or because he was mentally ill. He was not in despair. He made a deliberate, conscious decision to die. That's what Chaplain surmised, and he said the autopsy showed the cancer was very progressed. It would have been a long decline, and the pain would have been excruciating," Ag said.

"I never got to say goodbye. Ace never got to say goodbye."

"Maybe Tony couldn't wait. Maybe he hoped you'd understand. Maybe he couldn't say goodbye to you," Ag said.

Merit sat for a moment.

"I'll leave you alone unless you want me to stay," Ag said.

"No, yes, I would like to be alone."

As Ag left the room, Merit began to sob. She found crumpled tissues in her desk drawer and wiped her face. After she calmed down, she picked up the phone and dialed Ace's number.

Ace answered the phone laughing. Merit could hear other boys talking in the background.

"Hey, Mom," Ace said.

"Hi, Peaches. How's it going?"

"Great. I just got my history test back and I got a B plus."

"Coolio! That's a hard subject with all the reading. I'm proud of you."

Merit decided right then not to tell him about Tony. Ace had finally caught a break and she just couldn't give him that type of news just to make herself feel better by sharing. There would be plenty of time over spring break. She'd tell him then. It would keep.

"How are you, Mom? Did you need something?"

"Yeah. Uh. I got an email from your tutor. Seems there's a new font for dyslexia she wanted me to consider. She said we can buy some software to make it easy to change things over."

"She told me about it. It's called Dyslexie. I downloaded the font free from the Boer website, but the software will help with big things. I'd like to buy it," Ace said.

"What does the software do?" Merit asked. She wanted to get him talking so she could compose herself. Ace was very intuitive and she knew he'd pick up on her mood if he heard her voice.

"Well, the Dyslexie sort of tweaks letters. It puts all twenty-six letters of the alphabet through a process of adjustment to weight them down in a way. It makes it harder to confuse similar letters, so when I read, it won't be so easy to rotate and mirror the letters in my mind."

"Interesting," Merit said.

"It gives the letters fat feet by slanting the extenders and descenders. Also it opens up the circles to make bigger openings in p's, b's and so forth," Ace said.

"So it sort of deforms the letters? Can you read that?" Merit asked.

"Yeah, I've been playing with it. It's great. I just need the software to convert the books and stuff."

"Get it. Use your credit card," Merit said.

"Thanks, Mom."

"Let me know how it works out. Gotta run. See you over the break, Peaches Boy."

"Is everything okay?" Ace asked.

"Absolutely. I've got some research to do. Talk later?"

Merit returned to the computer and searched "physician-assisted suicide".

She found several websites on the top and clicked on one. She scanned down until she found something interesting.

It said: "The general public is overwhelmingly in favor of physician-assisted suicide. Many individuals are afraid of being kept alive by machines in hospitals, anticipating much suffering, both physical and mental. Modern health care is seen as being able to preserve the life of the terminally ill to a ridiculous degree with no regard for quality of life." She read on, not learning anything new and gave up trying to comfort herself through information overload.

Merit wanted wine. She did not want to feel the pain of Ag's information about Tony or what she was reading online. She did not want to process the information in the midst of all she had going on in her office and home. She did not want to feel. Anything.

A boy toy will get me out of this mood.

She called Tattoo to see if he could have a drink or dinner. When he answered the phone she could hear a jukebox playing ZZ Top and pool balls clacking together. He yelled into the phone.

"Hello!"

"Hi, it's Merit. What are you up to?"

"Hey gal. I'm in El Paso on my way to the Grand Canyon. Last minute road trip. I think I'll stay out west for a while. Sorry I didn't get a chance to say goodbye," Tattoo said.

"No problem. Have a good trip."

No help there. She knew he would eventually leave as quickly as he arrived, but she sure could use his special skills. Merit still wanted something to distract her from the pain she felt. Anything would do. She went down the hall to the break room and took a wine glass from the cabinet. When she opened the refrigerator, Betty appeared.

"Ag told me," Betty said.

"What?" Merit said.

"You know what," Betty said.

"No. No," Merit said.

Betty closed the refrigerator and looked at Merit. Tears puddled up in Merit's eyes and spilled over. Betty put her arms around Merit and rocked her back and forth as Merit wept for Tony and Ace and her lost home and her mistakes. They stayed that way a long time until Merit finally broke the embrace and plopped down in a chair like a deflated beach ball.

The Sunday after the big game, Merit drove about an hour out of Austin and arrived at Ag's second home in Briarcliff. The house was a rustic two-bedroom bungalow that looked halfway between a fishing cabin and a hunting lodge. The living room hosted a limestone fireplace that went up to the ceiling. The crackling fire made the room smell like mesquite. Ag was clean-shaven and smelled a little like pine needles.

"Beautiful drive out. Ever see Willie Nelson around here?"

"From time to time. I've seen him mostly around the golf course," Ag said.

"You. A golfer?" Merit said.

"You don't know everything about me," Ag winked.

"I think the IRS took most of his property around 1990. You should know this story. Darrell K. Royal persuaded Jim Bob Moffett to lend him $117K to buy Briarcliff Country Club. He planned to hold it for Willie. When the IRS found out that it was a friendly deal, they reimbursed the money plus interest during the right of redemption period. Later, the IRS re-sold it to some international investors."

"Didn't Willie eventually get it back?"

"Yep. Willie bought it back a few years later with the help of an entrepreneur out of Branson, Missouri. The recording studio had been auctioned off separately from the club and Willie's nephew, Freddy Fletcher bought it."

"Wasn't that used to start a music production school in town?" Merit asked.

"Right. It's still there. Those kids get to learn on all that wonderful old equipment steeped in history."

"Coolio," Merit said.

"I hear Willie and Freddy are going to shoot a movie around it," Ag said.

"I'd like to see that," Merit said.

"Let me show you the house," Ag said.

They took a brief tour through the inside and walked outside onto the large wooden deck. They looked out at Lake Travis, both mesmerized. The lake turned from blue to orange when the sunset colors reflected in the water.

They walked around the deck, checking out the deer in the brush and wound up near the barbecue grill. The fire was lit and the coals were burning down.

"I'm serving Longhorn steaks," Ag laughed.

"Hey don't dis my Longhorns just because you lost." Merit grinned.

"Okay. We'll have regular steaks. How about a glass of Italian red? That's your favorite, right?"

"Please."

They went back inside to the kitchen. The table was set and a bottle of red was breathing. It was so romantic.

Betty was right, Merit thought.

Ag looked at Merit with that moondog look Betty had described.

"Ag, we're friends."

"I think there's potential for more," Ag said.

"I admit, there's chemistry. I'm not ready for a relationship, and if we have sex, it's going to be awkward between us," Merit said.

"We could try having sex and see if it was awkward," Ag laughed.

"Ag, I'm not finished with the business with Tony."

"I'm sorry about that. I was trying to help," Ag said.

"No. I don't mean the business of the conversation we had about the suicide. We're fine on that. I mean that I can't commit to anything yet, and I don't see you and me having a fling."

He looked hurt.

"A fling would be nice," Ag said.

"Ag."

"How about just for tonight, we enjoy each other's company, have our steaks, let you bask in the glow of your UT win, and talk about it down the road," Ag said.

"Perfect. Now, may I have my wine?"

"Oh. Yeah. Sorry."

They both laughed.

41

Merit ran by Estevez Tire and Auto Shop on South Congress. She had a gift for Manny, and wanted to give Candy the news in person about her house and the status of the foreclosure. Business was good and the staff was bustling about talking to customers and returning cars at the end of the day.

Candy looked like Pippi Longstocking, in a Skunks t-shirt and candy cane striped leggings. At least she was covered and no cleavage was showing.

"Hey, Candy. Have a minute?" Merit asked.

Candy looked stricken. She fidgeted with her Jersey bangs that were curled into a tight red roll on her forehead.

"We can talk in the office. Bad news?" Candy asked.

"No, no, just the opposite. We checked, and there's been nothing posted for foreclosure yet on your home."

"Whew. Scared me," Candy said.

"There are a few things we need to do next," Merit said.

"Okay, shoot." Candy sat down at the desk, grabbed a pen and pulled over a tablet of paper.

"You qualify for a program that allows forgiveness of a payment. I spoke with your loan case officer. Your mortgage company has agreed to hold off any further action until you can fill out the paperwork if you complete it in the next few days. I had Val print it all out for you."

Merit handed Candy a file.

"I'll do it tonight."

"That brings me to the next thing. If we get you caught up, and you think you will not be able to make your payments in the future, let's get your house sold before you get into trouble again. That way, your fate will be in your hands, and you'll be able to get some money out of it and protect your credit from further damage."

"I understand."

"Okay. Can you drop those forms by to Val when you've completed them?"

"Sure thing. Thanks," Candy said.

"Where's Manny?" Merit asked.

"He's in the garage. I'll call him in," Candy said.

She picked up the phone and spoke over the PA system.

"Mr. Estevez to the office. Mr. Estevez to the office, please."

Manny came in wiping grease from his hands and smiled at Merit.

"This is a nice surprise," Manny said.

"I brought something for you," Merit said.

She tore the brown paper enveloping an eleven by fourteen picture frame and held it up for Manny to see.

"Tarantella!" Manny said.

"Yes. I took it one day when I was shooting pictures of the new equipment for the file on the loan."

The picture showed Tireman in his uniform with his name on the pocket. It was black and white and the light shone on his face in such a way to make him appear ethereal.

"Thank you," Manny said.

"I wish it were more," Merit said.

"The time will come," Manny said.

Next stop, back to school. Merit had gathered up all the research to date, both hers and Val's, on class action lawsuits and had it in her SUV. She found a good parking spot, a rarity on that end of campus, and entered the University of Texas School of Law.

"I'm feeling lucky already."

Walking through Townes Hall, a mausoleum of glass walls and granite floors, took Merit back to her time there as a first year law student. The smell of the place never changed, conditioned air, burning coffee from the cafe, and wonderful old books. A group of students laden with backpacks and paper coffee cups passed her. Their eyes were glazed over with late hours, too much caffeine, and fear. Law school was an intimidating place and any first year who denied this was a liar.

Merit was pleased to see her old study cubicle was empty. Walls of books made it semi-private. She set up her notes and questions and logged into the law library computer. She had modern day LEXIS in her firm library, but she was hoping to find some law review articles or case studies on fraud to expand the basics. The UT library had more extensive resources.

Merit reviewed the fraud issues in the memo from Val. She had used most of that in the Estevez trial. She would have another shot at those, and additional issues in the class action suit, if she were able to certify the class.

One of her stumbling blocks was getting information from Rooter. She knew that once the class was certified she could get all the records from him that she needed, but how much could she get before the hearing on certification? She did some quick research on discovery protocol. It appeared that usually, plaintiffs were given only minimal discovery prior to certification, limited to facts bearing only on the requirements for certification. So she would have to rely, for the time being, on the discovery from the Estevez trial for the rest.

Merit turned to part two of her task. Val had briefed the Private Securities Litigation Reform Act, or PSLRA, which was passed in 1995. Merit was hoping that Rooter would not be able to move the suit to State Court, but just in case, she wanted to have the research handy.

Under the PSLRA, plaintiffs were required to allege, in their initial pleading, exactly the way in which a defendant had committed an act of fraud. The statute tied the hands of the plaintiff's attorneys and kept the secrets of the defendants by preventing plaintiffs from gaining access to defendants' files until after the class was established. This standard would make it virtually impossible for Merit to establish the class. She had to fight tooth and nail to keep Rooter from transferring the case to federal court.

The act also required plaintiffs to allege that the defendant made misrepresentations with knowledge they were false or with dishonest recklessness. Proving a defendant's state of mind was always difficult, and they didn't have Boots King to testify.

Merit had operated under the assumption that Boots King could be compelled to tell the truth about his conversations in any court where she might find herself. She abandoned that notion. Since Merit had not had an opportunity to depose him, she didn't know what he might say, assuming Ag found him. Also the APD would certainly arrest him before he was brought into court. She removed Boots King from her witness list. Too many variables.

Merit flew down to Houston on Southwest Airlines, the bus in the sky. She wanted to work on her computer on the way, and couldn't do that from the BMW, no matter how well it drove itself. Also she didn't want to take a chance that Boots King or any other thugs hired by Nixon might get her alone on the highway. She felt safe in the midst of all these business commuter types.

It was the week before the class certification hearing, and she wanted to talk it over with Woody. She needed her mentor now, more than ever. She was nervous and concerned that she had taken on too much for her small firm. The Class Action Fairness Act, which was passed under George W. Bush in 2005, might allow Rooter to bump the case up to Federal Court. If he did, Rooter would not stop until he got all the way to the Supreme Court. There was a good chance the Supremes would bust the class if he could get them to hear it.

Republicans were always looking out for big business, but big tort cases had gotten so out of control that even fifty of the Democrats in the House had voted for the reform. Too bad the reform also hurt the cases that should be heard as class actions. Merit had grown up with a Republican father and a Democrat mother. She was politically schizophrenic, and usually wound up only voting when she had researched the candidate.

After takeoff, Merit opened her briefcase and took out her notes. She was worried because the Fed Courts could cut her attorney's fees. She had put a lot of time and effort into both cases, and Rooter had made sure she was covered with unnecessary paper to sort and respond to. She hoped that Woody had a few tricks up his sleeve for her to beg, borrow, or steal.

Merit made some notes about the need for her case to be heard in Texas. The Nixon case had exactly the type of class that the original class action laws were created to protect. She'd play that card if Rooter got too close to removal. She'd considered filing the case in Federal Court just to keep Rooter from moving it, but she thought she'd get a favorable jury in state court, and she bet she could keep Rooter from winning on the change to the Feds. One of the main criteria of moving the case was that more than two thirds of the class members were in different states than the primary defendant, in this case, Odell Packing. If Rooter wanted to move the case, he'd have to show that the class would expand beyond Texas, and Merit doubted Nixon would want to point out all the other signs in all the other states that might come into the class. If it got that big, she'd have to have a big tort firm come in and help, but for now, all she wanted to do was get the Texas group certified.

"One thing at a time," she said to herself.

She had to have the class established first. That was the big win. Once she had that, no matter what Rooter did, she at least had leverage over him and Nixon. She had some place to go. No class, no-go.

Merit landed safely and made her way via a rental down Allen Parkway to downtown Houston and Woody's office. She planned to stay with Joy and Tucker for the night before returning to Austin in the morning. It would be good to see her old friend. Merit shot Joy a text while waiting at a red light, to let her know she had arrived. Next, she called Ace to make sure he was confirmed for dinner at El Tiempo, his favorite restaurant in Montrose.

All activities scheduled, Merit went to her meeting with Woody. After hugs and howdies, they settled into chairs on the comfy side of his office. He wore his uniform of country gentleman attire. Merit loved the fatherly look of him.

"You didn't bring anyone with you did you?" Woody laughed.

"I can't believe you find that funny. How are you doing?"

"Great, let's get to work," Woody said.

Merit explained the case in detail, including her fears of removal to federal court and loss of attorney's fees.

"If you establish the class, you've won. The hardest part of a class action suit is to get the court to acknowledge that harm has been done to a group, and that the cost prevents them from suing individually. Once you've done that, the battle is pretty much over. Then, it's all about damages. Nixon may settle quickly if the class is established," said Woody.

"I can only hope," said Merit.

"You can't prove fraudulent inducement because you don't have this Boots King character as a witness. Nixon had to intend to cause the fraud, and you have to prove that Boots King carried out their wishes," Woody said.

"I'm hoping that Judge Hightower will take the word of our class representative, Odell Packing," said Merit.

"Won't it be his word against Nixon's word? You have no witnesses to the conversations. Isn't that where you lost before?" Woody said.

"Yes, and if it were only Mr. Packing, I'd say so. We weren't allowed to bring in other landowners in the first trial because we could not show it was relevant."

"What's different now?" Woody asked.

"Now, by nature of the class action, they are all relevant," Merit said. "We have over one hundred affidavits stating that Boots King and the other Nixon leasing agents all told them it was a simple lease. I don't think anyone would describe an option clause as belonging to a simple lease. Also all were prompted not to contact an attorney."

"Sounds like a class," Woody said. "How many do you have?"

"Over one-hundred and counting," Merit said. "The very number of those deceived indicates that it was by design and not a one-time event. There's not a single instance where a third person was privy to the conversations between Boots King and the landowner. What are the odds of that?"

"Sounds like res ipsa loquitur. The thing speaks for itself," Woody said.

"Now, don't go Latin on me," Merit said.

"The breach can be inferred from the nature of the facts. It is so obvious that even without a witness or other direct evidence, we can see how a party behaved," Woody said.

"Good point," Merit said.

Merit jotted notes on her legal pad.

"Go on," Woody said.

"I can also pull out the Italian Cowboy Partners case. Remember, it says that tenants can rely on the fact that landlords won't withhold material information. Concealing the option clause is a withholding of material information."

"That case was on point for landlords that withheld information, not tenants," Woody said.

"What's good for the goose is good for the gander," Merit said.

"You can fly that out there, but it might not work," Woody laughed.

Merit looked sheepish.

"What is your rationale on damages? I see you put ten million in the pleading," Woody said.

"What do you think?" Merit asked.

"You have to quantify that if it's compensatory damages to make the plaintiff whole. What was the quantifiable loss that the damages would cover?" Woody asked.

"I wasn't thinking of compensatory damages. I'm putting only one dollar there. We have to admit that the landowners received a fair rental rate, so they've already been compensated," Merit said.

"Right, and you don't want to give the court a way to give them compensatory damages, say they've been paid, and leave the option clause in the lease," Woody said.

"Right, and if Rooter has to fight compensatory damages, he'll call a host of experts to testify. It will cost me a fortune to depose them all and get ready for trial," Merit said.

"This way, you only have to prepare for punitive damages, which is very arbitrary and cuts against Nixon," Woody said.

"That's true. I'll stick with punitive damages for ten million," Merit said.

"Be sure and talk about punishment for wrongdoing and to deter other parties from acting in a similar manner as Nixon did. You also have to prove willful misconduct," Woody said.

"You're right. But I don't have to prove damages until the trial. First, I have to get the class established to even get to trial. Also if I don't prove willful misconduct, I can't establish the class anyway," Merit said.

"True. The damages don't really seem that high considering the deceit," Woody said. "Since you don't really want the money as much as getting rid of the signs, why appear greedy?"

"The value of the lands without the signs will go up drastically," Merit said.

"Ten million is still a lot," Woody said.

"Taking into consideration that the sign industry is a billion-dollar business, it's really not," Merit said.

"I like it, but it still gives the court only one option," Woody said.

"I'm worried about that too, but what else can I do?" Merit asked.

"All your eggs in one basket," Woody said.

"I don't see another way," Merit said.

"Neither do I. Excellent. You're ready, young lady. Merit, you've become quite the advocate," Woody said.

"It's easy with you. Now, if I can just do it in court."

42

Merit Bridges, Odell Packing, and Kim Wan Thibodeaux sat at the plaintiff's table in their Sunday best. Rooter, three associates, and Sonny Nixon sat on the defense side, all groomed to perfection. Old Man Nixon and Boots King were conspicuously absent. Everyone stood as Judge Warren Hightower entered the courtroom in his black robe. He settled into his chair, and with a gesture of one hand, settled the courtroom. The judge appeared stately in front of the old brass courtroom seal and flags of the United States and Texas.

"You're up, Ms. Bridges," Judge Hightower said.

Merit stood.

"As you are aware, Your Honor, today's hearing is for the sole purpose of establishing the class in Odell Packing, et al vs. Nixon Outdoor Advertising, Inc. The plaintiffs contend that first, Nixon fraudulently induced each member of the class into executing a lease by misrepresenting what was in the contract, second, that Nixon's representative was instructed to do so by Nixon, and third, the class members executed the contract relying on the misrepresentations. By its actions, the defendant caused injury to all the plaintiffs in the class."

Kim Wan handed Merit a copy Val had made of Johnson & Higgins vs. Kenneco. Merit asked to approach and when Judge Hightower nodded, she handed the case to him and a copy to Rooter on her way back to her seat.

"The Johnson case has been thoroughly outlined in our brief, which is on file with the court clerk. It asserts the standard for misrepresentation, which we have met."

"Proceed," Judge Hightower said.

"The class, after certification, is asking for relief in two ways. We beg the court to void the entire lease and give the defendant a specific amount of time to remove all the signs from the land-owners' property. If the court refuses to void the entire document, we plead in the alternative for the removal of the option clause from the lease."

"Anything else?" Judge Hightower said.

"Yes sir. We ask for one dollar in compensatory damages and ten million dollars in punitive damages, plus attorney's fees to be set by the court," Merit said.

"You want me to decide what's fair on attorney's fees?" Judge Hightower asked.

"Yes, Your Honor. We have attached to the brief our usual hourly rates and the number of hours we've spent on the case, as a suggestion," Merit said.

"A suggestion of attorney's fees? Clever, Ms. Bridges. Trying to keep the Feds from reviewing the case, I see. Putting that hot potato in my lap?"

"Fairness is the test, as you know. I trust you will be fair," Merit said.

"Thanks. Is that it?" Judge Hightower asked.

"Yes Your Honor. For these reasons, and those presented in the brief, we plead for certification of the class," Merit said.

She took a breath, as did Kim Wan and Mr. Packing. It seemed all to have come to a head. Hours and hours of work and strategy for such a short little speech. It was like cooking all week for Thanksgiving and eating in only twenty minutes.

Rooter stood up, ready to make his speech.

"Hold on Mr. Rooter," Judge Hightower said.

Merit stood waiting for permission to speak again.

"Do you have any witnesses?" Judge Hightower said to Merit.

"Yes, Your Honor, I have Mr. Odell Packing, the representative of the class, who will testify that he was fraudulently induced into signing the document by a Mr. Boots King, the agent for Nixon Outdoor Advertising, Inc. I also have my investigator, Mr. Albert "Ag" Malone who will testify that he and other staff members took affidavits from each plaintiff in the class stating similar circumstances."

"Do you have this agent, Boots King as a witness?"

"No, Your Honor, we have not been able to locate him."

"Mr. Rooter, can you produce this witness?"

Rooter stood. "No, Your Honor. He is no longer employed by Nixon."

"Ms. Bridges, is all of that in your brief?"

"Yes, your honor," Merit said.

"Then let's wait on the witnesses until we hear from Mr. Rooter after the break. We may not need them."

Merit took in a little gasp of air. Did that mean he was for or against the class already? She had no way of knowing.

During the lunch break, Merit and Kim Wan went back to Merit's office. Betty had barbecue from Green Mesquite waiting in the conference room with cole slaw and big iced teas. Betty always fed the crew like field hands during trial. Mr. Packing was sent out on his own so the two attorneys could strategize without overloading him with legalese before his testimony. He had been woodshedded by Merit the day before and was ready.

"What do you think?" Kim Wan asked.

"Great barbecue. Just kidding. I think old man Nixon is going to lie through his teeth on the stand," Merit said.

"I agree."

"How can he say he didn't authorize Boots King and the other leasing agents to lie or mislead?" Kim Wan said.

"He can't, but remember his course of dealings testimony in the Estevez trial?" Merit asked.

"By definition, Boots King was an agent of the company. He represented Nixon's interests with their permission and authority. I hope Judge Hightower swings more toward agency and away from course of dealing. There can be course of dealing, but it still doesn't negate the agency relationship," Merit said.

"It will be Nixon's word against Mr. Packing's about the misrepresentations. We need to have Mr. Packing stay calm and be convincing," Kim Wan said.

They nibbled on brisket and pondered their next moves while Betty refilled their drinks.

When Merit and Kim Wan returned to the courthouse, Mr. Packing was not at the plaintiff's table.

"I'll ask Ag to see if he's outside," Merit said.

"Check the men's room," Kim Wan said.

Ag exited the men's room with Mr. Packing looking pasty and wiping his mouth with a paper towel.

"Are you alright? The afternoon session is starting," Merit said.

"I don't like speaking in public. I didn't know the news reporters would be here," Mr. Packing said.

Merit shot Ag a worried look. She was kicking herself for not choosing the other plain-vanilla-white-bread good old boy on Ag's list to represent the class. Why hadn't she at least had a back up?

"Calm down, Mr. Packing. As Betty says, these people put their pants on one leg at a time, just like you do," Merit said.

"Just look at us when you're on the stand and tell us your story, Sailor" Ag said.

"Right. Most importantly, be yourself. The judge will believe you if you just tell the truth."

"I can do it," Mr. Packing said.

"I know you can," Ag said.

"Remember what they did to your business. Let's kick some Nixon ass," Merit said.

The color returned to Mr. Packing's face.

"That's right. I'm the one who's been harmed here. Let's do it."

The three entered the courtroom and Merit took her position behind the plaintiff's table just in time for Judge Hightower's return to the bench.

After the break, at the defense table there were only Rooter and Sonny Nixon, plus one associate. Maybe the David and Goliath look of the morning scene had caused Rooter to rethink his power strategy. Old Man Nixon sat in the gallery behind the defendant's table ready to testify if Judge Hightower decided witnesses were necessary.

At the back of the courtroom were several members of the press, including John Brewing, Merit's former lover, and Red Thallon, the short-skirted reporter from the fire at Estevez Tire and Auto Shop. Someone had been working the phones during the break. Judge Hightower went through the rituals and brought the courtroom back to order.

"Mr. Rooter, are you ready to make your statement?" Judge Hightower asked.

"Yes, Your Honor." Rooter stood.

"Proceed."

"First of all, we ask the court to address our Motion to Dismiss. We allege that the plaintiffs have failed to properly present their claims," said Rooter.

"What claims would that be?" Judge Hightower asked.

"The class is not appropriate for this type of suit because the defendants are all different, have different damages, and the case cannot be decided in one stroke based on the truth or falsity of the alleged cause of action. As you know, this is the standard for establishment of the class," Rooter said.

Judge Hightower leaned back in his chair.

"It seems to me," the judge said, "that if the members of the group were duped by this Boots King character or other deceitful employees of Nixon, and they all have the same lease clause, they are all of the same class."

Merit and Kim Wan looked at each other hopefully.

"We might concede that, Your Honor, if they were deceived. Putting that aside for now, and even if all of the allegations were true, they all have different property, and therefore different damages," Rooter said.

"What say you Ms. Bridges?"

"Your Honor, we are not stating that the damages will be the same dollar figure, as that is something that would be happening in the future, if the individual properties were sold. What we are saying is that the court can solve each of these plaintiff's issues with one ruling, an injunction to prevent enforcement of the option clause," said Merit.

Judge Hightower nodded at Rooter.

"The case law is clear that damages must be consistent," Rooter said.

Judge Hightower nodded at Merit.

"They are consistent, Your Honor. Just as in the securities fraud cases noted in our brief, there might be many defendants who bought stock in a company, but all did not pay the same price or buy the same amount of stock. Our case is very similar. All our plaintiffs want the same removal of the clause, and all are willing to take the same punitive damages. One lie, one penalty," said Merit.

"Motion denied, Mr. Rooter."

"Your Honor."

"Take it up on appeal if you like. Let's proceed to see if we can certify this class or kick it out. Make your case Mr. Rooter, in the event you don't win on appeal," Judge Hightower chuckled.

"The defense contends that the class should not be certified by this court. Setting aside for a moment whether fraud was committed, which my client denies, the class should not be certified for various reasons. First of all, as we said earlier, the damages allegedly suffered by the plaintiffs are not similar enough to form a class. Next, the civil courts offer each defendant a remedy on their particular cause of action and set of facts. If each member of the class would like to bring suit against Nixon Outdoor Advertising, Inc., we will face those issues one at a time, not in a group."

"Wouldn't it be more efficient to have one court hear all of the complaints at once?" Judge Hightower asked.

"No, Your Honor, that would be unfair to my client to defend such an action."

"Would it not be easier on your client?" Judge Hightower asked.

"In the alternative, we request that the case be transferred to Federal Court. As Your Honor is aware, the Class Action Fairness Act allows federal jurisdiction in cases where the amount in controversy exceeds five million dollars, and gives the courts greater scrutiny of class action settlements, especially those involving corporations," Rooter said.

"As I recall, that act was created to prevent forum shopping by plaintiffs in friendly state courts," Judge Hightower said. "Do you consider this court biased?"

"No, Your Honor," Rooter said.

"Do we have any out-of-state defendants here, Ms. Bridges?" Judge Hightower asked.

"No, Your Honor. Some may be added later, but at present, all defendants are Texas-based. May I go on?" Merit asked.

"Speak."

"The legislature also pointed out that the Class Action Fairness Act was, and I quote, 'the final payback to the tobacco industry, to the asbestos industry, to the oil industry, and to the chemical industry at the expense of ordinary families who need to be able to go to court to protect their loved ones. Critics charge that the bill makes it more difficult to bring class action suits, and may give the Feds some ability to control, through judicial appointments, outcomes that were previously under state control," Merit said.

"Mr. Rooter? What say you?"

"Your Honor, I would not, as a good Republican, attempt to take away any power from the sovereign state of Texas. However, the legislature in Washington has spoken and we must follow the law," Rooter said.

"Right you are, Mr. Rooter. I'll hear your witnesses this afternoon and go from there. Court adjourned."

The trial reconvened later that day. The participants looked a little weary except for Merit who had been waiting for this moment for a long time.

"All rise," the court clerk said.

"Call your first witness, Ms. Bridges," Judge Hightower said.

"The plaintiffs call Mr. Odell Packing," Merit said.

Mr. Packing took the stand dressed in a fresh suit of stretch fabric, which caught the light and appeared shiny. He lowered his eyes to Merit's face, and glued them there while he answered her questions.

After establishing Mr. Packing's full name, address, and place of business, Merit handed him the sign lease.

"Who brought the lease to your office?"

"A leasing agent named Boots King."

"What did he promise you in exchange for the execution of the lease?"

"Just what's in there, yearly checks and several month's free advertising for the storage company."

"Did he say anything else that you may have relied on when signing the lease?"

"Yes, he said it was a simple lease and that I could cancel it at the end of any lease year with written notice a month in advance."

"Did he say anything about the option clause on the back?"

"No, he specifically said it was a simple lease for the sign."

"Did he warn you to see an attorney before signing it?"

"No, he specifically said I didn't need an attorney. That it was a waste of money."

Merit took the lease from Mr. Packing and looked at the judge.

"That's all, Your Honor," Merit said.

Judge Hightower turned toward the defendant's table.

"Any questions, Mr. Rooter?"

Rooter stood.

"Yes Your Honor."

Rooter handed Mr. Packing another copy of the lease with highlighted paragraphs.

"How are you today, Mr. Packing?"

"Fine." Mr. Packing didn't look fine, but he kept his eyes on Merit's face.

"Mr. Packing, is this your signature on this lease between your storage business and Nixon Outdoor Advertising, Inc.?" Rooter asked.

"Yes, it is," Mr. Packing answered to Merit's face.

"Did you execute it freely and accept the consideration set forth in the lease?"

"Yes, I did," Mr. Packing still looked at Merit.

"No one held a gun to your head or prevented you from calling a lawyer?"

"No, but . . ."

"What about this clause that says it's the entire agreement of the parties. See, highlighted in yellow." Rooter pointed at the lease.

Mr. Packing looked down at the document then back up at Merit. Rooter stepped in front of the plaintiff's table, blocking the view of Merit.

"Did you read that when you signed the lease?"

"Yes, but . . ."

"Did you understand it?"

Merit stood.

"Your Honor. Please instruct Mr. Rooter to let him answer," Merit said.

"Mr. Rooter, give the witness a chance to respond."

"Yes, Your Honor."

Merit sat. Mr. Packing refocused his gaze on her.

"Mr. Packing, you've been in business for how many years?" Rooter asked.

"Over twenty, plus the U.S. Navy," Mr. Packing said.

"And, do you have an attorney?"

"Yes, but Boots King said I didn't need to call him. It costs money."

"Do you always do what strangers tell you to do?"

"No."

"And are you capable of making your own decisions?"

"Yes."

"Do you think of yourself as a smart man?"

"Smart enough."

Rooter placed his body between Mr. Packing and Merit again.

"Then why would you sign a document without reading it? Lazy? Not thinking?"

"I trusted him," Mr. Packing said.

"Trusted him?" Rooter asked, more contemplating than questioning.

"Yes, he seemed like a trustworthy person. I took his word for it. Took a quick look at the lease, and signed it. Foolhardy, I know, but it's the truth."

Rooter turned to Judge Hightower.

"Nothing further," Rooter said.

"Ms. Bridges, do you have any further witnesses?" Judge Hightower asked.

"Not at this time, Your Honor," Merit said.

"Mr. Rooter, call your witness," Judge Hightower said.

Mr. Packing left the witness stand as Rooter motioned to Old Man Nixon and called him to the stand.

Old Man Nixon swaggered past Sonny and the attorneys and asserted himself into the witness chair. His skin seemed to sag more than his last courtroom appearance, and his shirt was not quite so crisply pressed. After he was sworn, Rooter established his full name, address, and that he was the CEO and owner, along with Sonny Nixon, of Nixon Outdoor Advertising, Inc.

"Do you deny that Boots King and others were agents of Nixon Outdoor Advertising?"

"No, but I didn't tell Boots King or anyone else to lie. Just the opposite."

"What were your orders?"

"All sales agents were trained to use a script about the lease, and to tell the landowners to consult an attorney if they wished," Nixon said.

"Thank you. Release the witness," Rooter said.

Merit stood.

"When you say sales agents, you really mean contractors don't you? They weren't real estate agents, were they?" Merit asked.

"They were independent contractors," Old Man Nixon said.

"If they weren't realtors and therefore licensed to negotiate the option clause, weren't they outside the Texas Real Estate Commission regulations?"

"Well, technically, they worked for the company, so they didn't have to be realtors," Old Man Nixon said.

"Is technically your favorite word? Were they independent contractors or in-house employees? You can't have it both ways."

"Objection." Rooter was on his feet.

"Move on, Ms. Bridges," Judge Hightower said.

"You knew the sales agents were tricking the landowners by what they didn't say, didn't you?" Merit asked.

"No. It clearly says to consult an attorney," Old Man Nixon said.

"Why the small print? Why is the option clause on the back of the lease when it's one of the most important terms of the agreement? Why did you use a fill-in the blank form instead of a regular, legal-sized document? Isn't it trickery by its very nature?"

"Let the witness answer," Rooter said.

"Slow down, Ms. Bridges," Judge Hightower said.

"Okay, let's take them one at a time. Why did you use such small print on the back?"

"It saves space and paper. The leasing agents must carry the leases around with them when they travel. Having a notebook of leases allows ease in transport," Old Man Nixon said.

"Why would you put the lease parties and terms on the front page and the option clause on the back?"

"The main components are on the front, and the rest is on the back. It's just the way we set it up. It seemed logical at the time," Old Man Nixon said.

"Why did you use a fill-in-the blank form instead of a full sized legal document?" Merit asked.

"Same reasons. It was just easier for the leasing agents," Old Man Nixon said.

"Isn't it common practice to submit a document to a land-owner and have them get back to you later? Why should your leasing agents carry around a lease and insist that it be signed immediately?"

"It's our practice to sign up landowners on the spot," Old Man Nixon said, then realized his mistake.

"Really. No time to consult an attorney? Well that says it all, doesn't it?" Merit asked.

By this point, the judge was scrutinizing Nixon's face and looking perplexed.

Merit saw this as an advantage and marked a line through the rest of her questions on her legal pad. She had made her point.

After both sides had rested, the judge dismissed for the day.

"I'll take both your briefs into consideration. Court adjourned." Judge Hightower banged the gavel and it was out of Merit's hands. She turned to Kim Wan.

"What do you think?" Merit asked.

"I have no idea," said Kim Wan.

"What's next?" Mr. Packing asked.

"If the class is certified, we've won the battle and can proceed with the war. Then we'd be a real threat to Nixon. If the case is not certified, it's all over," Merit said.

43

Old Man Nixon, Sonny, and Boots King met at Texas Pie Company on the main square in Kyle, a small community off I-35 South, about twenty miles outside of Austin.

They each had a different slice, Texas pecan for Boots, buttermilk for Old Man Nixon, and strawberry rhubarb for Sonny.

"Your mother's favorite," Old Man Nixon said after Sonny ordered.

"That's right," Sonny said.

"You told me to leave town. I was halfway to El Paso. What's up?" Boots said.

"This suit is out of hand. Rooter lost the motion to dismiss. The judge is going to rule next week. We have five days," Nixon said.

"I thought the case was over," Boots said.

"It was, now it's back. Just like a wart that won't go away, recedes and returns. We need to kill it once and for all," Nixon said.

"Like Wart Away. This will cost extra," Boots said.

Boots watched Sonny cringe.

"The press is starting to get more involved. Make an example of Merit Bridges, and we'll settle cheap with whoever takes over her cases," Old Man Nixon said.

"Wait a minute there," Sonny said.

"What? You have a problem?" Old Man Nixon said.

"What are you talking about? Killing that tire salesman was

supposed to have been an accident. I'm not spending my life in jail to enrich your pocketbook, no matter how much you want to win," Sonny said.

"Look son, it's your pocketbook too. I sent you in here to get this thing under control and you've totally screwed the pooch. We have to get ahead of this, now!"

"Just look the other way, little boy," Boots said. "You always do."

"Rooter would not go this far either," Sonny said. "He's crooked, but he's not a killer."

"That's why he's not at this meeting," Old Man Nixon said.

"I can't be part of this," Sonny said.

While Judge Hightower reviewed the briefs in the class action, Merit asked Manny Estevez to meet at her office for a post mortem on the loss of his individual trial. He arrived in khaki slacks and a nice shirt, but he still had a touch of oil under his fingernails. It had been several weeks since they'd spoken, and Merit had researched the possibility of an appeal. There was a limited amount of time to file and she had to get Manny on board if she was going to do it. His individual case had been determined so she could not include him in the class action suit.

"I'd like you to consider going forward with your case," said Merit.

"We lost, what's left to do?" Manny asked.

"We can appeal," Merit said. "There are grounds."

"What grounds?"

"The issue of the fraud didn't go to the jury. It's not a matter of law, but a matter of fact. Judge Davis overstepped his bounds. We may be able to get the verdict overturned."

"What then, more lawsuits, more stress and disruption?"

"I know it's tough, but so much money is at stake with your business," Merit said.

"I don't know. I want to be finished with this. I want that Boots King monster out of my life, and I want my family to return to normal," Manny said.

"Well, don't say anything yet. Let me see if I can at least threaten them with the appeal," Merit said.

"What good would that do?" Manny asked.

"They're feeling the heat. If they think they'll lose on appeal, they may be willing to offer something. At least you won't lose your land. I think they were after the long-term lease all along," Merit said.

"Do what you can," Manny said. "I've got to get back to my business and my family. What's left of it."

Merit squeezed Manny's arm. "Don't worry about it today. I'll be in touch after I talk to Rooter."

Merit met with Rooter after work for a drink at the Cloak Room on Colorado. She wore a lovely new Kendra Scott necklace with her suit, and carried an Elaine Turner bag. Rooter had on an Italian pinstripe suit, costing at least five thousand dollars, with a yellow silk tie. His chunky gold Rolex looked just like Old Man Nixon's.

Maybe they got a fat cat discount for buying two, Merit thought.

"Aren't we the power couple," Rooter said.

"In your dreams," Merit said.

With the Texas State Capitol across the street and the clandestine underground location, it seemed a fitting place to strike a back door deal. There were several state senators and representatives already having a toddy. The dark wood on the wall and the close quarters felt like something out of a Patricia Highsmith novel.

Merit didn't enjoy the idea of socializing with Rooter, but she knew how the good old boys liked their schmoozing. Besides, it was tax deductible. Rooter was already seated and enjoyed a Johnny Walker Blue poured over a singular ball of ice. He raised two fingers to the bartender, ordering for Merit without asking her preference.

"You'll love it," Rooter said.

The bartender poured then served the highballs.

"Trendy," Merit said.

"Tasty," Rooter said.

Merit decided to ignore the chauvinism and save the fight for the lawsuit. Besides, she didn't mind if Rooter spent seventy-five dollars of Nixon's money on a drink. She raised her glass.

"To Judge Hightower," Merit said.

"And Judge Davis," Rooter said.

They clinked glasses.

"This is yummy!"

"Told you," Rooter wins again.

"Rooter, we've decided to appeal the Estevez case."

"Figured as much."

"We're going after the trial court's decision on the option," Merit said.

"Sore loser?" Rooter said.

"You know Judge Davis should have sent the question of fraud to the jury."

"Maybe. Maybe not. Want to wager a roll in the hay?" Rooter asked.

"Like that's going to happen," Merit said.

"Why are we meeting? You must have something in mind?" Rooter asked.

"Let's end this now for Manny Estevez. Nixon has hurt him enough," Merit said.

"Oh, I see. Still fighting the Estevez case," Rooter said.

"You've got your hands full with the class action suit," Merit said.

"We'll win that one too," Rooter said.

"Maybe. Maybe not. Why not go back to the mediation offer from Manny? It's a win for Nixon, and you'll look like a hero. They want the lease more than the land anyway, and you know it."

"Let me talk to Nixon. I'll get back with you."

44

Merit picked up Ace at school in Houston, released the security guard, and drove down to Port Aransas. She wanted to spend some time with her son while waiting on Judge Hightower to rule on the class action certification. Merit guessed they had about a week before the Judge would hold the hearing announcing his decision, and she needed a breather. She obtained permission for Ace to take a long weekend if he made up his homework when he returned.

"Thank goodness that jerk is gone," Ace said. "I couldn't take a leak without him watching."

"That's what I pay him for, to watch you take a leak. Seriously, this will be over soon," Merit said.

I hope, she thought.

"It better be. All this security is seriously inhibiting my moves on the women," Ace said.

"Yeah, right, ladies man," Merit laughed. She was delighted to see him and hear him joking like his former self.

Ag had helped her load her car in Austin and followed her to the Austin city limits to make sure she wasn't tailed by Boots or anyone else meaning her harm. She was fairly certain Boots King didn't know where Ace went to school. She'd had security on him from the first confrontation with Boots, just in case. There was even less chance that Boots or Nixon knew of her house in Port A. They'd be safe there, and she and Ace could take a break from watchful eyes and overly helpful advice.

Just in case, Ag had notified the Port Aransas Police Department, whose job was mostly giving out parking tickets and watching for drunk drivers. They had been very cooperative and had promised to keep a lookout for the distinctive truck and Boots King, but they were a small unit and couldn't make any guarantees.

Ag had also inspected Merit's gun. He'd swapped her target practice bullets for hollow points. The last thing he did was to place it in her case and into the map pocket in the door of her BMW. She may have bought a small pistol, but with the more destructive bullets, Ag made sure she had plenty of firepower inside it.

Merit and Ace cranked up Spoon on the sound system.

Ace sang along.

"Life is getting good again," Merit said.

Back in Austin, Boots King returned to his duties for Nixon and started tracking down Merit Bridges. He went to her office and watched the garage, but her car was not in her parking space. He went to her new high-rise and piggybacked on a car entering the garage under the building. He circled all three parking floors, not knowing where she parked, but did not see her SUV. He exited the garage, found a spot on the street, and looked inside at the doorman. He saw a security camera aimed at the reception desk, and loitered outside, smoking a cigarette. Sure enough, the doorman came out to see what he was doing.

"May I help you?" the doorman asked.

"No thanks. Just having a ciggy. Want one?" Boots asked.

"Trying to quit," the doorman said, then took one anyway.

"I'm trying to quit too," Boots said, making rings of smoke float upward with his exhale.

"I think I know someone who lives here. Merit Bridges," Boots said.

"She's out of town. Wait a minute, asshole. What do you want?"

"Just a smoke."

"Get out of here."

Boots flicked his cigarette in the doorman's face and left. He returned to his truck and drove down Seventh Street to I-35. In hindsight, it probably wasn't a good idea, letting the doorman see his face. Boots swerved and received a honk from another driver.

You're slipping old boy. He knew his time was short. Too many people could now recognize him. He was easily distracted these days. *Probably the joy of the hunt.* He wasn't sleeping much either. Odd hours.

"Where could she be?"

He'd had enough of this gig. It was time to take her down, wrap it up, and get out of town. He pulled over for a cup of coffee, looked at the pictures on his phone, and found the two pics he'd taken of her house files. The first was the address of Ace's school in Houston and the second was the Port Aransas beach house.

"I bet she's either in Houston with her kid and her lawyer buddy or she's at her beach house."

Boots took Highway 71 toward Houston, but when he arrived at the 183 cut off to Lockhart, he instinctively took it. It was all over the news about spring weather and he bet she and the kid were at the coast.

Merit and Ace enjoyed a sumptuous meal of plump shrimp with pasta, and rib-eye steak with gorgonzola at the Venetian Hot Plate. It had been Merit's favorite restaurant on the island since before Ace was born. It felt good to relax, have a great Tuscan bottle of wine, and visit with Linda, the Italian owner. It had been a hell of a year in Austin, and Merit particularly enjoyed being able to digest a meal without a clench in her stomach. The briny sea air mixed with the aroma of the grilled meat was more healing than any drug. She and Ace both loved the coastal lifestyle with its slow pace, excellent seafood, and beautiful sunsets.

They drove home along the beach to listen to the surf and watch the full moon rise. There were only two ways to go up and down the long peninsula, either along the beach or down 361. Driving in Port A was only accomplished by making rectangles. When they reached the sand and cleared the town lights, Ace aimed his phone app out the moon roof to identify a particularly bright planet, Venus, and then he located Orion.

When they arrived home, Merit parked in the garage and Ace took Pepper to the dunes for a pee. Merit curled up on the sofa with her latest download on her iPad, a John Grisham page-turner.

She could see Ace along the dunes with the leash in his hands. He was spotting planets and constellations with his phone app again. She saw a shadowy figure approaching him, but there were always people walking along the beach at night especially during the full moon. It was the best time to look for sand crabs. She wasn't concerned until she saw Ace turn and run up to the house.

She went onto the porch and called down to him.

"You all right?"

"Be right there," Ace yelled up at her, looking over his shoulder. "Come on Pepper."

He ran in the door and unclipped Pepper's leash while he caught his breath.

"That guy creeped me out. Something about him was off," Ace said.

"Where?" They looked down to the shoreline.

"He's gone. Must have been my imagination," Ace said.

"Never doubt your instincts, Peaches. I'll lock up," Merit said.

Her armpits prickled when the phone rang.

"Ms. Bridges. This is Sonny Nixon," the caller said.

"Yes?"

"I'm sorry to tell you this, but you're danger," Sonny said.

Merit froze.

"How?"

"My father has instructed Boots King to take you out. I've severed all ties with him. I want you to know I would never participate in harming you."

"I'm not in Austin. He doesn't know where I am," Merit said.

"He does. If he isn't in Port Aransas already, he will be soon. He has your address. He enjoys the hunt. He's not going to stop," Sonny said.

Merit grabbed a sweatshirt and her purse while yelling at Ace.

"Get Pepper. Put your shoes on. We have to go."

"Mom, what?"

Ace saw her face and went into action.

"Hurry. I'll explain in the car," Merit said.

"I knew it," Ace said.

They went into the garage, jumped into the BMW, and locked the doors. When the garage door lifted, Merit drove out to Highway 361 and toward town and the local police station.

A big black dually truck rubbed Merit's rear bumper. She gripped the wheel with both hands and swerved to get back on the highway. She felt the truck tag her again causing her to go into the drainage ditch and spray a rooster tail of water onto the road. Merit drove along the ditch and regained control just in time to swerve up on the shoulder and enter the Stripes on the corner of Beach Access Road 1A. She managed to avoid the gas pumps and took a right through the parking lot between the pumps and the store. She headed toward the beach hoping he would miss the turn behind her. It worked.

Merit thought he shot past the Stripes and 1A and she floored it to get to the beach before he could double back. In her rear view mirror she saw him make a U-turn on 361, cutting off oncoming traffic. He turned onto 1A behind her. She hoped he hadn't seen just her taking the right turn onto the beach. She followed the dunes but fell in behind a beach golf cart and could not go any faster. As she tried to pass the buggy, Boots swerved behind her upon the dunes, illegally passing a car on the right side and inciting a riot of horn honking mixed with seagull caws.

Merit swerved across the beach and drove down the water's edge. Her BMW kicked up sand and spun out in the loose ruts. Boots big tires gripped better than hers and he gained traction faster. She heard a loud pop and saw a muzzle flash in the rear view mirror.

"Duck!" Merit said.

She swerved closer to the shoreline and drove serpentine along the water's edge. She drove north toward mile marker twenty-five.

The hard packed sand by the water gave her more traction and she started making headway.

She could see the truck lights swerving behind her as Boots took out a port-a-can and sent it flying into the night sky. The monthly full moon bonfire party was in the distance at mile marker twenty-five. She had to get there before Boots could catch her and observe her plan.

"Ace. I want you to listen to me," Merit said.

Ace held his death grip on the door.

"When we get up here by the bonfire, I'm going to swerve over to the soft sand by the dunes. I want you to open the door and roll out. Take Pepper with you. I'll slow down, and the sand is soft, so you'll be okay. Roll toward the dunes when you hit the ground. Wait until the truck is clear behind me, then run over to the bonfire and look for a familiar face. See if you can find one of our neighbors and tell them what's happening. Tell them to call the police."

"No, Mom, I'm staying with you."

"This lunatic is shooting at us. I can't do what I need to do with you in the car," Merit said.

"What are you going to do?"

"This has to end. We'll never be safe with him after us."

"He's crazy. He'll hurt you, Mom."

Merit hit the overhead light switch so the light wouldn't come on when Ace opened the door.

"I'll be okay if I know you're safe, and you'll be helping me by calling the police. Ready?"

Ace grabbed the door handle and Merit swerved across to the edge of the dunes. She slowed the SUV, and pulled the wheel toward the highest sand she could see.

"Now!"

Ace held Pepper tightly, jumped from the car, and rolled into the high dunes on the right.

Merit passed the partiers on the left, gunned it, and caught some air coming off a ridge in the sand. She could see the big truck coming up behind her in the rear view mirror.

Merit held her breath until Boots drove past Ace. Apparently, he had not seen him leave the SUV, or didn't care. She swerved over to the beach road again and watched for the exit.

She hoped Ace stayed low in the dunes until the maniac in the truck passed him. There were about fifty drunk, but safe people standing around a roaring fire in the sand. He would be okay. They would help him.

"Please let him be okay," Merit prayed.

Merit saw that Boots was slowed by the full moon partiers and parked cars. She sped along the beach to the unpopulated end with less visibility. She killed the lights and pulled a U-turn into an indention in the dunes, facing out toward the beach road. She quickly unzipped her Ruger, blessed Ag for having put in the super bullets, slid the action back to put a round in the chamber, and waited for Boots to catch up. She could see him swerving and spinning down the beach toward her hiding place. She stood on the seat, popped her torso through the moon roof, and prepared to shoot. She shook so hard she had to steady her arms on the rooftop to hold onto the gun.

She could see Boots' headlights and then his head through the truck's windshield. Merit knew in that moment that if she shot him she would never be the same again. She would never think of herself in the same way, and her son would never know her as the woman she was. If she didn't shoot him, Boots might kill her, but Ace was safe. If she killed Boots now, she would never know if he could have caught her. She would only know that in a moment of choice, she had decided that her only option was to shoot a living, breathing person, regardless of the monster in his mind. She'd be an easy plot wrap in a clichéd paperback novel.

It all happened in a nanosecond. He was about twenty-five yards away as he drove by in front of her.

"Choose!"

Merit lowered the gun and emptied the clip into his dual rear tires, putting at least one into the sidewall. The outer tire popped and Boots swerved into the thick sand, sticking the truck and spinning to try to escape the rut.

Merit took advantage of the delay to pop down in her seat, zoom toward the beach exit and turn right back onto Highway 361. She dropped the empty clip and slid her backup clip into the Ruger, sliding the first round into the empty chamber. She dialed 911 and told the police where Boots was stuck in the sand. She was almost back into town when she heard a pop and the rear windshield exploded. She dropped the phone and swerved to the left as another bullet hit metal.

Merit ran the red light and took a sharp left onto Cut-Off Road hoping to come up on the back side of the police station off Avenue C. She saw Boots follow her around the corner with two now flat tires. His truck was wiggling out of control with the left rear side almost dragging the pavement. He bumped her again and she could not turn onto Avenue C. She floored it to keep him from hitting her again and barely made the left turn onto Cotter toward the ferry. She swerved at the last minute into Roberts Park Road and Boots missed his chance to avoid the ferry line. He swerved to avoid a parked car and plowed into the concrete barrier next to the ferry lanes. Merit saw him scrape down the barrier and bounce sideways. When the truck straightened, it was headed directly into the ship channel and went head first off the empty ferry dock and into the water. Pieces of wreckage tore away from the truck as it righted and started down the waterway.

Merit parked and ran back to the ferry. She could see Boots trapped behind the steering wheel as his big truck was sucked down by its weight as it filled with water. She saw him squirm to release himself from the collapsed dashboard, but he could not break free. The cabin filled and Boots slowly stopped struggling as the grill with the Playboy decal sank below the gurgling water.

TxDOT employees ran down to the water's edge. Merit watched as Boots' fire went out.

The Port Aransas Police Department drove Merit and Ace back to the beach house around four a.m. Merit's BMW was totaled, and she was too shaken to drive anyway.

Ace and Pepper collapsed in the bunkroom and Merit tucked them in and then drew a hot bath. She shot off a quick email from her phone to Betty and Ag. No sense waking them. They could learn about it in the morning.

Merit soaked in the warm bubbles and of course had a glass of wine. She stopped shaking after having to refill the tub three times with warm water.

It was over. Finally. Boots King was gone. She'd gone up against the devil's fire and she had won. She was alive, and Ace was safe. She'd emptied the hot water heater by the time she left the tub and went to bed with the sound of the ocean outside the window.

45

The next day, Merit and Ace flew out of Corpus Christi. They had decided to finish their short vacay in Austin. On the way to the airport, Betty called advising that Judge Hightower was ready to rule on the briefs in the class action lawsuit.

Merit found a rental car waiting for her at Hertz and drove Ace and Pepper downtown to their high-rise condo.

When they arrived at their new home, Betty was waiting with hot soup on the stove. She cooed and fawned over them, touching Merit periodically as if to make sure she was really there. Ace finally went to his room to stop Betty from hugging him again. Pepper scooted in and jumped on the blow-up bed as Ace closed the door.

The next morning, Betty stayed with Ace while Merit and Ag joined Kim Wan at the courthouse and braced themselves for the outcome.

John Brewing and Red Thallon were there again, along with an increasing number of newspaper and magazine reporters. Val crept into the back of the room and stood waiting with Ag.

Judge Hightower called the court to order and gave a long dissertation on the pros and cons of each side and his reasoning for reaching his conclusion. No one listened to the rhetoric; they could read that later in his printed decision. All Merit could do was stand at the plaintiff's table with Kim Wan, her splayed fingers holding her up against the gravity of the last few days and years.

Finally, Judge Hightower established the class.

"Unbelievable," she said under her breath.

She had won, at least the first battle. Her instincts had paid off and her hard work had carried the day. She smiled at her staff and associates with pride. As soon as the judge left the bench, she sat down. Hard. She would celebrate later for sure, but for now, she allowed herself to release her body and slump.

Merit sat in her office talking on the phone with Rooter. It sounded as if he were in his car, based on the echo. His threats sounded hollow.

"We'll appeal," said Rooter into the phone.

"No you won't," Merit said on the other end of the line.

"Nixon will not stand for this," Rooter said.

"I have some words for Nixon about his buddy Boots King. I may have a few for you, too."

For once, Rooter was silent.

"Besides," she said, "the publicity will bring all the other sign companies out of the woodwork. I've got Red Thallon on speed dial. So far, this has been a local fight, but with the class action, you know some national network will pick it up."

"Maybe," Rooter said.

"I looked into what happens after the class is established. Merits-based discovery means that the class is allowed to obtain info from the defendants or third parties relating to their claims. This time, I'll cover you with paperwork. This can last for three to five years, and the whole time you're answering discovery, I'll talk to the press every day on the status of the process."

"Beware of Old Man Nixon," Rooter said.

"Don't you threaten me. I've given the APD enough information to put him under the jail if he sends another goon after me. He'll be lucky if he's not in custody by the end of the week," Merit said.

"Maybe," Rooter said.

"Talk to Sonny. Let's settle this. Do you want to pull out every sign they have on I-35 while all their competitors keep theirs? Or even worse, do you think some other attorney is not going to jump on this bandwagon and investigate the other sign companies? Hell, we may go into phase two and pull in all your buddies on our class action. How would Nixon's cohorts feel about that?"

"I'm not threatened by you either," Rooter said. "The class certification will never stand up. You know the Texas Supreme Court or the Federal Court will bust the class. We have two shots at getting this thrown out," Rooter said.

"Maybe, but I can certainly educate the press in the meantime. If we lose the class, we'll sue you one sign at a time and I'll do the legal work for free. This stops now. Don't you see you've come to the end of the line on this?"

"I'll talk to my clients and get back with you."

"Wait, Manny Estevez' case is rolled in too. All wrapped. No loose ends," Merit said.

"Give me a day," Rooter said.

46

Merit stood at the doorway of her newly decorated high-rise in downtown Austin. She had spent a portion of the Nixon settlement money buying the condo and making it a home for herself and Ace. It was nothing like her old home in Tarrytown. It was modern and sleek and the view was of downtown, Lady Bird Lake, and the Texas Hill Country. A Saarinen marble table graced the dining room and the living room sported an Eames lounge chair and ottoman next to a charcoal sectional.

Merit had partially replaced her wardrobe, and planned to fill her new walk-in closet as time allowed. For the party, she wore a sexy red gown by Lauren Chester, a local designer that Val had discovered.

Austin had turned out for the occasion and the crowd over-flowed onto the balcony and into the hallway by the elevator. It was a combination celebration for settling the class action and house warming for Merit and Ace.

The room was festive and inviting with tiny white lights inter-twined with green plants and trees. Vases of fresh spring flowers were on almost every surface. There was a long bar set up with whirring blenders, tended by a trio of mixologists. The kitchen island hosted a variety of hors d'oeuvres, and the caterers passed through the room with trays of tidbits from Fonda San Miguel and snazzy napkins. On the balcony was a trolley cart with another waiter preparing Amy's Ice Creams for dessert.

Merit heard Ace talking to the D.J., getting tips on a new turntable that he was planning to put on his birthday wish list. Betty, in her only St. John's suit, bumped her gray helmet hair and swigged Jack Daniels. Merit knew this was a treat she allowed herself only on special occasions. Betty was sharing wisdom with Joy, who was wearing a tea length pink gown, and her husband Tucker, in a navy Tom Ford pinstripe.

Merit watched Kim Wan work the room and introduce his lovely wife, the brainiac from UT. Val was impeccably dressed in a white dinner jacket, a la Rock Hudson. He cringed at the sight of Odell Packing, who had on a fresh suit of slain polyesters in dark green.

Manny and his wife were talking with Candy who wore a little black dress that was understated and stylish. She also wore six-inch platform stilettos. You can take the girl out of Jersey, but you can't take the Jersey out of the Candy. She and Slag visited with Sonny Nixon who, after his father's incarceration, had taken over Nixon Outdoor Advertising, Inc. He was making steady improvements, and the first thing he did was to fire Richard Rooter. Rooter, Scooter, Roto-Rooter had not been invited to the party.

Merit observed Ag supervise security at the elevator. She saw him point to John Brewing and the bouncer escorted him back into the car going down. Ag allowed Red Thallon, in a dress cut up to there, to enter the room right in front of John.

Merit smiled at Ag, who walked over looking smug, having dispensed the former boy toy.

"Nice dress," Ag said. "Damn fine-looking woman you are."

"Hi there. Looking pretty snazzy yourself," Merit said. She straightened his tie.

Ag looked star struck.

Merit worked the crowd and made her way to the combo set up by the baby grand in the corner. She winked at the young male pianist and told the bass player to take a break.

"Let's give the D.J. a turn. Get yourself a drink," Merit said.

"Some things never change," Ag said.

"Some things do. Patience," Merit said.

"Really?" Ag said hopefully.

"No guarantees," Merit said.

Merit stood by the piano and raised her hand to quiet the crowd. Betty tapped her ring against her cocktail glass. Merit held a flute of champagne out before her. The group turned in her direction as waiters circulated with trays of the bubbly for the guests.

"Thank you for being here. It's a joy to see you all and share such a wonderful night with you in Austin. Thank you for all your housewarming gifts, especially the wine." She laughed.

The crowd gathered closer. Merit smiled at Ace. She sought out Betty, Ag, and Val with her eyes, locking onto each loved one with gratitude.

"I see a new family that we have created. I'm thankful for that."

"Hear, hear," the crowd responded.

"We have come through a lot this year, and hopefully we've seen the last of the danger surrounding our little firm."

"The last time most of us were together was very sad, as one of our family was taken from us too soon. Tarantella Estevez was a dear friend and good-hearted man. He will be missed."

Merit raised her glass toward Manny.

"To Tireman," Merit said.

"To Tireman," the crowd responded.

"No sadness tonight. We remember the good times with him. We all turn toward the future and know that all good things are ahead."

"Here, here," the crowd responded.

Merit felt a slight prickle in her armpits. Was that from the past or looking into the future? She shrugged it off for the moment and lifted her champagne.

"Raise your glass, lift your spirits, touch your soul," Merit said.

"Cheers!" the crowd answered.

Merit gave the thumbs up to Ace who cued the D.J. "The Eyes of Texas" blasted into the Austin night.

THE END

Want a peek at Music Notes? Read on . . .

MUSIC NOTES
Texas Lady Lawyer vs L. A. Baron

1

On a beautiful Texas spring day, Merit Bridges found herself in a situation she never thought she'd be—a fist fight. She wrestled against her attacker's six-foot frame and found herself overwhelmed by his strength. He grabbed her from behind with an arm around her shoulders. Merit spun free, ducked to avoid a punch to the face, and popped back up with a jab to his chin. He shook his head and steadied himself. Merit took advantage of his disorientation, grabbed him from behind in a bear hug with her legs around his waist and held his arms in place. He spun around and around until she lost her grip, detached and dropped to the ground. She hopped to her feet and swung. He blocked her jab and punched her in the stomach. Merit lost her breath and doubled over. Her attacker laughed at the amazed look on her face.

"You hit me!" Merit said.

"You hit me," Mayor Taylor said.

Both held their red boxing gloves in the air proclaiming

double victory and laughed out at the crowd of over fifty thousand. A banner above them displayed in huge red letters: TEXAS KNOCKOUT ILLITERACY!

"We're calling it a draw," Mayor Taylor said into the microphone. "Let me thank Merit Bridges, Austin attorney, fundraiser extraordinaire, and one of our favorite University of Texas Longhorns."

The crowd clapped as Merit made the Hook 'em Horns sign and joined Mayor Taylor at the microphone to address the audience. The sea of milling partiers spread from Barton Springs Road to Lady Bird Lake and covered almost every square foot of grass across the expanse known as Auditorium Shores in Austin, Texas. Attendees milled about between stages, lay on blankets in the grass, and perched in folding canvas chairs. They drank beer in recycled plastic cups and ate various types of food from barbecue sandwiches to food truck tacos to corn on the cob dripping with butter sauce.

Mayor Taylor and Merit bumped gloved fists, then she turned and spoke into the microphone.

"Thank you all for being here today and for supporting our three charities in the fifth annual music festival. Thanks to our sponsors, each of our musical performers, and the runners who participated in the 10K this morning. Last, but not least, thanks to Mayor Taylor for being our master of ceremonies and a really good sport."

The audience applauded and laughed. Television cameras zoomed in and drones snapped shots of the crowd from above. A small plane flew overhead trailing a banner proclaiming: TEXAS READS!

A second banner hung on the temporary fencing near the stage: Austin Charity Music Festival benefiting: Reading for the Blind & Dyslexic, Fresh Start for Kindergarten Readers, and Reading for the Incarcerated.

"Thank you Merit for chairing the event again this year. At last count, we've raised over one million dollars to be distributed among the three charities."

Merit stepped off the stage in her hot pink silk boxing shorts and white knee high socks. Her blonde ponytail swung from side to side as she climbed down the steps. Mayor Taylor, in black silks and "The Old Pecan Street Cafe" t-shirt, continued to work the audience, also known as future voters. Merit kept an eye on the mayor as she entered the VIP tent to check on the next act, a five-piece rockabilly band out of East Austin called Killer Delight. She nodded at Valentine Berry Louis, her law clerk, who was also a volunteer, as he gathered the rock group in a corner and went over instructions from a clipboard.

Bo, the lead singer, looked at Merit from bottom to top. He stopped at her eyes and they held there for a brief moment until a gel neck-wrap noodle interrupted his gaze when it passed before Merit's face and broke the spell.

Ace, Merit's teenage son and only child, smiled his million-dollar smile and handed out gel neck-wraps and bottles of water from a silver Yeti cooler. Ace wore the official t-shirt for the event which showed the black bats flying out from under the Congress Avenue Bridge and turning into music notes.

"Saw the mayor kick your ass, Mom," Ace said.

"Yeah, watch your language, Peaches. Give me one of those. I'm about to boil in this heat," Merit said.

Ace playfully hit his mother on the shoulder with the wet cooling tube and laughed. She'd been a single mom for some time now and the closeness of their relationship showed in their playfulness.

Merit wrapped the gel noodle around her neck and downed half a bottle of water until it flowed over her chin and down the front of her shirt.

"Easy, Mom, you'll get sick," Ace said.

"Who's the parent here?" Merit laughed.

Ace was in town for the event from his school in Houston for dyslexic students. It was good to have him home and Merit beamed at him like the proud parent she was. Joy and Tucker, Merit's best friends in Houston, had driven Ace up for the event. It was great having a houseful of fun loving guests.

Merit had been working on the festival committee for several years and had been an advocate for literacy since she'd discovered Ace's learning disability when he was in fifth grade.

A thin young man with purple hair walked toward Merit and Ace. Purple Hair looked like every other band member in the VIP tent—baggy jeans, t-shirt, no belt. Merit's armpits prickled ever so slightly. This visceral indicator of danger or intuition alert had been with her since she was a child. At this moment, she wasn't sure if something was up or if the Texas heat was giving her a heat rash. As Purple Hair got closer she saw that his clothes were dirty and his hair needed washing.

Ag, a tall, cool drink of water, with the kind of eyelashes women spent time and money to buy, stepped between Purple Hair and Merit.

"Where's your badge?" Ag Malone asked.

"I'm with the band," Purple Hair said.

"I don't think so," Ag said.

"I just want to talk to Ms. Bridges," Purple Hair said.

"You can't be in here without a VIP badge. Security reasons. You'll have to leave," Ag said as he escorted the interloper by his elbow to the nearest exit.

Merit was glad that Albert "Ag" Malone was doing his job. Ag was her private investigator for the Law Office of Merit Bridges, and coordinating security for the VIP portion of the festival. He wore his standard maroon shirt and jeans, a uniform of sorts for him, which showed his allegiance to Texas A&M University, his alma mater. Ag was long and lean with a quiet demeanor that was mysterious and attractive.

After Ag had ejected Purple Hair, Merit signaled to Val.

"The mayor is wrapping it up. Let's get Killer Delight up on stage as soon as he's finished," Merit said.

"All set," Val said and moved the band over by the stage entry ramp. He appeared almost too thin as he adjusted his vintage Tom Selleck type shorts and cropped Liberty Lunch retro t-shirt.

The crowd caught a peek through the tent opening at Bo Harding, the lead singer, and let out a roar.

On stage, Mayor Taylor got the hint as Merit moved back up the ramp toward him. Killer Delight held at the bottom of the stairs and the crowd roared again.

"Thank you all once more for your support this year for our very worthy charities. I'll now turn the mic over to Merit Bridges," Mayor Taylor said.

Merit stepped up to the microphone and raised her hand.

"Thank you all again for being here," Merit said. "We'll end the event with a killer local band that really needs no introduction.

Without further ado, here is the band you've all been waiting for, Killer Delight!"

The audience surged toward the barriers in front of the bandstand and attendees moved away from the other four stages around the lake and toward the main stage to see the lead act of the event and the hottest band in Austin.

Purple Hair tried to go against the crowd, was pushed about and fell. Several attendees helped him up and he worked his way toward the main exit on Barton Springs Road.

Red Thallon stood in the center of the festival crowd with microphone in hand. Her gimme cap had the Austin9Online logo on it. She continued her interview with a young woman with a large tattooed curl of barbed wire climbing out of her blouse and wrapping around her neck.

"Are you enjoying the festival?" Red asked.

"Loving it," said the young woman.

"How many acts have you been able to watch?" Red asked.

"I've seen six so far today including Solange, Erica Badu, and The Derailers. I'm looking forward to Killer Delight," the young woman said and pointed to the main stage.

The crowd roared as Killer Delight tuned up with a familiar chord and Red had to yell into the microphone to be heard.

"Thanks for stopping to chat," Red said and turned full face to the camera. "Catch us tonight on Austin9Online and at ten on KNEW nightly news. We'll have live interviews with Bob Schneider and Kevin Price. For now, let's have a listen to Killer Delight."

The camera panned the cheering crowd and moved toward the

stage settling on a close-up of Bo Harding. The tall muscular rock star was a wearing denim shirt and pants plus a pair of red leather and rhinestone cowboy boots. He shook back his long dark blonde hair and struck a strong riff on his guitar. The audience went wild again, and the concert began.

After Killer Delight had finished their set and the crowds had dispersed, Merit and Val sorted out the aftermath in the VIP tent and looked around for any remaining volunteers to help.

Liam Nolan, an aging, long-haired, tanned-faced guitarist with a purple guitar pick in the band of his tan straw cowboy hat stood outside the flap of the VIP tent. He put out a cigarette and chugged down a bottle of water. He looked like a worn-out rock star that some people thought they recognized but weren't sure from where. The seasoned music lovers knew him, of course. He was trying to redeem himself for years of alcoholism and drug abuse by giving back at the festival. His Narcotics Anonymous sponsor constantly reminded him that the twelve steps ended with service.

"Liam, if you're up for it, let's open all the flaps and let in the roadies," Val said.

"Glad to help," Liam said.

Merit saw Bo Harding and other members of Killer Delight walk over and shake Liam's hand.

"I grew up on your music, man," Bo said. "It got me through some rough times."

"Hey, thanks," Liam said and bumped fists with Bo.

"I saw your act at Stubb's once. Great show," Bo said.

"Those were good times," Liam said.

"If you ever decide to start writing songs again, keep me in mind. I love a good lyric," Bo said.

Merit had been helping Liam sort out his business affairs and put his financial life in order again. It was a slow process. Val was assisting by chronicling Liam's portfolio of songs from years of writing. Some had sold and some were still in old dust covered suitcases and boxes in her conference room.

"Just a minute Bo. Val, do I have anything left to sell?" Liam grinned.

Merit smiled and kept sorting through leftover t-shirts with Ace.

Val laughed. Merit knew he would never answer such a question even in jest if he wanted to continue to work in the law office. Confidentiality was her first rule for her staff. Integrity was her first rule for herself.

Merit recalled that while cataloguing and organizing Liam's songs, she and Val had discovered and hummed new tunes on the list that they recognized. They were surprised again and again that Liam had authored the songs that were part of the emerging portfolio.

Liam was the real deal. How he wound up barely surviving and in NA meetings every day was a story he didn't share with many except Merit. He had finally gotten control of his life. Liam's future was in his hands, or so he thought.

2

L iam sat at the edge of Lady Bird Lake near the statue of Stevie
Ray Vaughan at four-thirty in the morning. The crowds had
long cleared from the festival and the city was settled for the night.
The ember from his cigarette glowed in the pre-dawn light. He
looked at the skyline of Austin reflected in the dark water with his
Fender Stratocaster nestled in its case at his feet.

After the festival, he'd sat in on a set with some old classic
Austin musicians at the Saxon Pub before finding his way back
to the lake. He ran his hands over the guitar case and thought of
the horn shape that gave the axe its balance and distinctive look. It
was his favorite possession and one of the few he had not pawned
or sold to cover his former habit. His addiction to various drugs
culminating in Fentanyl had cost him everything except his life
and one remaining Strat. Fortunately, he got into recovery before
he could sell his entire portfolio of music. There were huge gaps
in his memory and millions of dollars lost who knew where. With
no family and a loveless bed, he was lonely but increasingly hopeful. His NA sponsor and a few remaining friends, including Merit,
were a big support for him and taking life one day at a time helped
him to manage his life in small bites.

Liam watched two teenagers with handheld controllers work
their way down to the water's edge flying their drones over the lake

and then under the bridges that crossed over the water at regular intervals.

Liam twirled a purple guitar pick between his fingers. It had a series of quarter notes on one side and L.N. on the other side. He thought of it as his business card. It was his signature gift to fans, and his talisman when he wanted a cool way to introduce himself.

He heard bits of conversation as the skinny male teens passed a joint back and forth. They laughed and played with their flying toys that looked like four legged spiders.

"Great light," said the first teen with ginger colored hair.

"Magic hour," said the other teen, sporting a mouth full of metal braces.

"Here come the cops."

"Throw the roach in the water."

Two extremely fit policemen on bicycles rode along the shoreline and spun gravel when they stopped beside the teens. Their uniforms were navy blue with shorts in lieu of long pants and they both had Blueguns tasers on their duty belts instead of a gun. Their bicycles were fitted with saddlebags holding first aid equipment.

"What are you two doing out here at this hour?" the older policeman said.

"We're capturing the light, officer," ginger teen said.

"Right," said the younger policeman sniffing the air.

"You have a license for that drone?" the older policeman said.

"No sir. I'm just taking pics for fun. No commercial use," ginger teen said.

"We don't need a license," braces teen said and giggled.

The two policemen looked at each other and appeared to make a non-verbal decision.

"Wrap it up and get on out of here," The younger policeman said.

"Yes, sir," ginger teen said.

The policemen rode on through the area, nodded at Liam, crossed over the bridge and then patrolled the other side of the lake. There was little activity, but the water's edge was never totally quiet in Austin.

Liam played the lyrics of a new song over and over in his mind. He smelled the wet earth at the edge of the water, listed the Twelve Steps in his mind, and lingered on gratitude. He felt light and unburdened now that he was finally turning his life around. He was grateful to be alive. Maybe he would write a song for Killer Delight, earn some money, and make a comeback. Possibly perform at Antone's or Guero's again. Maybe he'd meet a nice woman. Why not? Everything was possible again.

Liam got up, picked up his Strat, and walked along the lake on the hike and bike trail toward home. As he dropped down under the First Street Bridge, he looked up from his dreamy state to see a Pursuer coming toward him. The Pursuer was slight in stature, but backlit by the bridge and Liam could only see an outline.

"Hey, Liam," the Pursuer said.

"Hey. Who's there?" Liam asked.

"Don't you know who I am?" the Pursuer asked.

The voice sounded familiar. The Pursuer continued toward Liam until they were close enough for Liam to recognize the face.

"What are you doing here at this hour?" Liam asked.

"Looking for you. I followed you from the Saxon Pub."

"Well you found me. What do you want? I told you I have nothing for you," Liam said.

"Don't be that way. Let me buy you a cup of coffee. I want to talk to you," the Pursuer said.

"I don't want coffee and I don't want to talk to you. Leave me alone," Liam said and turned to go.

"Don't turn your back on me again!"

The Pursuer looked around and picked up a large rock from beside the path. Liam felt movement behind him. As he turned back, he felt a strong blow between his neck and skull. He fell, dropped his guitar case, then struggled to get up.

"You, asshole," Liam said.

As Liam pushed himself up from the ground, the Pursuer grabbed the guitar case and slammed it into Liam's head. Liam fell to the ground again and the Pursuer hit him with the case over and over until the latches broke and the case flew open, sending the Strat spiraling into the water.

Liam looked up to see the Pursuer freeze, blink, and begin to shake. A hand reached down by the dying face and gathered up the case handle and rock, and put them inside the broken case. The Pursuer ran along the trees and out of the park with the case. Liam's blood spread out over the trail, pooled at the grassy edge, and finally spilled over into the dark water.

No one came to help poor Liam or see the face of his killer. Dozens of purple guitar picks lay strewn along the water's edge.

The next morning, Red Thallon stood at the site of the murder of Liam Nolan. The serene water of Lady Bird Lake lapped quietly against the bank. Downtown Austin glistened in the background in the morning sun.

She raised the microphone to her mouth as the cameraman counted down five, four, three, then went quiet and held up two fingers, then one finger pointed at Red.

"We are at the site of the murder of Liam Nolan, an Austin favorite for his rock and roll hits of the Eighties and Nineties. Nolan was apparently assaulted in attempt to obtain his expensive Stratocaster guitar. The mugger was unsuccessful, as the instrument was found in the water after the incident," Red said.

Several lookers gathered around the yellow and black tape marking off the crime scene as the camera went to wide angle and showed the area. The cameraman scanned the audience and paused on each face. The young man with purple hair stared with wide eyes at the scene.

"Austin police are asking anyone with information to come forward. More on Austin9Online and at five on KNEW," Red said.

She made a slicing motion across her throat.

"That's a wrap."

**To continue reading, buy Music Notes
online and wherever books are sold.**

About the Author

M anning Wolfe, an author and attorney residing in Austin, Texas, writes cinematic-style, smart, fast-paced thrillers with a salting of Texas bullshit. Her award-winning series features feisty Austin attorney Merit Bridges.

Manning is a graduate of Rice University and the University of Texas School of Law. Each of her novels springs from a real-life case in her law firm. Her experience has given her a voyeur's peek into some shady characters' lives and a front row seat to watch the good people who stand against them.

Other Books in the Merit Bridges Legal thriller Series:
Green Fees
Music Notes

FOLLOW THE MERIT BRIDGES LEGAL THRILLER SERIES AND RECEIVE A FREE GIFT!

If you enjoyed Merit, Betty, Ag, and the whole Texas Lady Lawyer Gang, get notifications of their adventures and receive a free gift at: http://manningwolfe.com/giveway

You will also be notified of contests, drawings, and giveaways of free Kindles, Gift Cards, and Texas Lady Lawyer souvenirs.

www.manningwolfe.com

LEAVE A REVIEW

If you enjoyed this book, please leave a REVIEW on Amazon or Goodreads. Reviews are the lifeblood of authors and often determine whether other readers purchase books when they shop. Thank you.